GAME CHANGER

KAYT MILLER

Copyright © 2020 by Kayt Miller

All rights reserved. No part of this publication may be reproduced, distributed, or transmitted in any form or by any means, including photocopying, recording, or other electronic or mechanical methods, without the prior written permission of the publisher, except in the case of brief quotations embodied in critical reviews and certain other noncommercial uses permitted by copyright law.

This book is a work of fiction. All names, characters, locations, and incidents are products of the authors' imaginations. Any resemblance to actual persons, things, living or dead, locales, or events is entirely coincidental.

Editor: Hot Tree Editing

Proofreading by: Hot Tree Editing

Formatted by: Kayt Miller

Graphic Design: Book Smith Design booksmithdesign.com

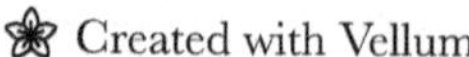 Created with Vellum

Hopeful Romantic

Thanks to Margie Dill (Coming soon.)

Chapter One

STELLA

Before I can reach into my bag for the key to my new dorm room, I notice the door is unlocked. Great. Brooke is home. Brooke is my roommate—not by choice, mind you. No, the person I'm supposed to be living with my freshman year at Northwestern University is my best friend, Lily, but circumstances being as they are—like a water main break in our real dorm building—I'm forced to live with an unfriendly upperclassman named Brooke. The only good part is I have my own bedroom, but we share a bathroom, a kitchenette, and a small sitting area. In Brooke's defense, she wasn't supposed to have a roommate this semester. She paid extra to live alone, but due to the accidental flooding of my dormitory, we're stuck with each other. In total, there were about seventy-five of us who were displaced "until further notice." Ugh.

Since Brooke is… not the nicest person, I've decided avoiding her as much as possible is the way to get through my time here. As I tiptoe into my room to gather up my things to shower, I hear the shower already running. Damn. I plop my tired body down into my desk chair to wait for my turn. At least I don't have to share a bathroom with an entire floor. See? I can think positively about my situation.

As soon as the shower shuts off, I hear voices—as in more than one voice. One of which sounds male. Oh, jeez, Brooke's got a guy there? In the shower with her? *I don't want to know.* I jump up from my seat to close my bedroom door before they can see that I'm home, but I don't get it shut in time. I catch Brooke backing out of the bathroom, attached at the mouth to a guy. It's all swirling tongues and moaning.

Bradley was right, that is gross.

It's then that I hear the guy say, "Come on, Brooke, let's go get dirty again."

I want to roll my eyes at the play of words, but I can't because I know that voice. I slowly look as Brooke giggles. The man and I make eye contact. He stops moving. I stop moving. There's silence. My heart stops.

"Stella? What the hell are you doing here?"

Standing in the doorway of my dorm bedroom, I see my boyfriend of one year half naked. I close my eyes tightly, hoping that when I open them, this bad dream will end. Opening them up again, I realize it's no dream. Bad or no. I'm not sure where it comes from because what I say next is so not me. "Me? What the heck are you doing here, Bradley? No. Wait. I know what you're doing. You've got your tongue down my roommate's throat. No need to explain. Now I know why you wanted to *wait*." I choke on my last words.

Bradley turns to my new roomie and asks angrily, "What's Stella doing here, Brooke?"

"What do you mean? I just met her. She's my temporary roommate. I told you that already," Brooke sputters as she rolls her eyes.

"I thought you said her name was *Stephanie*. You also said she was going to be gone all day."

"Stella, Stephanie, what's the dif? I told you she was some fat freshman girl. What do I care?" spits Brooke.

I squeeze my eyes shut in an attempt to make the scene before me disappear. When I open them again, I see Bradley glaring daggers at Brooke. It's at this moment when I think, *Run. Run, Stella, run.* I pull my bedroom door open the rest of the way and launch myself into our tiny kitchen. From there, I jerk the front door open and peer to the right at the elevators, then left at the door to the stairwell. I choose left. No way am I waiting around for an elevator. The sooner I can get the heck out of here, the sooner I can cry. *Just don't cry yet. Not yet.*

Moving as fast as my short legs will take me, I race toward the stairs. I can hear Bradley yelling for Brooke to help him find his pants. It's my chance to get a head start. I rush down the stairs, and as soon as I make it past the floor below, the tears start to fall. It's blurring my vision. I can barely see where I'm going. My goal is to get to the first-floor lobby before Bradley can catch up to me. Then, when I get to the lobby, I can run outside and hide in the bushes or something.

Honestly, I've got no real plan. Or stamina. This is one time in my life when I wished I exercised. The concrete steps are steep and long, so getting to the bottom from the fourth floor takes me too much time. As I descend, I mutter words to myself like, "lying, cheating bastard, asshole, and douchebag." What was he doing with me if he's attracted to someone like Brooke? We couldn't be more different. I'm short, chubby, and blonde. She's tall, thin, and a brunette. She's model gorgeous. I'm… well, I'm not.

I'm nearly to the lobby level when I hear Bradley yell, "Stellaaaa! Stellaaaa!"

Are you freaking kidding me? The movie called *A Street Car Name Desire* flashes through my head. There are times I really hate my name. Take now, for example. No, right now I really hate my parents.

I can't believe all of these things are going through my head. My mind is a blur of random messages, and I can't see because tears are flowing like crazy. As I tug open the lobby door, I hear Bradley's voice again; he's getting closer. I race through the door, looking back to make sure I can still get away from him, when I hit a brick wall.

Okay, it's not literally a brick wall, but it feels like one. I hit so hard that I bounce back a little. Before I fall ass over tit, big arms wrap around me, keeping me upright. The next thing I know, those arms pull me in until I'm pressed against an enormous body. His arms hug around me in a warm cocoon. My thoughts are muddled now, and the only thing I know is that it feels good to be against this person. I raise my arms and wrap them around his waist as I bury my face into his purple shirt. He's so big that my hands don't meet around his back, so I just clutch onto his clothes. He smells so good, like soap and man.

Breathe. Just breathe.

"Stella, listen, it's not what you think," Bradley exclaims from behind me.

I feel myself stiffen. Crap, he's caught up to me. I start to pull away from the warm embrace to escape Bradley once more, but the arms hold tighter. I don't fight it. It's strange, but I feel safe. Protected.

Panting, Bradley pleads, "Stella, it wasn't what you think. It was just a one-time thing. It meant nothing. You know you're the only person I care about."

I'm still shedding tears and snot, some of which has ended up on this poor guy's shirt. It's going to be soaked when this is over. As I press my face harder into his solid pectoral muscles, I hear a rich voice whisper above me, "Has this guy hurt you?" It's so deep, I can feel the vibrations from his body run through mine.

I nod.

"Has he hit you or hurt you physically?" the big guy asks.

I shake my head. "No," I whisper.

"What do you want me to do here?" he asks in a soft voice in my ear.

His whisper gives me goose bumps, but not because I'm cold. It's something else, something I can't quite explain. "Can you just hold me?" That's all I can muster. He pulls me closer, tighter than before, and I cling to him.

"I don't think the girl wants to talk to you right now, dude," states my knight in purple armor.

"Who the hell do you think you are? This is none of your damn business," spits Bradley.

"Who am I? I'm the guy that's here to make sure this gal is safe from you, jackass."

"He's a jerk," I whisper.

Apparently, I said it loud enough for my knight to hear. He laughs with a low rumble in his chest that I feel through my entire body, making my toes curl.

"I don't want to talk to him," I murmur.

"You heard the lady, beat it. She doesn't want to talk to you."

"This is bullshit. Stella, you need to give me a chance to explain," demands Bradley.

"No, I don't. Go away. I don't want to see you or talk to you." I finally turn to see Bradley standing there in only pants. They aren't even buttoned. That's when I remember the promise ring. I pull back from the big guy just enough to slide the ring from my finger. "Here." I toss the ring at Bradley. "I don't want this anymore." My chest aches at the loss. He gave it to me this summer in front of both of our families and our friends. He made a show of it at my parents' annual Fourth of July barbecue. It meant so much to me.

Our families sat together on the grass at my parents' annual 4th of July party, waiting for the fireworks to begin. We had a firepit going so people could make s'mores. Bradley stood and asked for everyone's attention. When he knelt in front of me, I was surprised. My eyes had to have been as big as saucers and my mouth agape. He reached into his pocket and pulled out a little black box. My heart sped up at the sight before me. I had no idea what was happening.

Bradley cleared his throat and spoke loud enough for everyone to hear, "Stella, you mean the world to me. You have an exciting future ahead of you as you start college, and I want to be sure I'm a part of that future. I want to give you this promise ring so that you know, when we're both finished with college, we'll get married and start our amazing careers as husband and wife."

There was a collective "awww" from the crowd around us. I slowly raised my left hand so he could slide the pretty little ring onto my finger.

I couldn't believe it. It was a pink heart-shaped stone with two tiny diamonds on either side set on a gold band. Typically, I only wore silver, but oh well. I was speechless, but everyone was staring at me, so I figured I'd better say something.

"Oh, Bradley, that is so sweet and romantic! Thank you so much! I love it!"

There was a smattering of applause, and then a few people approached me to give me a hug, one of which was my mom. Loudly, she stated, "Congratulations, Bradley and Stella!" But then she did what she always does; she ruined my mojo as she whispered in my ear, "Don't screw this up."

My smile dropped. Way to ruin the moment, Mom-devil. A few people patted Bradley on the back. I'd like to say he was smiling, but that wouldn't be the right way to describe his expression. Smug smirk was closer. Right then, the fireworks started, and that was that.

Chapter Two

STELLA

I shake my head and blink, bringing myself back to the nightmare in front of me.

"Stella, I know you don't mean this. You just need to let me explain."

I'm still looking at my ex—what was he? Boyfriend? Not really. Definitely not my fiancé. No matter, this is certain, begging doesn't look good on Bradley. This thought satisfies me for a second.

I lay my head back onto the hardest chest in the world. It's got to be carved from stone.

"Buddy, it's time to move along. You can talk to her another time."

"Who the hell do you think you are? You don't even know us," Bradley shouts. I peek back at Bradley because I can tell by his voice he's getting agitated. I can tell I'm right because he's running his fingers through his hair and pacing frantically

"I'm here for her"—*that must be me*—"and she wants you to go. So you need to go."

"Fine," Bradley snaps angrily. "I'm going, but I'll be back,

Stella. We *will* talk about this!" Bradley screeches as he stomps back to the doorway to the stairwell. It means he's going back up. To my dorm. Great.

The arms that were wrapped tightly around me start to loosen. Mine relax as well, and my eyes begin the long, long trek up from his hard chest, past his thick neck, up to the most beautiful man I've ever seen in my entire life.

"Damn!" he says.

"What?" I ask.

"You're beautiful!" he exclaims.

"Oh, no, I'm sure I look terrible." Fact: I'm an ugly crier. "But thanks for trying to make me feel better." I wipe the last few tears from my face. "And thank you for helping me get rid of him." Heat rises from my neck to my cheeks, most likely giving me a magenta-hued blush.

He reaches down with a gentle hand, wiping away one stray tear from my cheek. "Of course, I want you to feel better, but I meant what I said. You're a beautiful girl."

I shrug because it's not worth arguing about right now. I look up again at the gorgeous man. He can't be real. He has to be way over six feet. Not to mention, it feels like he's entirely constructed out of muscle and steel. He's got a baseball cap on backward. So cute. His brown curls peek out from the sides and on his forehead drawing my attention to the bluest eyes I've ever seen. They remind me of a summer sky. Below those is a strong, straight nose. Don't get me started on his amazing smile. It's addictive. So much so, it makes me smile right back even though I just caught my... Bradley with Brooke.

"Havin' a bad day, Pixie?"

Pixie? What does that mean? "You could say that," I mutter.

I let my eyes move back down his body toward his feet. He's wearing a purple Northwestern Wildcat tee. The shirt is working really hard to contain his extra wide chest and shoulders. He's got to be twice as broad as me, and that's saying something. His loose athletic shorts hang low on his trim hips. Michelangelo could sculpt this guy, and people would flock to see it. It'd be way better than the famous sculpture of *David*.

"Seriously, are you okay?" he asks.

I nod. It's then that I notice the crowd that's gathered around us, no doubt thanks to the scene created by Bradley and me. My face burns, which I know means it's three shades of red with embarrassment. My knight must notice this because he takes my hand and pulls me into a more secluded area of the lobby. We stop in a spot that is sort of a reading nook—like a place to study when your roommate is intolerable. It's a place I'm sure I will utilize my first semester here.

He leans his back against the wall while pulling me to him until I'm standing between his long legs. Next, he places his hands on either side of my face and bends so he can look directly into my eyes. My breath catches in my throat. He's so tall, I'm sure he's bent in half. I don't know why but I ask the dumbest question ever. "How tall are you?"

"I'm six foot four."

"Wowza. That's tall."

Luckily, he ignores my inane comment. He's close, but I don't mind his proximity. "Are you okay, Pixie?"

I nod and blink my bloodshot eyes at him. Needing to break the intensity of this moment, I'm tempted to ask him more stupid questions like, "How much do you weigh?" Because the guy is massive—but I really don't want him to ask me the same question.

"Your name is Stella?"

"Yes." I peer up at him and blink. "What's your name?"

"I'm Alex," he says with another brilliant smile.

I'm about to reach my hand out to shake his, but I decide now's not the time. So, I just say, "It's nice to meet you, Alex."

"It's very nice to meet you too, Stella. I'm just sorry it's under these circumstances. But I'm glad I ran into you no matter the reason."

I let out a relieved sigh. "I think *I* ran into *you*. I hope I didn't hurt you."

"Not possible, Pixie."

There it is again. What does this guy mean by 'Pixie'?

"What was the deal with you and that guy?" His smile is gone as he continues, "Did he hurt you?"

"Not physically. He's my boyfriend." I correct myself. "I mean, he *was* my boyfriend." Now he's my ex-boyfriend. "I just caught him cheating on me with my new roommate."

"Oh shit, that sucks. I'm really sorry to hear that."

He sounds so sincere, it makes my eyes water, but I will the tears back. "It's okay. I'll be fine." And I will be… eventually. "Thank you so much for helping. I just hope it was enough to keep Bradley away from me. I don't want to talk to him right now." Or *ever*.

"Well, he's pretty determined to talk to you. Maybe you need to let him. Once. Then you can let him loose."

"I don't know. We've known each other our entire lives. Our moms are best friends. I'm sure this thing isn't over until everyone has given me a piece of his or her mind." Why am I rambling to Alex about my history with Bradley? I'm sure he couldn't care less. "I'm sorry. I'm sure you have better things to do than listen to all of this drama." I start to pull away. "Thank you again, Alex."

"Where does that guy live? Does he live in this building? Do you think he's going to harass you?"

"No." I shake my head. Bradley's too busy with his fraternity and friends to spend his precious time "harassing" me. "And he lives at the Sigma Alpha Epsilon house."

"Figures," grunts Alex as he begins to pull his big body back upward. I practically have to crane my neck all the way back to see his face when he's at his full height. With his large hand, he reaches for mine, and I give it to him. My much smaller hand, literally, fits into his palm. I like how it feels. I can't seem to help doing what this guy wants. I'm drawn to him. He's so big, but not in a scary way. No, it's reassuring and safe.

"I'll walk you back to your room. Let's be sure Brad's gone."

I'm grateful he wants to go with me. I'm not ready for another confrontation with Bradley. As we walk over to the elevators, he rubs his thumb over my inner wrist, and it makes my entire body tingle. People are still milling about, watching us with curious stares, interested in the current drama, I guess. When we enter the elevator, a surprising number of people attempt to get on with us. Alex shakes his head slowly, and they stop and back away from the doors, leaving us alone in the elevator. Weird.

"What floor do you live on?" he asks.

"Four."

Alex pushes the button, the doors close, and the elevator begins the upward climb. "So, are you a junior or a senior?"

"Neither, I'm a freshman, actually."

"A freshman? How did you get a room in Shepard Hall?"

This dorm is ordinarily for upperclassman, but due to the flooding, they made exception. "I was supposed to room with my best friend, Lily, but our dorm flooded the day we were to move in. They reassigned all of us until they get the water issues worked out."

"It's probably good that it's only temporary. I doubt you'll want to continue to live with what's her name," he replies.

"Brooke. Her name is Brooke Clark, and no, I can't wait to move out of that room."

The elevator dings and the doors open to my floor. Alex

places his hand on my lower back, and it causes a shiver to run up my spine. Why does his touch feel so good? Bradley's touch never felt like this. I snort to myself, because the truth is, Bradley rarely touched me. In the short time I've known Alex, he hasn't *stopped* touching me. First it was the hand holding, then the wrist rubbing, and now the hand on my back. This guy makes me feel all kinds of sensations I'm not used to.

We reach my room, and I realize I don't have my key. Luckily, the doorknob turns easily. I take a deep breath for courage and slowly open the door, dreading what awaits me. I ease the door open and, thank goodness, the only person I see is Brooke. She's sitting on the sofa in the little lounge area.

"Stella? I'm so sorry. I had no idea." Brooke seems sincere, but I'm not basing that on anything concrete. I don't really know her.

"That's okay, Brooke." Obviously, it's not okay, but what else can I say? I'm not in the mood to talk about it. I'll never be able to unsee them together. "Everything is fine," I say with as much bravado as I can muster.

Brooke looks up and sees the man holding my hand. Yep, he's holding my hand again, doing that wrist-rubbing thing. I'm putty when he does that.

"Oh, hi," She giggles. "Aren't you Alex Emerson?" she asks, twirling a short strand of hair around her fingers.

"Yep," Alex says curtly.

"What are you doing here?" She turns to me, then back to him. "I can't believe Alex Emerson is standing at my door." She giggles again.

Ugh. I think I hate this girl.

"I'm seeing Stella home and making sure dick-face is gone," Alex mutters.

She puts her hands on her hips and nods. "Oh, he's gone all right."

"Good, glad to hear it." He turns to me. "Stella?"

"Yeah?"

"Can I talk to you in the hall for a second?"

"Sure." I walk back out into the hallway with him.

"Give me your phone." He's not asking.

"Why?"

"Well, I want you to have my number in case you need anything. Plus, I'm concerned about that guy coming back and bothering you. He seemed a little unstable, and sometimes guys get desperate. I just live two floors down, so I can be here in minutes if you need me. Okay?"

"Um, okay, thanks. But I'm sure I won't need anything. Bradley isn't the type to go overboard. I'm sure he thinks he can just talk his way out of this whole thing." And that's a true story. Bradley could schmooze his way out of anything.

"In any case, keep my number. I feel more comfortable knowing you can call me if you need help. Actually, call me if you need anything. Call me if you just feel like talking to someone who was there today. I'm a good listener."

During this entire conversation, Alex has his hand on my arm, making small movements up and down. It feels reassuring, but it also makes the little hairs on my arm stand on end. In a good way. Dang, he has magic hands.

I reach into my back pocket and retrieve my phone. Handing it to him, I say, "Thanks, Alex, I really appreciate it." I pause, watching him type on my phone. I feel like I need to say one more thing, so he knows I'm not going to bother him about any of this. It's over. Done. "I'm sure things will be fine."

"Good. Okay. Well, you have my number, call me if you need me. Have a good night. Sleep tight, Pixie."

There's no way I'm calling that guy. He's just being nice. And what the hell does he mean by 'Pixie'? I need to know. "Um, Alex?"

He turns. "Yeah?"

"Why do you keep calling me Pixie?"

"Because you're tiny, like a beautiful little fairy pixie," he says sweetly.

"I'm not tiny!" This guy is delusional.

"Yes, you are. And you're the prettiest girl I've ever seen." He winks as he says that last part and then strides off toward the stairwell.

When he's gone, I walk back into the suite where Brooke is waiting.

"How in the hell did you meet Alex Emerson?" she snaps as soon as I cross the threshold.

"I ran into him downstairs. He helped me get rid of Bradley."

"Well, aren't you a lucky girl?" she spits.

"Lucky? Seriously? I just caught my boyfriend, whom I'm supposed to be promised to, cheating with my new roommate. That's not lucky. That's terrible." I jam my hands on my hips for emphasis.

"Oh, come on. You know you'll take him back. Who else is going to date you?"

That's it. I can't stand here for one more second. I *knew* this girl was a mean girl the second I moved my boxes into my room, and I was right. I turn on my heel and storm into my room, shutting my door behind me and locking it. I need to keep the rest of the world out. I launch myself onto my bed as I try to prevent the memories of today from invading my thoughts, but it's impossible. Brooke is right, who else, besides Bradley, is ever going to date me? The truth is, I'm sad about Bradley, and I'm sad for myself. My one and only boyfriend is now history.

My phone dings to alert me to a text message. It's Lily. Oh, crap! I was supposed to meet her back in her new dorm room to hang out, but there's no way I'm going anywhere right now.

I write her back to apologize, telling her that something came up and I'm going to have to take a rain check. She doesn't seem to mind and, thankfully, doesn't press me for any details. After I finish the text, I lie down on my bed and think about tall, beautiful men. I fall asleep in minutes and dream of knights in purple T-shirts. *Alex Emerson....*

Chapter Three

ALEX

As the door to Stella's room closes, I stop to lean against the wall. "What the hell was that?" That girl took my breath away. She also made my dick hard as steel. She was, hands down, the most beautiful girl I've ever seen. Not to mention the fact that even with all of that crap happening to her, she still gave me the most amazing, dimpled smile. Her blonde hair was so shiny I wanted to touch it. Probably feels like silk. And her skin? Porcelain. She was rosy from crying but still glowed. And that body. My fingers itched wanting to touch her, everywhere. Damn, that little thing had curves—just how a woman should be. Shit, all of this imagining isn't helping my dick any. *Down, boy.* "Damn it. I feel like I've been hit by a Mack truck."

Shit. I hope no one is around to see me talking to myself like a lunatic. I've never felt like this after meeting a girl. As funny as it sounds, it sort of feels like love. Love at first sight? Is that even possible? Seeing her, feeling her little arms wrapped tightly around me, I knew she needed me. Not for my looks or my future in the NFL and all the potential fame and fortune surrounding me. She had no idea who I was. No, she just needed *me*—just a guy named Alex—to protect her.

Most of the women on campus know who I am, and they aren't shy. I can't walk across campus without chicks throwing themselves in my path. I'm not interested. My mind is on football and securing a place in next year's NFL draft. It's what I've always wanted. But meeting Stella has thrown a slight wrench into those plans.

Do I have time to pursue her? I mean, she's a freshman; plus, she just dumped her idiot boyfriend. Besides, I can tell she's special, which means getting with her would take time and patience. *Do I have that kind of time right now?* I don't know. Well, that's not true. There's no need to lie to myself. I want that little pixie. I'll just need to keep it low-key for now. The truth is, women have come so easily since I've been here, I'm a little rusty when it comes to the pursuit. Maybe some advice is in order. I decide to ask my roomie and best friend, Hank, for advice. He'll know what to do since he has to work to get a girl. I laugh to myself while thinking about teasing my roommate. Entering my suite, I yell, "Tank. You here?"

I spy him sitting on our tiny sofa doing what he does most days, playing a video game of some sort. "Fuck. Stop calling me 'Tank.' You know I hate it." He does hate it—with a passion—which is why I can't resist. "What's up? Where you been?" He looks at the clock we have hanging on the wall above our TV. "We left practice at the same time. I've been home half an hour."

"I met someone," I say, smiling from ear to ear.

At my words, he stops clicking away on his game controller. "What do you mean you met someone?"

"Let me ask you something. Keep in mind that this question may make you think I'm a pussy, but... do you believe in love at first sight?"

"Yep."

"You do?"

"No, I don't. But I do agree that the question made me think you were a pussy." He chuckles.

"Seriously, dude. Answer the question."

"Okay, let me think…. Well, it's never happened to me, of course, but I guess you could get zapped with something like serious attraction just by looking at someone. But I think love has to come with time. That's just my opinion though, Alex."

"Yeah, I guess that sounds logical. I don't know, man. I was helping this chick who was running away from her cheating, idiot of a boyfriend. Dude, he's in the Sig frat, so not a surprise there. But she ran right smack into me. She was crying and shit. Usually, I'd have stayed completely out of that scene, but she felt so good in my arms—all soft and womanly. Then, when I saw her face… Jesus, man, it felt like a punch in the gut."

Hank laughs loudly. "Well, I can't wait to meet the future Mrs. Alex Emerson."

"Be serious, Hank."

"I am. I can't wait to meet her! I wonder if she's got any friends. I wouldn't mind feeling something all soft and womanly right about now."

"Funny, dude. You keep your damn hands off this one. She's *mine*." At least for now. "Got it?"

"Got it, chief." Hank salutes me.

Smart-ass.

Chapter Four

STELLA

The second I wake up, I blink, trying to remember where I am. "Oh, right, I remember now. I'm in hell." That's when the dinging begins. Text messages. I don't even need to look at my phone to figure out who's texting. By now, Bradley will have called either Vicky, his mom, or my mom to garner support for whatever he's got planned. Sure enough, when I pick up my phone, I see there are multiple messages from all three people. That's just terrific. There's also one from Lily. *I should have called her last night.* She would have made me feel better. I was just too overwhelmed to talk to anyone.

Bradley's texts are what I imagined them to be. Things like, "Stella, call me." And "Stella, give me a chance to explain. I'll beg if I need to."

That one makes me snort, out loud. *If I need to?* "Yes, you jerk, you'd need to beg. That is if I had any inclination to take you back." Which I don't. My favorite one claimed, "Our parents are going to be devastated."

"Well, whose fault is that?" I grumble aloud.

Closing out my text messages, I see the indicator on the phone icon, which means I've got a voice message. Clicking that, I stare at my mom's name. Great. Dread fills me, but I want to get it over with, so I hit play.

"Stella, it's your mother. Please call me right away. We need to talk. What is this about you breaking up with Bradley for no reason? Are you out of your mind? You have no idea what you're doing. Who else is going to date you, Stella? I mean, you're a cute girl, but we both know you need more than a pretty face. Bradley is ambitious and driven. He'll be an excellent provider for you. Call me right away so I can talk some sense into you. Vicky is beside herself. What happened to make you do this? Did you spend one day in college and get too big for your britches? Well, we both know that's possible with you, now don't we? Get your head together, Stella. Call me. Now!"

Jeez, did the woman take a breath during that entire message? No. And did she call Bradley a "provider." Who says that? It's not the 1950s for goodness sake. I guess if being a lying, cheating snake is the kind of guy my mom wants for me, then I'm going to have to reassess Mom's taste in men because *she* is delusional.

I do my best to practice some yoga breathing exercises after that phone call. I need to calm down. So, I decide to do what I should have done last night.

Me: Hey, Lils.
Lily: Yo, Stella, what's wrong? I feel a disturbance in the Force.

Oh, Jeez, that girl is such a nerd. She must be psychic when it comes me.

Me: It's true! Bad things happened yesterday, but how did you know?

My phone dings right away.

Lily: Douchebag sent me a text telling me to talk some sense into you.

I don't even need to ask. Douchebag has always been her name for Bradley, even before yesterday.

Me: Did he happen to mention why I needed "sense talked into me"?
Lily: Nah, but he probably thought you and I had already spoken.
Me: Sorry, I wasn't in the mood to talk.
Lily: Tell me what happened. Do I need to kill me some little douchebag when I see him?
Me: Maybe.

Instead of typing it all out, I call her so I can tell her everything. Lily is my voice of reason. When everyone else in my life is completely off their rockers, she tells me what I really need to hear. Even though she never liked Bradley, she always understood what that relationship meant to me. I think she hoped that he would end up being the man I deserved. I don't bother to tell her about my knight in shining armor, Alex. He played a supporting role in the story, but I know she'd get fixated on him, which is a complete waste of time. It's not like I'm going to ever see him again.

Chapter Five

ALEX

I can't stop thinking about Stella, even though I need to be focusing on my workout. Since school doesn't start until tomorrow, the team is still required to have two-a-days, or two workouts per day. One is in the gym and consists of strength and cardio workouts. The second is on the field in full pads and gear. Our first home game is coming up this Saturday, so these practices are pretty serious and lengthy. But no matter how hard I push my body, I can't stop thinking about her. How could someone so sweet and beautiful end up with a tool like that frat guy? Granted, I don't know her at all, but from the little I gleaned from her yesterday, I can tell she's special.

The truth is, I'm worried about her. What if that guy came back? Of course, she didn't call me. I knew she wouldn't. It's like she didn't want to impose on me. She's very ladylike and feminine—gentle. My Stella was all soft and sweet. My Stella? I think I'm going half crazy. I either need to sweat her out of my system, or I've got to go for it with her. Run. That's what I'll do. I'll run my ass off for now, and then I'll check in on her after practice. Taking a deep breath, I increase the speed on the treadmill until I'm sprinting. No need to keep worrying about her and her douche of an ex. I'll see for myself that she's okay. Maybe I can talk her into going down to the dining hall with me tonight for dinner. Yeah, that's it. "I'm a freaking genius."

A guy in the weight room hears me and starts laughing. "Yeah, that's what we always say about you, Emerson. You're a fucking genius," shouts Kinley, our right tackle.

This time they all laugh.

Go ahead and laugh because I *am* smart. I'm no genius, but I have a 3.9 grade point average, and that's not from taking fluff classes like Geology 101. I'm working on my degree in Communications, and I plan to graduate on time—with honors. I need to be sure I have a backup plan in case I get hurt because I've seen what a career-ending injury can do to a guy firsthand. My dad was a great ballplayer, but he blew his knee out when he was a senior in college. He lost his chance at the NFL. He was smart, though. He finished up his construction engineering degree, and now he's got his own construction company. It all worked out for him, and I want to be sure I can land on my feet if I can't play football anymore.

The minute our workout is over, I jog back to the dorm. Unfortunately, I have to wait around for Hank to finish up his beauty routine before I can shower and shave. I don't want to frighten her with post-practice body odors. After I've showered and dressed in my nicest pair of sweats and a tee, I take the stairs up to her floor. When I reach Stella's door, I knock and wait. And wait some more. After what feels like hours, that chick, Brooke, opens the door. Her face has no expression until she gets a glimpse of me, then a fake grin slips into place. "Alex! Hi!" she squeaks. "What are you doing here? I wish I knew you were stopping by; I'm such a mess!"

"That's okay. I didn't come to see you. I came to check on Stella."

"Really? Why?" Her face scrunches up. She looks seriously perplexed.

I want to tell her it's none of her damn business, but I need to play nice with the roommate. "I wanted to see how she's doing after yesterday. She was pretty upset." Why am I explaining myself to her?

"Oh, she's fine. I'm sure she ate her feelings and she's all better. You know she'll take Bradley back. I mean, who else is going to want to date her?" she says with an evil cackle.

What a bitch. "What's that supposed to mean?"

"Well, just look at her. She's fat." She shrugs like she said something obvious.

I decide to ignore her because I'm only encouraging this girl to speak. "Can you please get Stella?"

Brooke looks dejected. "Get her yourself. There's her room."

She points over to the door closest to the bathroom. It's the same setup as our place. She's got the same room. Mine's just two floors down. As I approach, I can hear music playing softly. I knock on her door.

"Yeah?" asks Stella.

"Stella? It's me, Alex."

That's when I hear sounds of movement behind the door, things falling and furniture scraping across the concrete floors. I smile. The music stops playing, and the door opens abruptly.

"Uh, hi, Alex. What are you doing here?"

I nearly choke when I see her. She's even prettier today with her blonde hair pulled up and knotted on the top of her head. It showcases her face and rosy cheeks. She's so gorgeous, I can barely speak. "Um... well, I just came to see how you were doing and ask if you wanted to go with me to the cafeteria."

"I'm not very hungry today," she murmurs.

That's when I hear Brooke mutter from somewhere behind me, "Yeah, right."

Yep, she's a bitch. I look back over my shoulder and glare. She's eavesdropping on our conversation from the kitchenette. Stella leans her head out of her doorframe and gives Brooke a dirty look, one that matches my own. It makes me laugh. I half expect Brooke to take the hint, but she doesn't move an inch.

Choosing to ignore her nasty roommate, I turn back and look down at Stella. I'm dying to touch her, but I keep my hands to myself. For now. "I know you probably don't feel hungry because of what happened yesterday, but your body needs food. You need to nourish your body for school and everything else that's going on in your life. I'm an athlete; I know about these things," I say, smiling. "Please? Come down to the dining hall with me. I really don't like going down there by myself." I give her my most pathetic expression. It says, "Please?"

Am I begging? I guess I am. I hope it works. While I wait for her to respond, I take a good look at her again. She has beautiful blue eyes, like the Caribbean Sea. I let my eyes travel to her cute little button nose then on to her luscious lips shaped like little rosebuds and down to her full breasts. They're hidden beneath an oversized T-shirt that says, "I Paint Therefore I Am" with a picture of that sculpture of the Thinker guy holding a paintbrush. She must like art or something.

I'm broken out of my perusal by Stella saying, "Uh, well, okay. I'll go. I haven't been before, so it will be nice to go with someone who knows what to do."

Hot damn, my begging worked!

"Then I'm the man for you!" I say loudly. *Because I definitely know what to do; you just don't know it yet, Stella.* "Don't forget your Flexcard," I remind her. That's our meal card system. "If you don't have one, you can use mine." I smile down at her.

"No, I've got one."

"Of course she does," the roommate mutters. *Will she never leave?*

Ignoring her, Stella grabs her card, along with her keys from her desk while I wait at her bedroom door. When she reaches the doorway, I step back and let her go first. Out in the hallway, I point to the elevators. Walking side by side, the urge to reach down and take her hand is intense. Instead of doing that, I place my hand on her lower back. I immediately feel the touch down to my dick. This is going to be a long night. I do my best to concentrate on other things, like football, the state of the union, and what I'm going to eat for dinner. *I'd like to eat her for dinner. Crap! Stop thinking about Stella. Think about anything but the way she makes you feel.*

At the elevators, I push the down button, then smile at her. A few other people have moved closer too. "Hey, Emerson."

I turn to see a guy I recognize. He was in my English Lit class last semester. "Hey."

"You ready for Saturday?"

Seriously? He's gonna do this right now? "Uh, yeah." I mean, what else am I supposed to say? No?

"Cool."

I nod then ease in closer to Stella. Maybe he'll see I'm with my girl and leave me the hell alone.

"We gonna win?" the idiot asks.

We? Is he on the team too? "Hope so." This I say without looking at him. Instead, I stare straight at the purple set of elevator doors. When it dings, I sigh with relief—that is until we step on and Mr. Chatty steps on with us.

"You think our QB has what it takes?"

This time, I sigh, loudly. "Yep."

"Cool." The guy nods. "You going pro?"

I don't want to answer that question. I like the fact that Stella knows nothing about me. She doesn't know that I play football and that I'm a semi celebrity on campus. It's nice to hang out with someone who just knows me as plain old Alex.

When we finally reach the bottom floor, the doors open, and I let the guy out first. As soon as he's gone, she turns her head and looks up at me with big, doe eyes. "That guy was quite a chatty Cathy, wasn't he?"

I'm caught off guard by her comment, so I laugh. "He was."

"I could tell you were getting irritated."

"Nah." I shake my head. "I'm used to it."

"Still, kind of annoying."

I reach down and take her hand in mine. I'm tempted to lift it to my mouth and kiss it like they did in the old days, but instead, I gently squeeze her fingers and let it go. "It can be, but he meant well." That is until we lose, then guys like that enjoy telling me what I did wrong. It's all part of it, though.

"If you say so."

With my hand still on Stella's little back, I nudge her gently. As we exit, the small group of people waiting for the elevator move apart so we can pass through. I hear my name mentioned by a few people, but I ignore it.

Chapter Six

STELLA

I can't believe Alex came to my room to see if I was okay. Not only that, but I'm about to have dinner with him. I'm living in an alternative universe. My lower back tingles where his large hand rests. The elevator doors open, and when people see him, they part like the Red Sea. I now know he's an athlete. He must be pretty good if people treat him like he's royalty.

Before we enter the dining hall, I stop. Placing my hand on his forearm, I urge him toward the wall so I can ask, "Are you some kind of a celebrity around here or something?"

He looks down into my eyes and chuckles. "Something like that."

"Well, what is it you do here? What is your sport?"

"I play football," he says proudly.

My eyes drift down to his broad chest and shoulders. "Well, now that makes sense. What do you do on the football diamond?"

Alex laughs. "You mean field? The football field?"

"Oh, yeah, that's what I meant."

"I'm a tight end."

This makes me giggle. I'm tempted to ask him to turn

around so I can see if he's got what it takes. Instead, there's a rather lengthy silence. Am I supposed to know what a tight end does? Maybe Alex is waiting for me to comment, because he's just staring at me now. "I think I hear crickets."

Alex belts out a laugh like he's surprised I said something funny. *I can be funny.* He's got a great laugh. It makes my stomach flutter.

"Sorry, I was waiting for your next question. You know, something like, 'Alex, what is a tight end?' Then my answer would have been, 'Well, Stella, it's the hardest and best position to play on the football diamond.'" He gives me the cutest smirk, and I want to swoon. "Seriously, it's okay; I'll tell you. My position as tight end is on offense. I help protect the quarterback by blocking players from getting to him, but I also catch the ball like a wide receiver."

I blink. That's a lot of information about football in a short amount of time. I literally know nothing about football. I probably should have learned something from my dad, but I tend to tune him out when he's yelling at the television. So, I keep looking at him, nodding like I understand what the heck he's saying. It's interesting to watch because he's so animated. It's obvious that he's passionate about his sport. Not to mention the fact that he's easy on the eyes. I could probably look at him forever and never get tired of the view. Deciding to admit my lack of football knowledge, I say, "Well, it's a little confusing. I guess I'll have to google it. Or do they have *Football for Idiots* available at the bookstore?"

"I think there's an app for it." He laughs. His voice is rich and deep. His laugh is even better.

Entering the cafeteria, it happens again. Students part to let Alex pass. I'm staying close since I've no idea how any of this works. I look away from Alex to take in the famous cafeteria. Holy crap, it's packed with people, and it's huge. There must be fifty tables in the place, all various sizes. I'm not surprised when I notice all eyes have turned to look at Alex and, unfortunately, at me. It makes me feel self-conscious right away. My legs feel wobbly, and sweat appears on my forehead. He reaches down and takes my hand in his, making a sense of calm fall over me. How did he know?

His hand is warm and callused, probably from football, but I like it. It makes him real. He leads me to the entrance to all the different food areas. He explains how it's set up. "It's arranged by food groups, like soup and salad, main dishes, side dishes, then desserts, and so on."

I nod as I leave his side to look around at all of my choices. Everything smells delicious, and there's so many choices. On a normal day, I'd probably want one of everything, but honestly, I'm not that hungry. I wasn't making that up. I guess a breakup does that to you. Maybe I'll lose some weight over all of this. That'd sure make my mom happy.

Not only that, I'm not excited about eating in front of Alex. I mean, I know he can tell that I like to eat, but I don't want him to actually *see* me doing it. So, my solution to that is to only get a salad. I take a small plate and place a few carrots, some green peppers, and some chopped lettuce on it without dressing. Mom would be appalled if I used anything besides lemon juice on my salad anyway. Damn, she's over an hour away and I can still hear her diet advice. Next I check out the soup station. Nope, it has the potential to be too messy, and I don't want to make any strange slurping sounds and draw unwanted attention to myself. I guess it's too late for that since I've got a guy the size of the Hulk next to me.

Leaning over me, Alex grumbles as he points to my plate. "What the hell is that?"

I look up at him, startled. "What do you mean?"

"Are you a vegetarian or something?"

"No. Why?"

"Well, you need to eat more than rabbit food."

"I told you I'm not very hungry," I whisper, feeling embarrassed. I take the opportunity to look at his tray. It's heaping with food from every station. It appears he's grabbed one of everything. Wow! What would that be like, to be able to eat anything you wanted? A girl can dream, can't she? It doesn't hurt that he probably burns about 10,000 calories at football practice every night.

"Well, if you aren't going to eat much, make what you eat count. Come on, there's pizza over here. If you get one with vegetables on it, you've covered most of the food groups." He smirks.

"Alex, I don't want pizza. It's not good for me. Do you know how many calories are in a slice of pizza?"

"Yeah, I do."

I don't want to stand here arguing with him. People are still watching. I place the pizza slice on my plate. Next Alex shows me where the ice cream machines are.

"I'm not getting both pizza and ice cream!"

"Why not?"

"Well, do you know how many calories—"

"Yes, I know the calorie count, but ice cream will make you feel better. It's a scientific fact that if you eat ice cream when you're sad, the sadness disappears. It's true. I'm talking science here." He's giving me that toothy grin I'm starting to crave. "Besides, I won't take no for an answer; I'm getting you ice cream. Stop arguing with me. I'm Alex Emerson, star tight end of the Northwestern Wildcats. Don't you know who I am?"

That makes me giggle.

Alex laughs too. "I'm just teasing. I know you don't know who I am. Just do this for me this once so I can believe I made you feel better. Ice cream can cure anything, I swear."

Reluctantly, I agree to the ice cream. I choose chocolate, which seems to be Alex's favorite too. He tries to talk me into some candy bar toppings and hot fudge, but I only want the ice cream. "Thank you, Alex."

"For what?"

"For bringing me to the cafeteria and showing me how to navigate all of this. I was nervous thinking about coming down here alone."

"My pleasure. I'm glad I could help." And I believe he means it. "We should make this an every night kind of thing. I can stop by and get you after I get back from practice, and we can come to dinner together. How does that sound?"

"Oh, you don't have to do that. It would be putting you out. I wouldn't want to impose."

"No imposition. I like you, Stella Matthews. You're funny."

Oh. Right. Of course. I know what it means when a boy says "You're funny." I've heard it *many* times before. I'm the funny fat chick—every guy's dream friend. I'm the entertainment while the thin girls get all the good stuff. It figures. I knew he didn't really see anything in me. Why would he? I try to shake off the bad thoughts. Instead, I ask, "Hey, how did you know my last name?"

"I have my ways." He winks. "Okay, it's settled. You're my dinner date from now on. Now follow me, Miss Matthews, I'll show you to your seat." He raises his arm and bends at the waist like Prince Charming. I laugh as he grabs my tray and starts to walk. I'm relieved he's carrying my tray. People like to look at my plate when I'm out to eat. I guess they want to know what *not* to do.

He stops moving in front of a gigantic rectangular table. It's not just large; it's humongous. It looks like they put about three of those eight-foot tables together to make it big enough to house twenty people comfortably. "Here we are." He turns and steps back so I can take my seat. As I look around, I see a group of men—none of whom are average. They're all huge— really huge. I know my eyes must be bulging out of my head because I hear a couple of the guys chuckle. "Guys, this is Stella. Stella, these are the guys."

A few of them say, "Hey." The rest merely grunt.

I raise my hand slightly in a weak little wave and squeak, "Uh, hi."

"Okay, you sit here, and I'll get this jackass over here to move so I can sit next to you."

The guy in Alex's seat just grumbles and rolls his eyes, but he gets up, picking up his tray as he goes, saying, "I was done anyway, you tool."

Alex laughs. Feeling my legs shake with nerves again, I quickly sit down. Alex places my tray in front of me, and I pick up a fork and start to move lettuce leaves around my plate to make it look like I'm eating. Glancing around the table, I count about twelve football players and four girls at the table. I look at each of the girls one by one and smile. A couple of them smile back, but the other two give me nasty looks. *What did I do to deserve that?*

Just then I'm startled back to reality when a deep voice says, "So, how did Alex get so lucky to get you to have dinner with him?"

Lifting my head slowly, I see a blond guy, who is even bigger than Alex, staring at me. He winks at me with pretty gray eyes. He looks kind of like a big Viking—a Viking that's had his nose broken a time or two, but he's still very good-looking. His best feature is definitely his boyish smile. I bet he gets away with all sorts of things when he smiles.

"Um, I don't know," I say, blinking quickly.

"I'm Hank, by the way." He reaches his huge hand across the large table. His arm is so big and so long that he can almost reach from one side of the table to the other without leaning. I raise mine to meet his hand and find it is swallowed up in his massive paw. This is about the only time in my life that I've felt small—being at this table with these football players.

"It's nice to meet you, Hank." I smile back at him.

He grins, but he won't let go of my hand.

Just then Alex clears his throat. "That's enough, Tank. Hands off."

Hank smiles and winks at me again. "I meant nothing by it. I just wanted your girl to meet your best friend and roommate. I'm assuming I'll be seeing more of her...."

His girl? What the heck does that mean? "I thought your name was Hank?"

There's a collective laugh around the table.

"It is," another huge guy responds, "but we call him Hank the Tank because he's as big as one. He hates it, so that's why we keep using it. You know, to piss him off." More laughs from the guys.

"Oh, I see." I pick my fork back up and continue playing with my salad.

Alex leans over to whisper in my ear, "Didn't your mother ever tell you not to play with your food?"

Great. He had to bring up my mother? I know he has no idea what he's just said, but I've lost whatever appetite I may have had. I set my fork down. I try not to look upset, but it's hard holding back my grimace. I think Alex can tell he said the wrong thing because he quickly changes gears and says, "You haven't tried your ice cream. You'd better eat it before it melts."

I sigh and pick up the small bowl and dip into the melting chocolate ice cream. I taste the cold, creamy goodness and say, "Mmmm, it is good, Alex." When I look at him, his eyes are on my spoon, then my mouth. He has a funny look on his face. Is he breathing hard? "Alex? Are you okay?"

"Uh, yeah? Yep, your ice cream, it looks good. It looks really good," he says, nodding. He squeezes his eyes closed tightly before turning back to his plate to eat his pile of food while I finish my ice cream.

"So, is our football team any good?" I ask the group. That's when I hear a few laughs and a gasp or two, and see some people giving me blank stares. "What? I don't know anything about football."

A rather slim guy, at least compared to everyone else, sitting next to Hank replies, "Uh, yeah! We went to the Sugar Bowl last year. Have you heard of the Sugar Bowl, sweetheart?"

Another guy interjects, "And the year before that, we were the Big 10 Champions. Have you heard of the Big 10?"

I wait to reply because, in fact, I have no clue what a Sugar Bowl is. "Of course!" I sound so sure of myself. "Which one of you is the best player?" I ask to change the subject.

More laughter erupts. I'm so glad I'm the entertainment tonight.

Then Hank says, "It's all right, Stella. It's refreshing to meet a girl who isn't after Alex for his future NFL earnings."

"I'm not after Alex!" The heat of my blush rushes to my cheeks. Dropping my spoon, I push away from the table.

Now the laughs have turned into cackles and even a couple knee slaps.

"I'm not. He's just a friend." Tears start to burn right behind my eyes. This is not what I need right now, people thinking I'm after Alex. He must be so embarrassed. When I turn to him, concern lines his face. Oh no! This is too much right now. I whisper, "Alex, I'm so sorry. I didn't mean to embarrass you. I didn't mean to make you think I was after you."

I JUMP up from my seat as quickly as possible, grab my tray, then drop it back down. I don't know what to do with it. I dart out of the cafeteria, not daring to glance back, and head to the elevators, but then I think better of it. If I take the stairs, I can get back to my room much faster. I hope I've gotten enough distance between Alex and me. I just want to get to my room, shut my door, and put on some music. Music soothes me, and I'm in desperate need of comfort right now. Gah! This is ridiculous. I'm a frigging happy person normally. Is this what college is going to be like? Maybe I should find Lily. Then I'd have a friend with me at least. Things have got to be better tomorrow. They've just got to be. When I reach my floor and turn the corner to my hallway, Alex is leaning against my door. I'm sweating and panting from all the flights of stairs while he looks like it took him three strides to get here. Unfair.

When I reach my door, Alex asks, "What's going on, Pixie?"

"Nothing." I stare up at him and release a lungful of air. "I don't know." I shake my head, my fingers gripping the doorknob. "Everything has been so overwhelming, and I've only been here three days. Plus, I didn't mean to embarrass you down there, Alex."

"Why would you think you embarrassed me? The guys should be embarrassed. They made you feel bad. Don't worry, I'll kick their asses at practice tomorrow."

"No, don't do that! I know you must be embarrassed to have them think that I'm after you. You know, for your money and body and stuff."

"Why would you think I'd be embarrassed by that, Stella? I rather like the idea that you'd be after me for my body." He gives me another glimpse of his perfect smile.

"Well, just look at me!" I exclaim.

"Oh, I've been looking at you," Alex says as he looks at my face, then my chest, then back at my face.

"I'm definitely not your type, Alex."

"And what type is that, Pixie?"

"Stop calling me Pixie. I'm not little!" I say, frustrated.

"Yes, you are."

"I'm short, but I'm definitely not little."

"Stella, I could pick you up with one hand."

"No, you couldn't. Plus, you'd get hurt if you tried. I weigh a lot." But he isn't listening anymore. Nope, he's wrapping his huge, muscled arm around my waist. He then lifts me off the ground like I'm a small child. He's lifted me just high enough so we're face-to-face, inches apart. I'm not sure what to do with my legs because right now they're just dangling, so I wrap them around his waist.

"See, I told you I could lift you with one hand."

He moves my body back until it's up against the wall. "Please put me down, Alex. You're going to get injured!"

Alex doesn't listen; instead, he uses his other arm to wrap around me, pulling me even closer.

"What are you doing, Alex?"

"Well, Pixie, I'm about to kiss you. What do you think about that?"

I don't have any words after that, and apparently, neither does he because his lips brush against mine in a gentle, sweet kiss. My body comes alive in his arms just from that little kiss. I wrap my arms around his neck and lean into him. I turn my head to get a better taste of his full lips and nip at his bottom one, which produces a sexy moan from him.

Where did I learn to do that? I've only ever kissed Bradley, and his kisses more closely resembled a grandpa kiss.

When Alex's tongue slides into my mouth, my first instinct is to pull back, but I quickly change course and meet my tongue with his. He swirls his around in my mouth, and I feel a connection so deep, so powerful my entire body tingles. I press my center into him to feel some relief down there. His big palm slides down and passes over my butt, squeezing gently. Wow. I think I get it now. I see what all the fuss is about.

Just then, the door to my dorm opens abruptly. "Stella!

What are you doing?" Bradley practically screams. "Put her down! That's my girlfriend you're kissing!"

Slowly, Alex loosens his hold on me to enable me to slide down, but it's like slow motion. In the process, I feel every single one of his hard muscles against my soft ones. My nipples harden to the point that I know that he knows. Alex winks at me, and I'm mortified. Please kill me right now. After my feet are solidly on the ground, I turn toward Bradley and say confidently, "I'm not your girlfriend, Bradley, *and* I'm not talking to you right now."

Brooke peeks her head out of the doorway, but her expression only reads bored—well, bored and pissed, so that's something. I'm the one who should be angry. Why did she let Bradley back into our dorm? I suspect the answer to that is because she clearly likes to stir the pot.

"Come on, Stella, you know it was just a misunderstanding. We need to talk. Our parents want us to work this out. Your mom is heartbroken and very upset with you right now."

"Upset with *me*? Do they know what you did?" I ask defiantly.

"Not exactly. They just know that you broke up with me and that you're being unreasonable."

"What the fu—" Apparently, Alex is just as shocked at his words as I am.

"That's ridiculous. Please leave, Bradley." I take a deep breath, tired from all the drama. Alex places a comforting hand on my lower back and slides his palm around to my front, gently guiding me back into his chest so that I'm in a cocoon of protectiveness.

"What the hell is going on between you two, Stella? Doesn't he know you already have a boyfriend?" Bradley demands.

"I don't think it's any of your business, and frankly, you lost the right to call Stella your girlfriend when you screwed around on her."

"Seriously, dude, what the fuck? You need to keep your damn nose out of our business." Bradley is flailing his arms around like a crazy person.

He's gone off the deep end. I decide to try to defuse the situation. "Alex, maybe you should go now." I don't want him to see this crap again today. It was embarrassing enough yesterday.

"I'll leave when this dick leaves. I want to be sure you're okay."

Bradley grunts and looks first at me, then at Brooke. Her bored expression is long gone. Now, there's murder in her eyes. The question is, who's the target?

"Bradley, you need to go. When I'm ready, I'll call you. But we aren't getting back together. Not that we were ever really together. At least not like you were with her." I use my thumb to point at Brooke.

Bradley looks shamefaced. He should. I walk past him and around Brooke to get into the dorm. When I turn to go into the sitting area, I nearly run into Alex. "I'll go, but I'm taking him with me." He's pointing right at Bradley.

I touch Alex's arm. "Thank you."

With a nod, Alex turns to Bradley. "Come on, Brad. Let's get out of here."

"Oh, come on, Stella! What are you doing? He's using you. He knows you're vulnerable right now."

I've had about enough of Bradley. Enough for a lifetime. "This is none of your business, Bradley, and besides, Alex is just being a friend."

"It didn't look like he was just a friend out in the hallway," sputters Bradley.

"Well, he is, and it's none of your concern. It's time for you to go, Bradley. Alex wants to walk you out apparently."

"I don't need that dumb jock to walk me anywhere. This isn't over between us, Stella!" he bellows as he heads out the door toward the elevators.

"Are you gonna be okay?" Alex asks quietly.

I sigh. "I'll be okay. Thanks for helping, again. I bet you're getting tired of saving the stupid damsel, huh?"

"I'm not tired of anything about you, Stella. I'm not sure I'll ever get tired."

I let out a small gasp because, well, that was so sweet.

"Will you send me a text so I've got your number?"

"Sure."

"Promise? Will you do it as soon as we go?"

I don't know why he needs it, but I'm not going to argue with him right now. I want Bradley out of here. "Yes. Promise."

"Then, I'll text you later." As I walk him to the door, he leans down and gives me a light kiss on my cheek. "Talk to you soon, Pixie," he whispers in my ear.

"Night, Alex."

As he leaves, I shut the door and turn around to face Brooke. She's glaring at me. What's new? I cross my arms and wait. I know something is coming.

"What?"

"Oh, I don't know. I'm at a complete loss. Has something happened to the space-time continuum? I just can't figure out how you have two guys fighting over you. You!" she scoffs. "You're fat!"

In my experience, girls like Brooke are predictable. All they have going for them are insults and hurtful remarks. "I don't know what you're talking about. I don't have anyone fighting over me. Well, Bradley is hanging on to something, but I don't know why. What I don't get, Brooke, is why you're still hanging out with Bradley."

"I'm not hanging out with him," she snipes. "I just don't

care enough about any of this to give a damn about him or about you. It's perplexing that he's trying so hard to win you back. I mean, did you even question why a guy like Bradley wanted to date you? It didn't cause any alarm bells to go off in that fat head of yours? You can't possibly believe that someone of Bradley's caliber really wants to be seen with you." Her scowl turns into something much more sinister. "I'll tell you why he was with you. It's because you're his ticket to getting a job at your dad's law firm. Not to mention, you're going to make it super easy for him to make partner in record time."

I've thought about our relationship a lot in the last twenty-four hours. He used to do everything he could to avoid being seen with me, except around our parents. I had already figured out that he thought marrying me would get him a job, but I hadn't gotten to the partnership part of the equation just yet. It all fits, though.

But Brooke isn't finished. "The truth is, Stella, you disgust him. He told me he was dreading the time when he was going to have to see you naked and have sex with you."

Okay, that hurts. A lot. Deep down I know that guys aren't attracted to me, but I thought Bradley was the exception, that he really cared about me and loved me. He knows how insecure I am. I figured he was sensitive to my feelings.

My thoughts are interrupted when she says, "I don't know what game Alex Emerson is playing with you, though. but believe me when I say, you are not his type either." She's silent for several seconds. I'm not sure what's she waiting for. "Well, aren't you going to say anything, or are you just going to go into your room and eat your feelings? That's what you do, right? Eat your feelings?" She snorts, and it's as unattractive as her personality. "You must have a lot of feelings."

In a surprising twist, Brooke's offensive words don't make me cry. Nope, they make me angry. I want to tell her to go fuck herself, but that's not the way I was raised. Instead of engaging with her anymore, I walk toward my bedroom, but before I enter, I turn to Brooke. "You know, I don't understand why you're so angry and hateful and why that hate is directed at me specifically. I can't imagine what made you the person you are right now. Were you abused psychologically? Beaten? Abandoned on the side of the road as a child? Raised by wolves? I just don't get it."

I don't know anything about Brooke, but I suspect that her life was not filled with tragic moments but with a lot of overindulgence by her parents. Brooke is a bully, a mean girl, and a bitch. There's nothing I could ever say to change her now. "The thing is, Brooke, I don't care enough to try to figure you out. That ship has sailed. I just plan on avoiding you from now on, and I hope you can do the same for me. I've only got to live here a month, thank goodness. While I'm here, I plan to spend that time focusing on other things—not on you." I don't wait for a response. I just walk into my room and shut the door. Leaning against the door, I sigh with relief. Living with that woman is so dang stressful. No matter how much bluster I show, the truth is I'm not up for dealing with her for a month.

That's when I hear her yell, "Fuck you!"

Nice. *Real nice.*

I collapse onto my bed. It's been one awful day—no, it's been two terrible days. Tomorrow *has* to be better. That's my new mantra. Tomorrow will be better! Pulling my phone out of my pocket, I stare at it. Then I hear Alex's voice in my head. *Promise me you'll text me.*

"Shoot." Before I overthink it, I search my contacts for his name. I laugh when I see what he used for his contact name. "Alex Emerson, Football God." He'd put his number in my phone yesterday, and this will be the first and probably only time I'll bother him.

Me: Hi Alex Emerson, Football God. This is Stella Matthews, average girl.

Yeah, sounds lame, I know.

Next, I decide the only thing that will actually make me feel better about all of this is talking to my best friend. It's strange, we only live across campus from one another, but it feels like miles. In my contacts, I press Lily's name. When she picks up, I start talking, and I don't stop until I get to the last thing Brooke said to me as I shut my door.

"Holy shit, Stella. Poor baby. I can't believe the crap that's been going on over there. My life is boring compared to your drama."

"I wish my life were boring. Trade ya."

"I'd trade you on some of that but not all of it. Bradley is a grade-A asshat. You know I've always felt that way about him."

Lily has known Bradley as long as I have, and she's always thought he was a self-serving whiner. She doesn't restrict her censure to just Bradley though. She has extended it to include his entire Northwestern University Sigma Alpha Epsilon fraternity. According to Lily, ΣAE is the douchiest frat on the planet. Seriously, if you google "douchiest frat," Sigma Alpha Epsilon was listed number one by *Rolling Stone* magazine. No joke.

"I know. I… well, I was just hopeful. You know I'm a dreamer. I prefer to see the good in everyone until they show me otherwise."

"I think you've seen otherwise from both Bradley and Brooke. She sounds like Satan."

"She is. She's a beautiful Satan."

"She may be attractive, but no way is she beautiful. Beauty comes from within. I know it sounds cliché, but I believe it wholeheartedly. My grandma used to say that to me as she tried to untangle my wild, red curls. I'd be crying because it hurt so much and spewing how I didn't care if it was beautiful or not. She'd remind me that it had nothing to do with my hair and everything to do with my soul. Your roommate has a black soul. I can tell without ever meeting her."

Lily is beautiful though, her hair especially. It's a vibrant auburn that lights up like fire when the sun hits it just right. Not only that, she's got a head full of curls that people pay huge sums of money for at the salon. They aren't tight little curls, they aren't big waves; they're the perfect mix of both. The curls flow halfway down her back when she lets them free. But most of the time, she's either got it in two braids or up in a tangled bun on the top of her head.

Lily's nearly the exact opposite of me. She's tall and lean, and I'm short and fat. She's five foot eight inches, and I barely reach five foot three. She's got no boobs or ass to get in the way of life or fashion, and I'm pretty much all boobs and ass. Honestly, I'd kill for her bod. Of course, she's adorable. She almost exclusively wears black, she's outspoken and loyal, and I'm so, so lucky to have her as my best friend. "So, all of a sudden you're some sort of clairvoyant?" I ask.

"Yeeessss, my lovely. And I see your future so cleeaarrllly," she says with a wavy, ghostly voice.

"I'm pretty sure clairvoyants don't sound like ghosts, dork."

"Thiiissss one does. I see your fuuuuttture, my beautiful Stella, and it's got a big, strong athlete in it."

Lily has always been able to make me giggle. "Stop. You know nothing. If you want to predict anything, predict whether or not I'm going to oversleep tomorrow. I need to hit the hay, doll. I'm beat."

"Fine. Whatevs. Go to bed like a loser," she says with a giggle of her own. "See you tomorrow in Life Painting. Ooh, maybe you'll finally get to see a peen in real life." She giggles some more.

I hang up on her after that comment. Peen? What's a peen? Oh, wait… I think I know.

After pulling myself up from my bed, I pack my bag for my first day of college—after all, that's why I'm here, right? I need to focus on school—and prepare for bed. Just as I'm finishing up, I hear my phone beep. Ugh, I hope that's not a text from Bradley. I can't take much more of that.

Alex Emerson, Football God: Hey, just wanted to check on you, Pixie.
Stella: Wait, is this Football God?

Yes, I'm teasing him.

Alex Emerson, Football God: Who else calls you Pixie? Tell me and I'll kick their ass.
Stella: You sure are in the mood to do some ass-kicking today, aren't you?
Alex Emerson, Football God: When it comes to you, Pixie, I'd slay dragons.

Oh, that's sweet.

Stella: That's sweet. Maybe I should come up with a nickname for you too?
Alex Emerson, Football God: Better than Football God?
Stella: Well, that one is hard to top, but since you seem to be my knight in shining armor, how about Sir Lancelot? I could just call you Lance for short.
Alex Emerson, Football God: No thanks, I know a guy named Lance from high school, and he's a real tool.
Alex Emerson, Football God: How 'bout Adonis?
Stella: LOL
Alex Emerson, Football God: LOL? Really? You don't see me as Adonis?
Stella: Can I call you Donnie then?

Alex Emerson, Football God: Sigh. Never mind. We can keep working on it.
Stella: No, I really LOVE Donnie!
Alex Emerson, Football God: Funny. Wait, if you LOVE Donnie....
Stella: ;)
Alex Emerson, Football God: Did you just wink at me, Pixie?
Stella: Maybe
Alex Emerson, Football God: I like it. You can wink at me anytime ;)

Wow, it feels like he's flirting with me.

Stella: Well, I need to get to sleep. Big day in Stella-land tomorrow.
Alex Emerson, Football God: Stella-land, huh? I'd like to live in Stella-land.

Hmmm. What does he mean by that?

Stella: Sleep well, Donnie!
Alex Emerson, Football God: Sweet dreams, beautiful Stella.

What is going on here with Alex Emerson? What's his story? I should google him and the football team. And I will. First thing tomorrow. Before going to bed, I change Alex's contact information from "Alex Emerson, Football God" to "Donnie." As I drift off to sleep, my mind wanders back to that kiss. Wow. That kiss. Kissing Alex Emerson was a life-altering moment. I mean, who knew French kissing was so amazing? Oh, right, everyone. Everyone except Bradley.

Chapter Seven

STELLA

I wake up excited to start my first day of college. Peering at my phone, I see several texts. It's pretty early for people to text, but I see one from Mom and one from Bradley. Ugh!

Mom: We need to talk!

I'm not going to deal with that one right now.

Bradley: When can we talk?

Nope, never if I can help it. And then the phone beeps. It's a text from Alex.

Donnie: Have a great first day of class, sweet Pixie. I'll pick you up for dinner at 5:30. Be ready! And don't start thinking of excuses why you can't eat in the cafeteria with me.

None of the guys meant anything. Plus, The Adonis has dealt with them!

Stella: "The" Adonis, huh?

Donnie: That is correct, milady.

Stella: If you say so.

Donnie: You don't seem impressed. What does a guy have to do to impress Stella Matthews?

Stella: Honestly? Just be kind, sincere, and trustworthy.

Donnie: Check, check, and check. I'm set.

Stella: Gotta go get ready. Don't want to be late for my first day of college!

Donnie: I'll pick you up at 5:30.

Stella: Um, I'm not sure.

Donnie: I told you, Pixie, I've kicked the guys' asses. They'll be on their best behavior.

Stella: OK, I guess. C u then. Have a great day!

Donnie: You too -- have a great first day, beautiful Stella.

It's funny, neither my mom nor Bradley wished me luck today. Alex is so sweet. What is he really doing talking to me? Someone that good-looking, that built, that popular, who has so many exciting things happening in his future should want nothing to do with the likes of me. I need to remember that he's just a friend. I do *not* want to lose my head over Alex Emerson—no matter how tight his end is. I'll do my best to forget his little kiss last night though. I know he was just trying to make me feel better. I need to get advice from Lily. She'll be able to put things into perspective for me. We have class together later today. I'll do it then.

Enough of the daydreaming, it's time to get ready for the first day of the rest of my life. I shower and do what I can to my wavy hair. I dab on some lip gloss and mascara and put my dad's old Nirvana T-shirt on. Yeah, he used to be cool. I decide on a pair of cutoff jean shorts. I also choose my yellow

Converse low tops. I'm going for comfy casual, so I can blend into the crowd. The last thing I want to do is draw attention to myself, and looking like a typical Freshmen is definitely a no-no.

My first class, psychology, starts at nine thirty. I had a similar course in high school, so it shouldn't be too difficult. My second class, the one I'm the most excited for, is Life Painting. It runs from noon until three. Most classes last about an hour and a half, but studio art classes run twice as long. It's a good thing, because once you get all of your paints out and start working, you don't want to stop.

I'm a little nervous about the "life" part of this class because we'll be painting people in the nude—as in real, naked people. I'm not sure how I feel about painting someone's you-know-what. I must remember I'm a grown-up now and an artist. I can do it. While we will paint both women and men, I'm most nervous about the men. I haven't actually seen a guy naked before—the internet doesn't count. My artist's heart tells me it's important to learn how to draw and paint both sexes in the correct proportions. I feel my face flush just imagining the classroom and a nude male model. I know! Maybe I can find a way to draw the male models from the back.

All of my other classes meet on Monday, Wednesday, and Friday. Those include English Composition, Introduction to Business, and Geology 101. They call geology "rocks for jocks" because it's supposed to be easy enough for the college athletes to pass. I hope they're right because I know absolutely nothing about rocks.

After my first class, I have some time to spare before Life Painting, so I take a long stroll through campus to people watch. I brought a sack lunch since going to the cafeteria this morning was not an option. It's still very intimidating down there. I pull out a granola bar to munch on as I walk.

Around me, I see a few familiar faces from my first class

and the dorm. When I turn a corner to make my way to the Art and Design building, I see Alex across a large grassy area. He can't see me though. He's standing with some other big guys and a few girls, really beautiful girls. That's not a surprise. A couple of them are clinging to Alex like Velcro. One of the girls goes up on tiptoes to whisper something into his ear, but he makes no move to bend closer. I can't decide if I feel relieved by that or not. I shouldn't feel anything. He's out of my league. I see one of the girls laughing with her head thrown back, and Alex has a smile on his face, but he's not looking at her. Nope. He's looking right at me. I hope he didn't see me staring. He smiles the best smile ever and waves at me. His wave is animated, like he's really happy to be doing it. I smile and wave back, then turn and head to art class.

Art class. If I had my choice, I'd be an art major. I love to draw and paint. It's something I could see myself doing every day for the rest of my life, painting especially. When I paint, I feel the weight of the world lift right off my shoulders. I get so immersed in the work I forget my troubles. It's not only that. I feel like I *need* to create. The problem is, my parents don't see it that way. My dad wanted me to go pre-law, but that's not me. Since I said no to law, my mom decided my major would be business, that way I could choose to work for a company doing whatever business majors do or I could start my own business—a little shop or something. Ugh, I hate the idea of doing either of those things unless the little shop is an art gallery. It's no use arguing with Mom, though, so I submitted and listed my major as business. Choosing my battles is the key to surviving life with my mom.

As I approach the best building on campus, the Art and Design building, I see the one person I'm trying to avoid. It's going to be impossible though. I just need to deal with him. "What are you doing here and how did you know I was going to be here, Bradley?"

"You showed me your schedule like twenty times this summer, remember?"

That's right, I did. I was so excited about everything. I probably drove him crazy repeating all of the details. "Whatever. What are you doing here?"

"I wanted a chance to talk to you without King Kong interrupting."

"King Kong?"

"Yeah, that huge guy. Anyway, I think you should come home with me this weekend so we can sit down with our parents and talk about all of this."

"Why is this any of their business? I don't want to sit down with your mom and my parents and discuss my love life, or lack thereof."

"You know why it's their business. They want us to be together. They want us to get married. They're never going to accept that you broke up with me."

"Bradley, I think you ruined any chance of us ever getting back together, don't you?"

"I told you, Stella, it was a mistake, a one-time thing, and not what you think it was about."

How does he know what I thought? I didn't confide anything in him, nor will I. "I've got to go, Bradley; I'm going to be late for my class." I turn to leave and start to move away, but a hand grabs my arm roughly and yanks.

"Just wait one damn minute, Stella. You owe me the opportunity to talk about this."

"Ouch, you're hurting my arm, Bradley."

Just then, a huge shadow falls on Bradley's face.

"Let go of her arm!" growls Hank, Alex's roommate. "Stella, is this guy bothering you?"

"She's my girlfriend. This is between us, asshole," barks Bradley.

"I don't think so, little man," chides Hank.

"Little man? I'll have you know that I'm the president of ΣAE," spits Bradley.

"Hank, it's okay," I say, hoping it calms Bradley down.

"The hell it is, Stella," Hank protests. "Dude, you have one second to get your hands off her before I pound your sorry ass into the ground."

"I was just trying to get Stella to listen to reason." Bradley is practically whimpering.

"You don't get a girl to listen to you using force, fucker." Hanks voice has gotten so deep and ominous I'm a little scared. For Bradley.

Releasing my arm, Bradley takes a step back from both me and Hank, sputtering, "I-I wasn't forcing her to do anything. I was just trying to get her to stop walking away from me so she'd listen. But I'll leave. For now." Hank growls again as Bradley backs away, but he can't seem to stop himself from saying, "Jesus, how did you get mixed up with these asshole jocks anyway?"

Hank steps closer to Bradley with fists clenched.

Raising his hands up like he's getting robbed, he takes a step backwards. "I'm going. I'm going." Jogging away, Bradley shouts the rest, "Stella, this conversation isn't over."

"Stella, what the hell was going on there?"

"That was my ex. I caught him with my new roommate the second day I was here, and he's trying to tell me that I misunderstood the situation."

A chuckle erupts from Hank. "Well, I hope you stay the hell away from him. He's bad news. I don't like that he had his hands on you, and Alex is going to burst a blood vessel when he hears about this."

"Why would Alex care?" Seriously, why would he care?

"Oh, giiiirrrlll... you are clueless, aren't you?"

"No, I'm not clueless. I'm actually quite intelligent."

"I'm sure you're smart as a whip, but this thing with Alex

will all become clear to you very soon. It will be illuminating for you."

"Whatever. What are you doing here anyway? This is the art building."

"What? I can't be artsy-fartsy?" defends Hank.

"I didn't say that. It just surprises me to see you here."

"Well, I'll have you know that my mom is an artist and she instilled in me a great love of the arts," he says with a flamboyant hand gesture. "So, I volunteer to model for a professor friend of my mom's. Some of the professors have to pay for models out of their own pockets, so this is my way of helping out. I do it for free, hence the volunteering. It's a great way to share what God gave me with the art world. I mean, have you looked at me?"

I giggle. But then my jaw drops. "Wait, which class are you going to model for this term?" *Please don't say Life Painting, please don't say Life Painting.*

"Life Painting."

"Oh? Really?" Aw, crap! I'm going to see Hank naked? "I'm taking that class this semester."

"Well, it's your lucky semester, little Stella. You'll get to see me in all of my naked glory." Leaning a little closer, he whispers but it's loud and sounds sort of conspiratorial. "You'll thank me later."

"Uh-huh." I chuckle as I do my best to not picture Hank naked. He's ginormous. I think he may be bigger than Alex. Alex is taller, but Hank is definitely broader. He's got sandy blond hair is cut short, almost in a military style. He's got at least one tattoo running down his right arm that looks like it's made up of thick, dark, vine-like lines. He's handsome in an angular kind of way with his strong jaw and nose and high cheekbones. His lips are full, and his eyes are gray and kind. Yep, I like him. I just don't want to see his you-know-what.

"On second thought, Alex probably won't like that you're

going to see all of this." Hank gestures up and down his body. "But he's going to have to deal." He winks at me again.

"Okay, well, on that note… I need to get going. I'm going to be late for my favorite class."

Hank quickly moves next to me so we're walking side by side. "Is it your favorite because you know you'll see me naked?"

I roll my eyes, but I'm laughing inside. This guy is funny. Picking up my pace, I walk as fast as I can to class. I hope I get a seat next to Lily and far away from Hank. Lily will enjoy hearing about all of this, and I'm positive she'll enjoy having a naked football player to paint. By the time I get to the Life Painting classroom, I'm late. Everyone in class turns to see me walking in, followed by Hank. I search quickly for Lily and spot her across the room. She waves and points down. She's saved me a place, thank goodness. We hug and settle in for class.

"So, two questions: one, why were you late? And two, did it have anything to do with that hunka-hunka man with you?" Lily raises her eyebrows up and down like a dork.

"That's Hank. He lives in my dorm. He's going to be our model in this class. Naked. Nude. Sans clothing," I explain.

"Sweeeeet!" Lily squeals.

"That's okay for *you*." I groan. "You don't have to see him every day."

"Oh, I wish I did. *Daaayum!* That man is hot, hot, hot. So, why were you late?"

I explain that Bradley was lying in wait for me—that he wants me to go home this weekend to talk with our parents about our breakup.

"Oh, damn, girl! When will he leave you alone? He must be desperate. What's his deal anyway?" Lily asks.

"No idea."

Just then, a tiny woman in an apron covered in paint splatters moves to the middle of the room and clears her throat.

"Well, well, well, isn't this a great class! Welcome to Life Painting, everyone!" she says with a smile. "This is going to be a great semester. You will learn so much about the human body, proportions, and composition. Don't worry if you haven't painted the figure before; that's why you're here now, isn't it? Now, let me introduce our first model for the year. Come on up, Hank. I lean forward and pull my body up so I can see above the head of the girl in front of me. I watch Hank saunter into the middle of the room with a broad smile on his face. "Everyone, say hello to Hank."

In unison, the class says dryly, "Hiiii, Haaaank."

"Hi, everyone. I look forward to getting naked for you all." He chuckles, as does the rest of the room.

I stare as Hank looks around the room. I hold my breath when his eyes stop on Lily. I watch as his smile widens to massive proportions; then he winks at her. What's with the winking? I turn to see Lily wink back at him. *Damn.* That girl has confidence to spare. I love that about her.

In a loud whisper, Lily says, "This is hands down my favorite fucking class. I already *love* Life Painting."

"Uh-huh," I mutter. "It's gonna be awesome." *Not.*

Professor Willis breaks our little private moment, reminding us to bring all of our paint supplies to class next time because we're going to jump right in and start painting. She excuses us early from class, stating, "Boys and girls, this will be the only time we will get to leave early, so enjoy it."

Lily and I begin to say our goodbyes when a smiling Hank saunters up to us. "Hey, ladies. Stella, are you going to introduce me to your beautiful friend?"

Oh, boy.

"Tank, this is my friend and future roomie, Lily Smith. Lily, this is Hank the Tank." I wink at Hank and see the scowl on his face. "I'm sorry, I couldn't resist."

Hank extends his huge paw-like hand toward Lily. She

places her tiny hand in his and says, "It's really nice to meet you, Hank. I can't wait to see you naked."

I choke out a laugh at that. Her confidence is remarkable.

Laughing as well, Hank says, "And I can't wait to get naked *for* you, little Lily."

Wait for it. Wait for it. There it is… the wink. I knew it. He just can't resist.

"Okay, you two, enough of the flirting. I think I just threw up in my mouth a little bit. And for the love of Pete, quit with the winking."

"Whatever you say, Stella," Hank says, winking again.

At that, the three of us part, each heading in different directions, or so I thought. By the time I've reached the dorm, Hank is walking next to me again.

"So…." He pauses. "Lily?" asks Hank.

"Yes? Is there something you'd like to know about my best friend?"

"Sure, lots of things, like will she be, uh, visiting you here at Shepard at all?"

"I suppose. Do you want me to work on that or something?" I've stopped walking and have turned to face the mammoth guy. "Are you asking me to set you two up, because if you are, I don't think my help is necessary. I think we should just let that happen organically."

"I guess we could go that route. That might be time-consuming, though. Any help you can give to nudge things along would be appreciated." Hank winks. "And thanks! See you around, Stella," he shouts as he heads into Shepard, adding, "I owe you one."

Chapter Eight

ALEX

At exactly five thirty, I knock on Stella's door. No answer. I knock again. No answer. Shit, I hope she hasn't changed her mind. I told her I took care of the jackasses on the team. Maybe she's hurt. It's possible. Tank told me that dick, Brad, had his hands on her today, which proves my earlier claim. That guy is dangerous. Either way, I need to be sure she's okay. I try the knob. Unlocked. Damn it, that's dangerous too. The girl needs to lock her damn door. I'll talk to her about that later.

I slowly open the door to see a dark lounge area. Brooke's room is also dark. Good. That girl is nothing but trouble. When I look toward Stella's room, I can see her door is a jar and hear music playing. I walk closer and realize that she's listening to that Meghan Trainor song "All About the Bass." At least it's upbeat. If she were listening to some sad music, like Adele, I'd be worried she was upset about her ex.

I knock. Nothing. I know she's in there because I can hear her singing. Pushing the door open just enough to peek in, what I see makes me smile. Stella is dancing and singing at the top of her lungs. And let me tell you, the girl cannot sing. I'd go so far as to say she's tone deaf. But, damn, she can dance. It's hot as hell. Stella is twerking and shaking her ass to the music. Suddenly, she stops. It makes my attention change from her ass up to her face. That's when she shrieks, "What the hell, Alex! Ever heard of knocking?"

"I-I did," I say, but she doesn't look convinced. Her hands are on her hips and she looks pretty damn pissed. I've got to say, I like this feisty side of Stella. "Seriously, Stella, I knocked a bunch. You must not have heard me. Your music was pretty loud," I say, attempting to yell over the music.

"Fine." Her arms drop to her side in defeat. Then, she reaches over to her desk and turns down the music.

Now that it's quiet, I add, "Oh, and great moves, by the way. It was hot."

She practically slaps herself when both of her hands cover her face. "Oh my gosh, I'm so embarrassed! You saw me dance? You heard me sing?"

Her face turns every shade of red and pink.

Choosing not to mention her singing voice, or lack thereof, I say instead, "Stella, you can dance for me anytime." I step out of her personal space. "Ready for dinner?"

"I'm not going. I'm too embarrassed now."

"Please don't be embarrassed. I thoroughly enjoyed the show, and I'm going to do everything in my power to get another one. A very private one," I say with a wink. "Come on, let's go." I've muddled her to the point that she just sighs, grabs her stuff, and walks toward the front door with me. I peer down at her. "One other thing, when you didn't answer your door, I tried the knob. It was unlocked. That's unsafe. You never know who'll walk in here. Luckily, it was just me, Pixie. Promise me you'll lock up from now on." I run my finger down the side of her face. Her skin is as soft as silk. I'd love to let that finger continue its journey, but her eyes look wary. "Lock it up, Pix. Yeah?"

"Yes. Brooke must have left it unlocked. I'll be sure to check next time." Good girl. As we make our way to the elevator and down to the lowest level of the building, I keep my hands on her in some way. If my palm isn't on her back, then I'm holding her hand in mine or touching her arm. No matter what, I never stop touching her. I stay with her while she chooses food, making certain she's actually eating something other than dry rabbit shit. She does a better job tonight, selecting a small cup of mac and cheese, a side salad, and mini pudding cup.

I decide to help her out a little bit, screw her stupid calorie counting. "Here." I place a piece of double chocolate cake on her tray.

"I don't need any cake, Alex."

"Need? Who said anything about *need*? Besides, we're going to share it. It's for both of us."

"Okay," Stella groans.

"That's my girl." As we make our way to the team table, Stella remains pretty quiet, so I take over the conversation by telling her about my day and asking her about hers.

"You need to come to one of my games, Stella. It's the best way to learn the sport."

"Um, I didn't get student tickets this year."

"That's okay, you can use mine. Each football player gets four tickets a game for family and friends."

"Alex, I wouldn't want to take any tickets away from your family and friends."

"You wouldn't be. My parents usually go, but my little sister only comes to games occasionally. She's too busy for her big brother."

Stella looks like she's trying to come up with an excuse to turn me down.

"Look, the tickets just go to waste when no one uses them.

I'd love for you to come to one of my games. We have a home game this weekend." *Please say yes, little one.*

"I can't. It's Labor Day weekend, and my parents always have a big barbecue. My attendance is required, unfortunately. Plus, I'm sure they're planning on an intervention."

"An intervention?" I ask perplexed.

"Uh-huh, a Stella and Bradley intervention. They're going to try to get me to take Bradley back."

Damn. Is she going back to that douchebag? Over my dead body! "You're not going to take him back, are you? That guy is dangerous."

"He's harmless, but no. No way am I taking him back," she says it with determination.

Good. I don't want to come off as too controlling, so I switch back to the topic at hand. "So, what about the following weekend? We have a home game then as well. Actually, we have three in a row, which is nice."

"Um, I guess. My dad would probably love to go with me. He's a big sports nut."

"Awesome. It's settled. I'll get you two tickets to the second game." Fucking awesome is what I should have said, but instead, I say, "I'm going to love looking up into the stands and seeing you, Pixie."

Her blonde brows are furrowed. She looks confused. I know she doesn't understand what's happening here. She's been through a lot in just a few days, but she'll see soon enough that I'm serious. That I've got feelings for her.

We take our seats at the table with the guys and a few of their women. I promised her the guys would be on their best behavior, and they start off by smiling and greeting her. This time, dinner in the cafeteria is much better. After dinner, I take her hand as we walk back to her dorm room. Once at her door, I take the key from her hand to unlock it for her. I want to check her place out to be sure there aren't any idiot frat boys lurking around. Sneaky fuckers. Scanning the place, I see it's still empty. Her roommate must be out. Before we walk in, I pull her gently to me. "Thanks for going to dinner with me, and thanks for saying you'll come to one of my games. That means a lot to me, Stella." I lean down to press a soft kiss on her neck, just below her ear.

"Sure." Her voice is so soft, I barely hear her words.

Shifting my focus, I give her a lingering kiss and feel her lips quivering beneath mine. "I've got to go, Pix. I've got a bunch of homework tonight. I wish I could stay. But I'll text you later."

When I get back to my room, I get right to my homework. I need to get shit done so I can spend time with Stella. Before I settle in for the night, I send her a text.

Me: Hey, Pixie. You there?
Stella: Yes. I'm here.
Me: Good, I wanted to make sure you were safe and sound. Did you lock your door?
Stella: Yep, all locked up. Safe and sound here.
Me: What are you up to now?
Stella: Just getting things ready for tomorrow. You?
Me: Same. Finished up my homework. Going to get to bed early. Practice was brutal today.
Stella: I bet. I can't imagine what you have to do to get ready for a game.
Me: It's a lot of working out, running plays, watching film, etc.
Stella: Watching film? What, do you guys watch sports movies?

That makes me laugh. God, this girl is adorable.

Me: Ha-ha. No, we watch film of the team we're

gonna play next week, so we know what to expect. If we can figure out what they're going to do, we can anticipate it and try to stop them.

Stella: Oh, I see. It sounds complicated.

Me: Nah. I'm used to it. It's actually fun to try to figure out another team's defense. So, what classes are you taking this semester?

She lists all of her classes but quickly changes direction by asking me about my classes this semester.

Me: Changing the subject, I see. ;) Fine. Today I had Comm St 335: Philosophy of Language and Communication and RTVF 321: Radio/Television/ Film Authorship. Tomorrow I'll have Calculus and Abnormal Psych.

Stella: Wow, what's your major?

Me: Communications: Broadcasting – Radio and TV

Stella: Oh, like you'd want to talk on television? What would you talk about? You'd be good at that, by the way.

Me: Why do you think I'd be good at that, Pixie?

Stella: Well, your voice is amazing, but I'm sure you've heard that before. Right?

Me: I don't care about anyone else. You like my voice?

Stella: Um, yeah, it's really deep and rich.

Me: Hang on.

I stop texting and give her a call. She answers on the first ring.

"Hello?"

"So, my voice is sexy, Stella?"

She laughs. She has a beautiful laugh. I could listen to it forever.

"I didn't say sexy; I said it was deep and rich sounding. I can get you the text transcript so you can see that I said nothing about sexy."

"Sexy, rich, same thing. The important thing is that you like it."

"I do. But I'm sure I'm not alone. Is that why you called? So I could hear your voice?"

"It is. I wouldn't want to deprive you of hearing that richness and sexiness that you obviously crave." I've got her really laughing now.

"Whatever, Alex. It's true, though. It's kind of sexy," she admits.

"Now, that wasn't so hard to admit, was it, Pix?"

"Whatever," she says, exasperated. "Well, I need to get to bed, Alex—another big day tomorrow."

"All right, Stella, sweet dreams."

"Night, Alex."

She disconnects the call. I lie back on my bed and think about her. She's so frigging beautiful—so soft, curvy, and sexy as hell. As I recall her dance moves, I feel myself get hard. Hell, I've been hard since the second I met her, but this time, I can't ignore it. So, I don't.

Chapter Nine

STELLA

This first week of school has flown by while the homework has piled up. I like all of my classes, but Life Painting is, by far, my favorite. Hank has been modeling in class, but he hasn't been nude yet, thank goodness. He's just been wearing loose shorts and no shirt. That's plenty of nudity for me right now. Not for Lily, though. She's disappointed that she hasn't gotten to see "his goods" yet. She and Hank have been making goo-goo eyes at each other the entire time, and I can't decide if it's cute or annoying. When he poses, I'd swear to you he intentionally positions himself so he can see Lily. She's barely gotten anything on canvas yet because she can't stop staring at him. It's sickeningly sweet. Truthfully, I'm really happy for her.

"Are you going home for Labor Day weekend?" I ask Lily. It's Friday, and school is out for a long weekend.

"Nope. The folks are going out of town. You going to your mom's over-the-top soiree?"

"Yeah, I have to head home tomorrow afternoon, but what are you doing tonight?"

"Nothing." Lily sighs. "My roommate is a complete bore. Did you want to do something?" Lily asks excitedly.

"Well, I thought we could have a slumber party tonight. Do you want to come over? You could come early and eat dinner in the cafeteria with me, and then we could hang out and watch Netflix or listen to music or whatever."

"That sounds awesome, but what about your evil roommate?"

"I'm sure she'll be going out. She's rarely there at night. I'm pretty sure she's a vampire. Besides, I have my own room with a door. We don't have to interact with her at all."

Lily agrees to come over right after she's finished with classes. I can't wait. I miss bonding time with her.

"Ooh, and maybe I'll get a sighting of Hottie Hank while I'm there!" Lily claps her hands together.

"Maybe you will." No doubt she will. They'll all be eating at the big boys' table in the cafeteria. But I don't want to tell her about that in case he has other plans. It *is* a Friday night, after all. I'm sure those guys have parties to go to and are in demand with the ladies. As I exit the Art and Design building, I spot a large man leaning on the bicycle rack. To say I'm surprised, well, that's an understatement. "Alex, hi, what are you doing here? Are you waiting for Hank?"

"Nope, I stopped by to walk you home. After that deal with Brad, I wanted to be sure you got home safely. Then there's the fact that Hank has plans to get naked in front of you. I've got to say, I don't like it. Not one bit," he grumbles.

A laugh escapes me. "I'm not excited about seeing him naked either."

"Well, I'm glad to hear it. I hope I'm the only football player that you see naked in the near future."

That does it. I start to cough and choke at that last comment.

"You okay, Pixie?"

"Um, yeah?" I say, still coughing.

Alex reaches down and takes my small hand in his huge

one and pulls me toward home. His hand is warm and comforting. I feel safe whenever I'm around him. I don't know why that is. It isn't like my life's been dangerous or anything. My parents have always provided me with a safe environment. I have friends who don't do crazy stuff. So, what is it I'm feeling about him? Maybe "safe" isn't the right word. Maybe it's that I sense that he genuinely cares about me, he wants to be with me, and he won't let anything bad happen to me. Plus, he wants to touch me. That's completely new to me, and I like it.

Heading back to Shepard Hall, hand in hand, I can't help noticing how many people are watching us. Maybe they're just watching Alex. The man is a magnificent specimen. It doesn't matter who you are, your eye finds this guy. But I also get the feeling they're looking at me too, no doubt wondering what Alex is doing with *me*—why he's holding the fat girl's hand. It makes me uncomfortable, but the more I squirm and try to remove my hand from his, the tighter his grip becomes. He's not hurting me, don't get me wrong, he's just gripping me more firmly.

My thoughts are interrupted when a beautiful blonde woman approaches Alex. She's thin with extremely long legs, which are accentuated by four-inch stilettos. Who wears high heels to college classes? Seriously, we walk miles and miles to get here and there. Wearing heels all day is asking for all sorts of foot issues. The blonde says his name as she saunters closer. When she's a breath away from him, she leans into Alex, pressing her impressive breasts into his arm. She doesn't acknowledge me at all. Why would she? This girl has no qualms about messing with a guy who's standing next to a girl, holding her hand. What happened to us girls sticking together? What about girl power? Sisters before misters—oh wait, not that one.

It's then that she squeaks, "Hiiii, Alex. Remember me?"

Alex nods and mutters, "Uh, maybe?"

"It's me, Jules!" She jumps up and down, making it so her chest rubs on his arm. "What have you been up to lately? I haven't seen you in, like, foreeevvveeerrr." She draws out the word "forever" forever.

"I've been going to class, playing football, and hanging with my girl."

"Oh, well, that's nice." She ignores everything Alex said. "You still have my number, right? You should call me. I'd love to see you again."

That's it! I can't take any more of this. It's bull crap. First, she's talking to him like I'm not there, and second, he's letting it continue. I know girls like her. I live with one. Now I kind of get what the football guys were talking about that night in the dining hall. Girls like her only want him for his future NFL earnings, like Hank said. No matter, Alex is letting this continue, but I don't have to. I yank my hand away from his. It takes some serious muscle power, but I free myself and start to walk away from Alex and his new blonde friend as quickly as I can. I swear I do not need this crap. Men are clueless. I know there's nothing between Alex and me, but it still stings to be treated like I'm not even there. It's hard telling how long that conversation is going to last anyway, and I've got to get back. Lily will be at my place any minute. Just as I turn a corner on my way back to the dorm, big arms wrap around my middle, lifting me off the ground.

"Put me down! You're going to hurt your back. Not to mention that I don't want to talk to you right now, Alex."

"Aw, come on now, Pixie. You aren't hurting my back, but you are breaking my heart. Why'd you run off?" Alex doesn't let me down. I'm suspended there in his big arms. It's surprisingly comfortable.

"Seriously? I didn't want to hang out with you and Blondie

as you reminisced over your last date and made plans for your next one," I grumbled.

"Are you jealous, sweetheart? There's no reason to be jealous. There has never been nor will there ever be *plans* with Blondie. Not that particular blonde anyway."

"Well, whatever blonde you end up with, I don't want to hear about it. You guys acted like I wasn't even there," I growl. "It was very, very rude."

"Pix, I'm sorry." His voice sounds a little remorseful. "I didn't mean to be rude. She was some girl I met through one of the other guys on the team. He was seeing her, and I may have talked to her at a party or something, but that's it. I haven't seen her since. You're the only blonde I want to be with, babe," Alex pleads.

He called me "babe." That is the single hottest thing I've ever heard in my life. I've seen it written in my romance novels, but hearing Alex call me that? It literally made me tingle.

"I'm sorry. It's none of my business, Alex. This week has been a roller coaster of emotions. I don't expect anything from you. You should be with someone like the girl back there. She's gorgeous."

"No, *you're* gorgeous, Stella. How many times do I have to tell you how beautiful you are?"

"Excuse me?" I squeak.

"You're beautiful. You're the prettiest girl I've ever seen in my life. You're sweet and kind, funny and spirited. What's not to like, Pix?"

My mouth falls open. I have no words. Alex doesn't seem fazed by my silence, because while I've been staring up at him, he has gently set me back down onto the ground. He wraps his arms around my back and coaxes me forward so that I'm flush against him. It feels amazing to be this close to him. We fit together like puzzle pieces. He's so big and warm, and I'm small in his arms. I watch him as he lowers his face to mine, his lips to mine.

"I'm going to kiss you now, Stella. Okay?"

"Okay." When his lips touch mine, warmth spreads through me. He opens his mouth, and his tongue touches my lips.

"Open for me, sweetheart," he whispers.

I open my mouth slightly to give Alex enough room to slide his tongue between my lips. Not to be outdone, I move my tongue against his, trying to mimic his movements. He moans in my mouth. Wow, could anything sound hotter than Alex moaning? The kiss gets even more intense as he turns his head to deepen it. My body vibrates against his. I can't believe this is happening. Heck, we're standing on a sidewalk in the middle of campus. I'm sure people can see us. That's when I feel it— something hard against my belly. I'm pretty sure I know what that thing is, but I'm not ready to figure out for sure right this minute. Off in the distance, someone shouts, "Get a room!"

That jolts me back to reality. I pull away slowly and say, "Um, Alex?"

"Yeah?" He pants. His eyes are almost smoky, and his eyelids are only slightly open as he looks down at me. It's sexy. *He's* sexy.

"I think we should stop. We're standing out here in front of everyone."

"I don't care." He leans down to start the process all over again, and I pull back a step.

"Well, I do. Don't get me wrong, that was an amazing kiss, but we need to get back to the dorm. Lily is coming over tonight."

"Oh. Okay." He's still staring at me. He's looking into my eyes, then down to my mouth. I swear he's inching closer, but I back away a little bit. "That kiss was incredible, wasn't it, Pixie?"

I nod and smile up at him as we start to walk toward home. I nearly fall over because my legs are so shaky. Alex must have noticed my current state of Jell-O legs because he smiles and wraps his arm around me to give me support as he leads me to the dorm.

When I enter my suite, Brooke is coming out of the bathroom completely naked. Luckily, Alex dropped me off at the door without needing to check on any break-ins. I'm glad, the last thing I need is for him to see Brooke's perfect body.

"Stare much?" she spits.

I ignore her and walk into my room, shutting my door to her angry sneer. I start to chant to myself silently. *Focus on my fun night with Lily. Forget about my roommate from hell. Think happy thoughts.* I repeat this in my head until I've had a chance to turn on my music. I unpack my book bag and organize my school stuff on my desk. A loud knock on the front door brings me out of my mantra. I run out to catch the front door before the naked Lucifer gets there.

"Lily!" I squeal. "I'm so glad you're here. This is going to be so much fun. I need time with friends. And, boy, do we have things to talk about!" I say this louder than I normally would so Brooke knows that I have company.

"I'm excited too. I brought my tunes and some old DVDs. I didn't know what you wanted to watch, but I brought some of my favorite horror movies."

Ugh. "You know I hate horror movies, Lily."

"I know, but I chose some classics, so you shouldn't get too scared, my little chicken," she says, tickling my side.

"Whatever. You know I don't sleep well afterward—and when I say that, I'm actually saying that I don't sleep for like a week." I'm utterly childish when it comes to those movies, but I can't help it. I sigh and add, "But you're my guest. If you want to watch a horror film, we will. But I can't guarantee that I won't be hiding under my covers during the entire movie. Deal?"

"Deal. Now, show me to your fancy private room, Miss Matthews."

I show her my private room while she unpacks her little overnight bag. We talk about school and our favorite classes. Hers is Life Painting too but for obvious reasons. I encourage her to speed up her unpacking process, as we need to get ready to go to dinner; Alex will be here soon to walk us down to the cafeteria.

"Ooh, Alex? Is he the guy that's been saving you from Bradley this week?"

Lily knows everything there is to know about Alex. "That's the one. He's been really great. He doesn't need to keep escorting me down to the cafeteria, though. I can go it alone. I think he wants to be sure that no one bothers me, but he should stop worrying about me."

And I mean that. He should stop worrying because; I'm used to it. I'm used to the way people talk to me—how they perceive me. When you're built like I am, fuller figured, people think they can comment on your body, especially as it relates to food. True story, one time I was working a cotton candy booth for my high school art club fundraiser. I was happily spinning the cotton candy and selling it like crazy, having a great time with my fellow art friends, when a guy stepped up to our booth and asked me if I "was eating all of the profits." I was struck completely mute by his words. It ruined my entire day. I don't even like cotton candy. I have a million stories just like that one —some more painful than others. There's a saying that I find to be true: *Tell a girl she's beautiful, she'll remember for a moment. Tell a girl she's ugly, she'll remember it for a lifetime.* It's been several years, but it still makes me wince whenever I think about that guy and his remark.

While we wait for Alex, we chat about school and plans for

the semester, that is until we hear a knock at the door. I'm tempted to make a run for the door, you know, to beat Brooke to it, but her room is dark and things are quiet which means she's gone, thankfully. Lily beats me to the door. Opening it, she squeaks with surprise, "Hanky!"

I giggle at her name for him. *Hanky?* I'm not surprised to see him. No doubt Alex told him that Lily was coming over. So, it makes perfect sense. When I spy Alex behind Hank the Tank, I wave. "Come on in, guys."

As he steps in the door, Hank says, "I heard there was a hot little art student down here for a slumber party. I thought I'd offer to escort her to dinner." Hank continues, "I also wanted to hear more about this slumber party. Will there be naked pillow fights? If so, I'd like to volunteer to referee that match. I wouldn't want anyone to get hurt. Fair play and all that."

Lily titters, "Oh, Tank, you're hilarious."

"Tank? You called me Tank? Oh, Lily-kins, you know I hate that name. You're very naughty today, aren't you? Do I need to punish you?" He stalks toward her.

Lily giggles again. "Punish me? I hope so! And if you do, I can start calling you Spanky instead of Hanky."

Hank reaches out, taking Lily's hand and pulling her out of the dorm room. "Let's go sweet cheeks, I'm hungry." Hank swats Lily's bottom as they walk down the hall, which causes her to shriek with delight. What a pair.

I look at Alex as he says, "I had no idea they knew each other when I told him you were having a slumber party with her. When did they meet?"

"In Life Painting."

"Oh, *that's* the girl."

"What about her?" I ask, concerned.

"Nothing, except I think old Tanky is in loooove."

"It doesn't surprise me. They spend the entire time in class making googly eyes at each other. And from what I've seen already tonight, I'd say they may have already seen each other outside of class as well."

Alex nods knowingly.

I guess I was right. Which means Lily's got some explaining to do.

As we step onto the elevator, I peek over at Lily and Hank. She's gazing up at him, and he's smiling down at her. While part of me is thrilled for my best friend, another part of me is a little sad, maybe even envious of the ease of their friendship. I honestly don't ever see that happening for me. No, I seem to make everything harder than it has to be. Look at me and Bradley. Nothing was easy for us. Example, I thought Bradley was *the one*, but now I know nothing could have been further from the truth. Heck, we weren't even friends.

I look over at Alex who's preoccupied with his phone. Alex and I are friends. Friendship is nice, but I want something more. I don't dare wish for more with a guy like Alex, though. He's way out of my league.

Chapter Ten

ALEX

As we walk to the cafeteria, I place my hand on the small of Stella's back. Hell, I just love touching her. As we walk through the buffet line, I notice that Stella is up to her old tricks again. She's got a plate full of lettuce and a lemon wedge. Who eats that shit?

"Babe? If you get a piece of grilled chicken, you can cut it up into your salad for a boost of protein. It's light, and it tastes good. As a matter of fact, I think I'm going to have that. Care to join me?"

"Yeah, that sounds good. Where do we get the chicken?"

I lead her over to the grilling station and order us two grilled breasts. As she waits, I head over to the dessert station and grab a slice of strawberry cheesecake. When I return, she spots my sweet treat and rolls her eyes. "Hey, I can't help it. I've got a sweet tooth. Besides, I was gonna share."

"Alex—"

I don't let her finish because I know she's going to turn me down. "Who doesn't love cheesecake? You're going to share it with me, right, Pixie?

"You can just eat the whole thing yourself," she mutters.

"Now, what kind of boyfriend eats all the dessert without sharing with his girlfriend? A selfish one, that's who. And, Stella, I am not a selfish boyfriend." I look down at her with a determined expression. When I see her brows furl, I have to wonder if she missed me labeling us. Hmm, I think she did.

I hear Lily whisper in her ear, "Holy shit, girl. You've got a live one there!"

Stella looks dumbfounded. "I'm not sure what you mean."

"Oh, you will. I promise you that," Lily responds.

I chuckle. They're a pretty entertaining duo. This is going to be fun.

"So, what do you girls have planned for tonight?" Hank asks after we all sit at the football table.

Lily tells us about their plans to watch horror movies and hang out.

Hank's pretty excited. "I love horror movies. What are you going to watch?"

"I brought the classics because little Miss Scaredy-Pants can't take the good ones, so there's *The Night of the Living Dead*, *Psycho*, and *Scream*."

"Those are classics, but have you seen *Paranormal Activity*? What about *The Ring*? Ooh, *Saw* is crazy too," replies Hank.

"I've seen *The Ring*, but I haven't seen the other two," Lily says.

"What about you, Stella? Have you seen any of those?" asks Hank.

"No. I don't really care for horror movies. I plan to spend the entire time underneath my blanket."

Damn, I'd love to join her under there.

"Well, I have the best idea ever. As in e-v-e-r," says Hank. "Why don't you girls come down to our place tonight, and we'll watch those scary movies *with* you? That way Alex can protect you, Stella."

"Oh, I don't know."

What's this? Stella's trying to get out of hanging with me?

"Yeah, that sounds great," Lily says. "What do you think, Alex? Want to help keep your girl safe tonight?"

Stella starts to make excuses. She reminds us that it's Friday night and that we probably have better things to do. I've heard enough. "I don't have any plans. Big game tomorrow and all that; I don't like to go out the night before. Besides, there's nothing I'd like more than keeping you safe from the boogie man, Pixie."

She sighs, but I see a slight smile play on her lips. "I guess." She shrugs.

"Well, don't sound so excited," Hank deadpans

"Can you please at least pick something that isn't completely terrifying?"

"Oh, we'll pick something good. We promise." I give Lily the stink eye because I know her better than anyone and she's fibbing. She's going to work with Hank to choose something extra scary.

I cough in my hand, so Stella doesn't catch me laughing because Hanks philosophy about horror movies? The bloodier the better. No worries, if Stella doesn't want to watch the movie, we can just go into my bedroom. Alone.

After we finish up dinner, Hank asks the girls to come down to our place in an hour. That will give us time to pick up some snacks and straighten up our place. It's a pigsty, and I'm pretty sure it stinks like old socks. What do you expect? We're football players. We smell.

"What's your room number?" Stella asks.

"We're in 273. We'll see you there in sixty. Yeah?" I smile and give her a quick kiss on her lovely lips as I drop her off at her door. Lily and Hank aren't far behind.

Back in our dorm, Hank works to straighten the living room up while I make my bed and shove my junk underneath. I'm nervous. How in the hell can I be nervous? I feel like this is my first date ever with someone I want to impress. Part of me thinks I should say "fuck it" and leave the mess, but the other part of me says she's worth it. She's worth the effort of making a good impression. "Yo, Hank. Clean the bathroom," I yell out my door.

"It's your turn," he yells back.

"Nah, I did it last year." I hear him laugh from his room as I chuckle too. I switch on some music from my playlist and work my way out of my bedroom into the kitchen. I make a list of things we need from the store before I wipe down everything and shove the dirty dishes into our tiny dishwasher and turn it on. "I'm going to the store. Back in twenty."

"Right on. I'll keep cleaning."

"Good." Because I want to make a good impression.

Chapter Eleven

STELLA

When Lily and I get back to the room, we scurry around looking for something to wear to movie night. We could just stay in what we're wearing now, but it's important to be comfortable, right? Lily finds her gear and opts to put on her pajamas, if you can call them that. She's brought a tiny tank top and even smaller boy short bottoms. I recognize them. They're black and covered with kittens. The shorts are so short that they reveal some of her ass cheeks. She's got the body to pull them off and, like I said, this girl is dripping with confidence. After dressing, she pulls her long hair back up into a messy bun and reapplies some of her makeup. She looks really cute. That is until she pulls out the biggest, ugliest pair of slippers I've ever seen.

"No! Not the beavers, Lily. Those things are disgusting. I think they actually smell like a real beaver now. Plus, is that gum stuck to the side of Lefties head?" Yes, she named each of them.

"Stella, you know damn well they're bears not beavers, as in Da Bearz, you know, Chicago Bears? I've had them forrrreeevvveeerrr, and they're my favorite and they're perfect. If you can't handle them, then tough."

"Whatever. You still look cute, Lily-kins, even with the roadkill on your feet," I say in a little teasing tone.

"So, is that what you're wearing over to Alex's place?"

I show her my black yoga pants, my black tank top, and my white, oversized slouchy sweatshirt, a la *Flashdance*, circa 1983. "Yeah." I look down at myself. "Is it okay?"

"Absolutely. It's sexy yet demure. I like it," she says, nodding. "It's just loose enough for Alex to have access," she says, raising her eyebrows up and down quickly.

"Oh, is it too loose? I don't want Alex to get any ideas."

Lily chokes out a laugh. "Why the hell not?"

"Because I'm not ready for anything like that."

"Stella, you don't need to hang on to that V-card so hard."

"I know. I'm just not ready. Just because you lost yours at prom...."

I maybe could've lost mine at prom too, but I didn't go to prom. Bradley couldn't get back home because he had some fraternity function to attend, so I stayed home and read a good book and ate a half gallon of double chocolate chip cookie dough ice cream. The same was true with the homecoming dance, winter formal, Valentine's Day, my birthday, my graduation, and my gallbladder surgery. Yeah, he was always too busy.

"Yeah, and it was very anticlimactic, let me tell you. That's why I can't wait to be with a *real* man. You know, someone who's older, who knows what he's doing," Lily says, nodding.

"That's what I said about Bradley, but he wanted to wait until *I* was ready." The truth was, I was ready last summer. "I liked the idea that he'd know what he was doing." I thought I was doing the right thing. Now, I'm definitely glad I didn't give him that part of me.

Lily snorts. "You think he would have known what he was doing?" She rolls her eyes.

"I know he's not a virgin." Especially now after seeing him with Brooke. He was definitely more experienced than me.

Lily steps over to me and places her hand on my shoulder. "It wasn't meant to be. He wasn't the one who's supposed to pop your cherry, but maybe Alex is."

I roll my eyes. I can't comment. I don't think anyone is ever going to want to pop anything on me, to be honest. As we finish getting all dolled up, I get more and more nervous. Lily seems to be buzzing with adrenaline while I'm sure I'm going to vomit. This is a first for me. I've hung out with Bradley at my house, and I've been to Vicky's house before just not to see Bradley so technically, I've never gone over to a boy's house before. I hope Alex doesn't expect me to do sexy stuff with him tonight. I'm not ready for that.

We take the stairwell down two flights and enter onto the guys' floor. Our building has both coed floors and floors with just girls and floors with just boys. My floor only has girls, and Alex's only boys. The floor between is coed. As we enter the hallway from the stairs, it feels strange. It smells completely different than my floor too. I wouldn't say it's an unpleasant smell, but I wouldn't call it pleasant either. It's a mix of cologne, body odor, and other scents that shall not be named.

"Boys kind of stink." Lily has her nose scrunched up as we walk down to the other end of the hall. When we reach the correct door, Lily knocks. I take a deep breath and the door is suddenly wrenched open by Hank.

"Ladies!" he says loudly. Raising his arm, he gestures toward his small living area. "Welcome to chez Hank and Alex."

"Oooh, French. Do you speak fluently?" Lily giggles.

"Si," says Hank.

"That's Spanish, dingus," jokes Lily.

"What can I say, I'm multilingual." Hank shrugs.

Lily and I both laugh at that.

"Here, let me show you to our theater room." He points to the small lounge area again. Their suite is just like mine. It's the exact layout since it's on the same side of the building. The only difference is the way they have their lounge area set up. Instead of one big sofa, they have two smaller love seats. I guess that's so they each have a place to sit. They aren't long enough for either of them to lie on, but I suppose it's better than trying to sit two big guys that size on one couch.

The rest of the suite is the same, though. On the right is a bedroom that must be Hank's. The center has the lounge area and the kitchenette, and on the right is a bedroom across from the bathroom. The door to the room that would be mine opens up. Alex walks out wearing those loose athletic shorts and a tight black T-shirt with the word LANY printed in simple white letters on it. He looks so damn good.

"What's LANY?" I ask, approaching him.

"Oh, it's a great band out of California."

"I've never heard of them."

"Well, I'll have to play some of their music for you later. One song in particular."

We just stand there smiling at each other like idiots until Hank breaks us out of our spell, telling us to pick a movie. He gathers snacks together for us while keeping an eye on Lily. I'm surprised he can function. He seems to be fixated on her bottom in her tiny shorts.

My thoughts are interrupted when Alex whispers, "You look beautiful, Stella."

"Thanks, so do you."

"Can I get you something to drink? Want a beer? Soda?" asks Alex.

"Soda please."

Alex heads to the fridge and lists out their drink options.

"We have Pepsi, Diet Coke, Mountain Dew, Diet 7Up, Dr. Pepper, and Snapple."

"Wow, you guys must like a variety," I say.

"Well, no, we typically don't, but I wanted to be sure I had something that you would like, Stella. I figured you'd probably ask for diet soda because regular soda would have too many calories, but I picked up regular too so you could choose one of those instead."

That is such a sweet thing for him to do. I smile and request a Dr. Pepper. He grabs a Mountain Dew along with a can of soda for Lily and Hank, then takes my hand and leads me to one of the love seats. He plops down onto the couch, grabs me by the waist, and pulls me down onto his lap. I stiffen up because I know I'm going to break his legs. But he doesn't seem to mind.

He pulls me back until my shoulder is up against his chest, his arms still wrapped around me. I turn my head and smile at him. I've got the urge to kiss him, but I can't do it. What happened earlier was probably just a fluke—the heat of the moment after my little tantrum over the blonde girl. No, I need to just play it safe.

"Well, ladies, what would you like to watch first?" asks Alex.

"I'll defer to Lily. I told her she could choose," I reply.

"In that case, I pick, drum roll please, *Paranormal Activity!*" Lily exclaims.

I groan.

"Don't worry, Pix, I'll protect you." Alex's breath tickles my ear. I close my eyes, lost in the sensation. Then he squeezes me tightly around my middle, and I almost moan in response to being so closely pressed into his body.

From the kitchen, Hank says, "Go ahead and start up the movie, I'll make us some popcorn. Who wants butter?"

"Me!" yells Lily.

I remain quiet.

"Don't you like a little butter on your popcorn, Stella?" Alex is still practically whispering in my ear. It's giving me chills. The good kind.

"If you want it, sure," I say, shrugging.

"Well, I'm fine either way. I really want to know if *you* want butter."

I agree to the butter, surprising myself a little bit. My mom would die on the spot if she knew I was going to have butter on my popcorn. But Alex wants butter, so we'll have butter. If I gain a little weight, I'll have cut back on things next week.

"We'll have some butter on our popcorn, Hank," yells Alex.

"Coming right up."

Alex lifts me up off of his lap and sets me down so he can start the movie. I mean, he literally lifts me up. He didn't even grunt in pain when he did it. I'm shocked. He returns to the seat, and we're both squeezed onto the love seat side by side now. He reaches his big arm over my shoulders and scoots me closer. I rest my head on that spot between his shoulder and his chest. My head fits there perfectly. He smiles down at me, and I look up and smile back. It's so cozy, I snuggle up even closer to him. From this spot, I can smell him. My gosh, he smells amazing. I inhale deeply.

"Are you sniffing me, Pixie?" whispers Alex.

"Maybe. You smell good."

He leans his head down and inhales deeply. "You do too, Pix. You smell like sweetness and summer."

The previews start, and I curl closer to Alex. I hate the previews as much as the actual movie because they preview even scarier movies than we're about to watch. I should resign myself to burying my face into Alex's chest. I hate being scared. Alex wraps his arm around me tighter.

"Pixie? If you really hate these movies, we can watch something else. I don't want you to be scared," he whispers.

"No, it's okay. I just have to get used to the idea. I'll be fine."

"Okay, but if you change your mind, just say the word and I'll turn it off," Alex assures. "Or we can go into my room."

A shiver runs through my entire body. Go to his room? Alone? I'm not ready for that. So, I promise him that I'll alert him if I can't take it anymore. As the movie plays, I find I can't get close enough to Alex. This stupid movie's the scariest thing I've ever seen. It seems to be based on a true story about a couple that thought their house was haunted and they filmed the evidence at night. I swear I'm going to cry I'm so scared. I bury my face into Alex's chest so hard I'm sure I'm leaving bruises. At some point in the film, I actually climbed back into his lap. Without thinking, I wrap my arms around his neck and snuggle in close. He must not mind because he hasn't asked me to move. He keeps asking me if I want him to stop the film. I just say "No" each time.

Honestly, I have no idea how the movie ended because, by that time, my hands were covering my ears and my face was plastered into his neck.

"You're shaking. It's over now, Pixie. It's okay."

"I just really hate horror movies." I breathe slowly, calming my body. As I do, I heat up at when I realize where his hands are. One of them is resting on my lower back and the other one... well, it's on my bottom. Lifting my head, I look back at the other sofa. "Where are Lily and Hank?"

"Oh, they went to his bedroom about thirty minutes ago."

"What? Why didn't you tell me? We could have stopped watching."

"I did tell you, but you were intent on staying on my lap, apparently," he says, smirking.

"Oh, God, I'm so sorry." I attempt to scramble off of him. "Your poor legs, they must be asleep."

"My lap is good. More than good, actually. Stay put. I like having you so close to me."

"You do?"

"My poor, little Pixie," he coos in a sweet voice. "I'm sorry. I'm clueless. I thought you were okay with the movie. I'm sorry I didn't stop it sooner."

"It's okay. It really is. I'm just childish about horror movies," I admit. As I reassure him, I feel something hard between my legs. I try to stay completely still because I have no clue what to do. If I move, I could hurt him. He slides his hand that was on my lower back up to my cheek, then it goes to wrap it around the back of my neck beneath my hair. He uses his new position to pull my face closer to his.

"I'm going to kiss you now, babe."

"Okay," I whisper. Oh shit, he said "babe" again. Why does that word turn my body into molten lava?

He doesn't start off tentatively when he kisses me this time. It starts off more passionate than earlier today. I don't need for him to tell me to open my mouth. I do it on my own. I want this kiss as much as he does. The kiss gets deeper and more frantic, and I feel him get even harder beneath me. I have the urge to press into him, but I scoot away instead. He seems to get that I'm hesitating because he wraps his arms around my waist, and as he stands, he picks me up like I'm light. With my feet still off the ground, Alex slides his hands around to my bottom. "Wrap your legs around me, Stella." I do as he asks as he begins to walk toward his bedroom.

"Alex?" He must sense how unsure I am.

"I'm just taking us into my room to lay on the bed. It'll be more comfortable than that little love seat. I promise you we won't do anything you aren't ready for. I just want to hold you and kiss you. Okay?"

I believe him. I really do. "Okay."

Once we're in his room, he sets me gently on his bed.

"Scoot back and lie down. I promised you I'd play you some of LANY's music."

While he's setting up his playlist, I take that opportunity to look around his room. I notice that he's got the same desk that I do, the same closet, but he's got a bigger bed. It's longer and wider than mine. It makes sense since the guy is humongous.

"Here it is. It's called 'ILYSB.' It's a great song." He walks over to his bed and lies down, sliding his body next to mine before reaching over and pulling me close. He grabs his quilt and throws it over both of us. We lay and listen to the song.

"It's beautiful," I say.

It's a simple song, but you can tell the guy means what he's singing. It's filled with heartfelt emotion.

"When I listen to this song, I think of you," he says.

"You do?" My mouth feels dry, suddenly.

He nods in reply. I remain quiet, so I can hear the words "*I Love You So Bad.*" That's what the letters stand for. Does he *love* me? That can't be possible. We just met. He pulls me closer until I rest my head on his chest. My head is in that perfect spot, the one between his shoulder and his chest. I swear it was made just for me. We fall asleep like that, listening to his music play softly in the background.

IT'S EARLY. I can tell because of the soft light coming from the window. Not only that, I feel well rested, probably due to the best sleep I've ever had. It takes me a few minutes to realize that I'm not in my own room. I feel a big arm wrapped around me and hear Alex snoring softly. It's game day. I wonder what time he's supposed get to the stadium.

Before I wake him up, I take the opportunity to really look at him. I haven't felt comfortable enough to do that before now. I notice that his facial hair has grown a lot overnight. He's on his back, but he's got his arm beneath me while his other hand rests on his chest. His fingers are long and thick. I hold my hand close to his to compare them. His hand is, literally, twice the size of mine.

I feel a chill and look around for a blanket. We must've kicked the quilt off onto the floor during the night. Heat is radiating off the man, so I snuggle closer. Next, I look down his long body. The guy is built like a Greek god—or like I imagine a Greek god to look like. It's obviously built for competition with the muscle definition on his arm and legs. Gah! I can't believe I'm sleeping next to this guy. My eyes travel down his legs to his huge feet then back up to his shorts. Something is poking up. Oh dear, I know what it is. I've just never seen one firsthand. I stare at it for a few minutes and nearly choke when it moves. Oh my. I think it's getting bigger!

"Pixie?"

Crap on a cracker. I hope he doesn't realize I was staring at his, um, manhood. I pretend to be waking up. "Huh? What?" I say in a faux sleepy voice.

"What are you doing, sweetheart?"

"Me? Nothing. Why do you ask?"

"Well, you seemed pretty interested in my morning wood." He grins.

Busted.

"What?" I practically choke on the words. "I was, uh, just looking for some water."

Lies. All lies.

When he offers to go get some, I shake my head. I don't think he should be walking around the suite sporting that big thing. What if Lily is out there? Well, she'd probably like it, but I wouldn't want her seeing Alex, um, like *that*.

He interrupts my internal meltdown by saying, "It's not uncommon for a guy to wake up a little bit excited. Especially when there's a beautiful, delicious-smelling woman next to him. It's only natural."

"Okay, well… I really wouldn't know."

"Why is that? Didn't douchebag ever wake up like this?" He nods down at his shorts.

"Well, I never slept with Bradley. We didn't sleep together, I mean. Oh, shoot. We never slept in the same bed together. We didn't sleep, sleep together either." Crud, I think I'm making it worse.

"Are you telling me that you didn't have sex with Bradley? Weren't you together for over a year?"

I'm not sure I like his tone much. "Yeah, so, what's your point?" I question defensively.

"My point? My point is that he had the prettiest woman on the planet for a year and he didn't do anything with you? Ever?"

"I guess not. I've, uh, never, uh… you know."

"You're a virgin, Pixie? Is that what you're trying to say?" Alex says this rather angrily.

"Yes?" I attempt to scamper out of bed. This is so humiliating. I just admitted to a guy I barely know that I'm a virgin, and he seems to be pissed about it. I feel those frigging tears coming back. I swear, I've cried more in the last few days than I have in my entire life. College is stressful. Guys are stressful. Evil roommates are stressful. I honestly don't know how much more I can take.

"Hang on, hang on, Stella." He grabs me before I can roll over him to escape. I'm now lying directly on top of him. His arms are wrapped around me so snuggly that I can't move any further.

"Don't be upset. I didn't mean to sound like a dick. I just can't believe what an idiot that guy is. He's an even bigger dumbass than I gave him credit for."

"I don't know what you mean. Why are you surprised that

I'm a virgin? Have you looked at me?" I sniffle, doing my best to keep the tears at bay.

"Yes, I have looked at you, and I want to see more. Honestly, I'm fucking ecstatic he didn't touch you. Stella, I'm really glad because that makes me hope that I will get to be the guy that shares your first time with you, Pix."

Alex is looking at me with the most serious expression I've seen from him yet. His eyes are intense, and his mouth is drawn tightly closed. I lean up, slowly crawling up his chest just enough to look directly into his eyes. "That was the sweetest thing anyone has ever said to me, Alex." I move my lips closer to his and kiss him. He kisses me back with so much passion I feel tingles all the way to my core.

"Angel, you are so damn sexy," he pants.

I can't talk. It's too much. I just want to kiss him. I can't seem to get close enough to him. I clutch his T-shirt with my fists. I'm still on top of him, and now I push myself up a little so I can straddle him. He reaches around with one arm holding my waist while his other hand reaches back, squeezing my bottom. It feels amazing. So much so, I moan. He must like that because he flips me over onto my back so that he's on top of me, growling as he goes.

"Baby, I want you so much. I know you're not ready, but let me touch you, please?"

I'm not sure what he means by that, but I want to find out, so I nod. I want him to touch me. He reaches up and rubs his thumb over my breast. My nipples are already hard little nubs. His thumb brushes the tip of my right breast, which makes me arch my back like I'm trying to get closer to him. I moan my approval.

"You are so gorgeous." He's breathing even harder now.

His other hand slides into the waistband of my yoga pants. Oh, God, he's putting his hand down my pants. What under-wear do I have on? No time to think of that, he's moved his hand down into my panties until he's touching me... down *there*. My mind is working overtime. Even though this is a first for me, I've read plenty of romance novels, and in those, the women are always bare. Crap! Should I have waxed? I had no idea this was going to happen, so there was no special, you know, preparations made. I should stop him, I really should, but I don't want to. He doesn't seem to mind my hair situation. He slides his hand through my center, and I feel his fingers brush down further.

"Oh, God, Stella, you're so wet."

He's got magician's fingers. How is he doing that? Nothing has ever felt so good. "Mmm-hmm" is all I can say right now.

His fingers move back and forth between my legs. He spends extra time in the front, and whatever he's doing is making my body hum. I've never in my life felt anything as good as this. His finger moves further back to my center and slips inside of me, in and out. I'm the one panting now. He hasn't forgotten my needy breast either. He's pinching my nipple with one hand and using my own juices to move his fingers enough to make me squirm with the other. My goodness, he's talented.

When he chuckles and says, "Thank you." I know I must've said that out loud.

Oh, who cares? Because right then, Alex finds my spot. The one I called my golden ticket. Yes, I know it's called a clitoris, but that's too embarrassing to even think about. So, golden ticket it is. He must be able to tell that I like it because he starts to rub it in earnest now, moving faster and circling around it. With a mind of its own, my body moves with him as he rubs and pinches. Oh, God, what's happening to me? I can feel something happening to me.

"Don't stop. Please don't stop, Alex."

"I won't, Stella. Come for me, angel. I want to see you come for me."

So, I do. When I explode, I swear I see fireworks. My eyes are pressed so tightly together that I'm not sure I can open them again. Holy smokes, I think that was my first orgasm. Alex Emerson, star football player and all-around hottie, just gave me my first orgasm. The sweetest, nicest, and sexiest man in the entire world just made me see stars. "Oh, Alex," I say breathlessly. "That was unbelievable. I've never felt anything like that before."

"Stella? You've never had an orgasm?"

"If that was an orgasm, then um, no, I've never had one, but I'd like to have lots and lots of them in the very near future."

Alex laughs. "You will, and I plan on being the one giving them to you. I loved watching you come. You were beautiful, Stella."

I can feel Alex's erection pressing into me. "What about you, Alex? Do I need to, um, do anything to help you?"

"I'm okay for now, Pixie. Next time." He smiles.

I know he's got to need relief; I mean, I can feel how much he needs relief.

"Is it painful?" I ask.

"Nah, it'll be okay. I probably should move though. The closer I am to you, the harder it is. No pun intended." He chuckles. "I'm just going to hop up and go to the bathroom for a minute or two. Okay?"

"Okay. I need to go get Lily anyway. I still have to pack for home. Don't you need to get ready for your game?"

"Oh shit, I totally forgot." He laughs, sounding surprised. "See what you do to me? I forgot all about football. That's not easy to do, but when you're near, I only have you on my mind. Just hang on, I'll be out in a sec," he says casually.

He jumps off the bed and jogs across the hall to the bathroom, closing the door behind him, I hear the shower start. I begin to worry that I'm a distraction for him. He should be focusing on football and school. What if having me around impacts his chance to make it to the NFL? I would hate to be responsible for him losing that opportunity. I don't even know what we're doing here. He seems to like me, but why?

I need to get out of here. I probably made him late for his game. I hurry over to Hank's door and tap urgently. "Lily? It's Stella. We need to go. Now!" The door opens a crack to reveal a very disheveled Lily Smith.

"Give me a couple minutes. I'll be right out," she says in a husky voice.

I wait by the door, hoping to get out of here before Alex finishes up in the bathroom. Five minutes later, we're out the door and heading back upstairs. "Did you have fun last night, Lils?"

"Oh yeah! Did you?"

"Yeah. Fun," I say flatly.

"Well, don't sound too excited."

"I'm just confused about everything right now, Lily." And I am. Confused about Alex. Confused about Bradley. Confused about all of these feelings that Alex is eliciting in me. I mean, my first orgasm. It was incredible. No wonder everyone is always talking about them.

Lily nods knowingly. "I get it. But, damn, that boy is hot. Just remember that when you're contemplating your life's choices and stuff."

Oh, I will. When we get to my place, I hear voices coming from inside my dorm. I open the door to see Brooke standing in the kitchenette wearing only a little tiny T-shirt and panties while Bradley sits at the kitchen island. Great. Just great.

"Ugh, what are you doing here, Bradley?" I snap angrily.

"I came to drive you home. You are going home this week-end, right? Your mom will pitch a fit if you aren't home for their Labor Day barbecue," he says, crossing his arms. He looks like a know-it-all. And no one likes those.

"I'm going home, but I'm driving my own car."

"Your own car? You have your car here?"

"I'm renting a car today. Then I'm going to drive my own back on Sunday."

"Sunday? You're not staying through Monday?"

"Nope. I've got too much homework, and I need the library here to finish a paper."

"Well, there's no need to rent a car. You'll just ride with me. It makes more sense, economically."

Just then Brooke makes a sort of grunting noise and walks to her room.

"Is that a freaking thong?" Lily yelps.

"Yeah, what's it to ya, nerd?" Brooke snaps back.

Lily looks at me then rolls her eyes. "Wow, she really is precious, isn't she, Stella?"

"Yep. Precious," I mutter. I look back over in Bradley's direction. He'd been watching Brooke walk away too—not surprising since she's practically naked. "Bradley, I'm not going to ride home with you. I'm not leaving until later this morning anyway. You go ahead and go."

"Now that's just silly, Stella!" Bradley exclaims.

"No, it's not silly. I don't want to spend over an hour in the car with you."

"Come on. We've known each other for fifteen years. You can't spend an hour in the car with me?"

"I think she said, no, dude," Lily defends.

"Who the fuck asked you, Lily?" Bradley retorts.

"No one. Just like no one asked you to come over here and no one asked you to give Stella a ride home," snaps Lily.

Ignoring their spat, I say, "I'll just plan on seeing you back home. I'm sure you have some type of intervention intended for me. That'll be soon enough for me."

"What the hell happened to my sweet Stella? It's because you're spending time with those idiot jocks, isn't it? Is that where you were last night? Already sleeping with other people?" he sneers.

"Sleeping with other people? That would mean that I had slept with *you*, Bradley, which I know you didn't want to do. Brooke told me all about your aversion to seeing me, erm, that way and being forced to have sex with me." I can't believe I just said all that aloud.

"What? I never said that! She's just jealous that I want to be with you instead of her, that's all."

With that statement hanging in the air, Brooke's door flies open and slams against her bedroom wall. She steps out, still only in underwear. "Really, Brad, that's your story? Stella, what I told you was the absolute truth. I could give two shits what happens to you and this idiot, but that's exactly what he said about you. Shit, I may have even sugarcoated it a little bit. I think he was even more explicit than I was," says Satan's mistress.

"That's bullshit, B, and you know it."

"Whatever," Brooke says while she stomps back to her room, her tiny ass jiggling.

"Girl, get some damn clothes on. I don't need to know that much about you," Lily bellows.

Brooke flips Lily off and slams her door again.

"Wow, what a sweetie. If she wasn't the princess of darkness, we might have been friends," states Lily.

I roll my eyes. Bradley called her "B." That's a pretty familiar way of addressing someone you only slept with once. I turn to Bradley, point to the door, and tell him I'll see him at my intervention tonight. Because I know my family and there *will* be an intervention. The thing that my family doesn't realize is that nothing will change the fact that Bradley and I are finished. I could never take him back. Not now.

Bradley looks sincerely dejected and sad as he leaves, telling me he'll see me at home. I'm sure he's just upset that he's not getting his way. The guy could sell ice to an Eskimo, so he's probably confused about my resistance. I almost feel a little sorry for him, but I'm sure he'll rebound. He always does.

Lily decides to shower at my place so she can have a bathroom to herself for once. I start packing up my overnight bag for home. I'm not looking forward to the conversation tonight, but I need to get it over with. After my bag is packed, it's my turn in the bathroom. I shower and pack up my toiletries.

"Let's see, which one of my graphic tees should I wear today? I don't want to antagonize my mom; she hates my tees," I explain to Lily. Graphic tees are the staple of my wardrobe—tees along with jeans and my Converse. But my mom h-a-t-e-s them. If she had her way, there would have been a huge bonfire made entirely of my T-shirt collection.

Lily looks in my closet at all of my tees. "What about this one?" She holds up a navy blue scoop neck T-shirt that says, "Come to the Dark Side. We have cookies."

I laugh. "Any reference to food or drink of any kind is strictly prohibited by Mrs. Matthews."

"Okay. How 'bout this one?" "Glitter: The herpes of craft supplies."

She and I both laugh at that one. It's one of my favorites. Ironically, the text is made of glitter. But I have to say no.

"Okay, last try," says Lily.

She pulls out a red V-neck tee with "Life without art is just… meh."

Yeah, that one is safe. I slip the T-shirt on with my tan shorts. "This will be fine. Nothing I wear will really make her happy, so I might as well be comfortable. Right?"

"Right!" Lily agrees. "Okay, I'm taking off. Have a safe trip home. Call me when you get back or call if you need to talk while you're there."

"Yeah, I'm not looking forward to any of this, but I need to get it over with. I'll talk to you on Monday, okay?"

"Okay. See ya."

"And, Lily-kins? When we get back, I want to hear about you and *Hanky*," I yell after her.

"Definitely! I can't wait to tell you all the gory details." She laughs.

I grab my bag and pick up my phone to order an Uber to take me to the car rental place. As I leave my room, I see that Brooke's door is still closed, thank goodness. I open the front door quietly and tiptoe out into the hallway and come face to chest with an enormous guy.

"Alex?" I say, surprised.

"Stella, you left without saying goodbye. I had to stop and think what I'd said to you before my shower to make you take off like that. I still can't figure it out," he says sadly.

"Oh, I'm sorry, Alex. I didn't want to make you late for the game. I don't want to distract you from football or from school. I would feel terrible if I had anything to do with—"

"Pix, you misunderstood my meaning when I said that. You are not a distraction for me. You make everything better."

"But you need to focus if you want to go to the NFL."

He chuckles. "I'm not a Neanderthal, sweetheart. I can focus on multiple things at once." He smirks while reaching out to wrap his arm behind my back. "Besides, it's nice to think of something beautiful, soft, and sexy."

I roll my eyes because his words are sweet, but they make me nervous. "Well, I—"

"Listen, Pix. Yes, I love football, but I know there's more to life than that."

"You do?"

"I do." Leaning down, he kisses me softly. "I've gotta say, though, I can't wait for you to see me play."

"Oh? Why's that?"

"So you'll finally admit that you're with Alex Emerson— Football God."

I snort out a laugh. "All right. If you say so."

"And…" He pulls me closer. "If anything, you make me more determined than ever to strive for the NFL. I want to make you proud to be with me," he says, resting his hands on my hips.

He wants to make me proud? "I have no doubt you'll make it."

"I'll miss you this weekend, Pix," he whispers sweetly.

"I'll miss you too, but I'll be sure to watch the game today with my dad. He's a rabid fan, and he'll be tuned into the Big 10 Network. If I have questions, he can answer them for me." When he asks when I'll be back, I tell him about my parents' annual Labor Day barbecue and that I won't be back until Sunday night. "This barbecue is a Matthew's family tradition."

"I wish I could go with you. I'd like to make sure dumbass stays far, far away from you."

I laugh. "He's not going to do anything. He was already here this morning."

"What? Did he touch you?" Alex asks angrily.

Shaking my head, I pat his forearm. "It's okay. I sent him away."

"Okay, good. Hey, be careful driving. I hate to think of you driving all that way there and back alone."

"I'll be fine. It's not far, and I know how to drive."

"I'm sure you do, but I can't help worrying."

"I'll be safe, *Dad*. No texting and driving and all that. I know the drill."

Alex growls, "I am not your dad," bringing his hands around to my ass.

"Oh, I know that." I smile as he leans down to kiss me softly while squeezing my bottom with his big hands. His touch makes my nipples come alive. They rub against his chest as he kisses me, and that sensation alone makes me want to climb him like a dang tree. Oh, hell's bells. What have I become?

"I'll text you tonight." He smiles and winks, knowing what he's doing to me.

"Have a great game today!" I squeak, trying to seem composed.

"If I know you're watching me, I know I'll have a great game."

"I'll be watching."

With a quick kiss, Alex turns to go. I stare after him as he jogs to the stairs with his gym bag in hand like I've never seen a hot guy before. "I hope he's not late because of me."

Chapter Twelve

The trip home goes too fast. I've been enjoying the solitude for a while. Since moving to campus, there always seems to be someone with me or at least nearby. The good part is that I can think about everything that has happened in the short time I've been at Northwestern. The bad thing is I can think about everything that has happened in the short time I've been at Northwestern. No matter, I need time to collect my thoughts and to prepare for the confrontation that I'm sure I'm about to face at home.

When I arrive at my parents' house, I park the rental car, grab my bag, and text the car rental place to arrange a pickup time. According to our agreement, they'll stop over and get the car tonight. Easy. Then, when I head back tomorrow, it'll be in my old compact car, the one I've had since I was sixteen. Boy, it'll be great having my own car at school. Sure, parking on campus is a hassle, just like it is parking in a city like Chicago, but it will give me some freedom that I don't have right now. Besides, I love my little Civic. It's the perfect car for me because it's small and economical.

When I walk into the house, I notice that it's quiet. "Mom? Dad?"

"In here, pumpkin," Dad yells in response. His voice sounds like it's coming from the kitchen. My parents' house is amazing. The kitchen probably belongs in one of those home design magazines. Mom designed it herself, taking things she liked from all of her friends' kitchens and from magazines and from some of those home improvement shows she loves.

Walking into the kitchen, I see Mom leaning over whispering into my dad's ear.

"Oh, hi, Stella," Mom says sweetly—too sweetly.

"Hi, Mom. Hi, Dad. All ready for the big barbecue?"

"Getting there," Dad says.

"What can I do to help?"

Mom pipes up in a chipper voice, "Oh, we're ready to go. Why don't you go up and settle into your room and rest? You're probably tired from your trip."

"Uh, okay." What the heck? Aliens must have abducted my mother and replaced her with a kinder, gentler version of Candice Matthews, because it's bizarre that she doesn't immediately jump down my throat about Bradley nor does she tell me to get to work helping with the barbecue or to change my graphic T-shirt. I swallow the hard lump that's now in my throat. This is going to be worse that I suspected.

"Be sure to change before dinner, though. You know I hate those T-shirts of yours," she says.

That's my girl. I knew my judgmental mom was in there somewhere. "Yeah, sure, Mom." I turn, grabbing my overnight bag as I go, and walk up the grand staircase up to my old bedroom. Honestly, it's great to be home, but dread is seeping into my bones. Once I'm in my old room, I decide to turn on the television see if Alex's football game has started. Kickoff is at three, and it's now two forty-five. Shoot. I forgot to ask him about his jersey number. No worries, I'll just google it. I've meant to google Alex Emerson all week but never got around to it. I'd thought about it a number of times but, if I'm being honest, I was afraid what I'd find out.

Digging my phone out of my purse, I type his name into the search engine. I watch as page after page with Alex Emerson's name begin to appear. I gasp at all of them. "It's worse than I suspected," I mumble to myself.

Reading through some of the information, I discover he's number eighty-five. Not only that, he's an all-American tight end and an All-Big 10 Academic Honoree. Not once or twice, but three times. Something I already knew was the Northwestern Wildcats have won the Big 10 championship three times in the last ten years and have gone to the Sugar Bowl once during that period. I scroll down my phone in amazement. There are so many links to articles about Alex it makes me a little lightheaded. Reading on, I see many experts are projecting Alex will go in the first round of the next NFL Draft, probably as a top fifteen selection overall because there are lots of teams looking for tight ends. That's good. That's what Alex wants. *They aren't the only ones*; I joke to myself.

Because I'm a glutton for punishment, I click on a few more links, and holy crap, they estimate his first contract could net him over eight million dollars, and that doesn't include the signing bonus. That's amazing! I'm so happy for Alex. He's so deserving of all of this. A tear comes to my eye when I realize... *I can't get in his way.* I just can't. I hope he really meant what he said, that I was helping him and not a distraction.

Just then I hear the television announcer say, "Number eighty-five, Alex Emerson, starting tight end."

I look up to see him running onto the field. Holy moly, he looks amazing in his outfit. The crowd goes wild when he runs up to his teammates. I should really get a book about football so I understand some of this lingo or... I could just go pick my dad's brain. I trek back downstairs to the family room. Sure enough, my dad's in his usual spot, poised and ready to start yelling at the television.

"Can I watch the game with you, Dad?"

"Sure, pumpkin! I'd love that." He gives me a broad smile like he actually likes my company.

"Do you mind if I ask you questions as they play? I'd like to know more about football."

"Uh, sure, honey. I'll do my best."

So, that's what I do. I watch Alex all while paying attention to things Dad is saying as the game goes along. Alex is doing amazing things on the field.

At least that's what my dad keeps saying. I'll have to take his word for it. Things like, "I think that Emerson kid is having the best game of his career."

"Really?" I perk up.

"Yeah, really. He's spectacular anyway, but something must really be making him push even harder today."

"I wonder what that could be," I say with a sly smirk. I know what that is.

It's me.

"I don't know, but the better he is, the better place he'll end up in next year. Maybe Dallas or San Diego."

Alarm bells ring in my head. "As in Dallas, Texas and San Diego, California?"

"Yep, that's where those teams are based, sweetheart." He nods as he turns his head and smiles at me.

"Oh." I hadn't given that any thought. He's going to be gone soon. As in far away.

"What about the team in Chicago, Dad? The Cubs?"

"I think you mean the Bears, Stella. It's a possibility, but I'm not sure they need a tight end, but anything's possible."

Okay, don't panic, Stella. There's a chance he'll be nearby. I'll just cross my fingers and hope it all works out for the best. It's all I can do.

Oh, who am I kidding. By then, Alex will have moved on to someone new. I doubt he's thinking about anything long-term with someone like me, especially now that I know he's got a chance to go to some place like California.

"Why the sudden interest in football, honey?"

"Oh, you know, being at Northwestern made me want to root for my team. That's all. I'm really only interested in Wildcat football."

"I know the feeling, pumpkin." My dad and mom are both Northwestern alums, so it's natural he'd root for his alma mater.

We sit together in companionable silence as the game is played. I ask questions periodically and listen to him as he talks to the television. It's funny to see my dad like this. He's usually so collected and calm, like a seasoned lawyer should be, but he lets loose during these times. I like it.

The game is still on the television when Bradley and his mom, Vicky, arrive for dinner. Bradley steps into the family room to say hello. When he sees what we're watching, a scowl appears on his face and he turns toward the kitchen.

"Brad, the game's on," my dad yells.

"Yeah, I know. I'm just going to see if they need any help in the kitchen. I'll be in later."

Bradley never makes an appearance in the family room, and in the end the Wildcats beat Penn State handily. Not surprising. Alex had an amazing game. Dad said he caught ten passes for over a hundred yards. He also scored a touchdown. I'm proud of Alex, and I'll be sure to tell him when I talk to him tonight. It's something to look forward to—unlike the family firing squad that I'm about to face.

Mom has outdone herself tonight with the dinner. It's hard to believe she had time to cook dinner with all of her barbecue party planning she has going on, but she made lasagna with salad and breadsticks.

In front of everyone, Mom says, "Stella, I warmed you up a Lean Meal. Don't worry, it's lasagna too so you don't feel like you're eating something different than the rest of us. Plus, there's fat-free dressing in the small dish next to your plate."

"Great. Thanks, Mom," I say in the most insincere, monotone voice I can muster.

"You're welcome," she says sweetly—way too sweetly. "You need to be careful of the freshman fifteen, Stella. But knowing you, it'll be more like the freshman twenty-five." She snorts.

And… there it is. My mom just can't help herself when it comes to how I look. And why does she have to do that in front of company? Granted, it's only Vicky and Bradley, but could it be any more embarrassing? Seriously? Does everyone at the table need to know that I get special diet food or that she predicts I'm going to gain twenty-five pounds my first year of college? Her passive-aggressive way of talking to me is getting old, but it's not worth arguing about right now.

The dinner conversation is going on like it usually does. Dad and Vicky talk about the office since Vicky works with my dad at his law firm. Mom talks about the party and all of her other activities. They ask Bradley how things are in his fraternity and how his classes are going. They avoid me like the plague. That is until the dinner portion ends and Mom brings out a double chocolate layer cake.

"Stella—" she starts.

"Yeah, I know, Mom. I'm eating something else," I say snidely.

"Watch that smart mouth of yours, young lady. You definitely don't need cake," snarls Mom.

"I know, Mom."

She hands me a tiny fruit cup.

"Since you brought it up, why don't you tell us why you decided to end things with Bradley?" asks Mom—not so sweetly this time.

"I didn't bring it up."

"Getting snippy about your fresh fruit cup was a start if you ask me," grumbles Mom.

"Fine, let's get this over with then. I'm not getting back together with Bradley," I say defiantly.

"Why in heavens name would you break up with someone like Bradley, Stella? He's the perfect boyfriend, and he'll be a great provider for you once he starts working at Jim's law firm."

There it is again. *Provider.* Ugh.

"I'm not looking for a 'provider,' Mom!"

"Of course not," Mom barks. "You're not thinking of anyone but yourself, young lady. Or are you expecting your father and me to support you forever? So selfish," she mutters under her breath.

"Candy, let's let Stella explain herself," says my dad in his normal calming voice.

"I met someone else," I say cautiously. I don't want to be the one to tell them that Bradley cheated on me, and I wasn't going to mention Alex tonight, but they've left me no choice here.

"Who? Who is this new person you're seeing?" Mom asks in a disbelieving tone.

"You don't know him. I met him in my dorm."

"So, you're expecting us to believe that you met another boy the first week of school and decided to dump the man you're supposed to marry for no reason?" She takes a bite of cake, making sure I notice.

"I don't expect you to believe anything I say. You think the worst of me automatically."

"Well, at least you understand where I'm coming from. I find it hard to believe that you could meet anyone else."

"What's that supposed to mean?" I know what she's insinuating.

My mom sighs like explaining this to me is a chore. "You know what I'm saying. Look at yourself, Stella. Men just aren't going to be that excited about dating someone of your, um, size. Bradley can, at least, see past all of that. Whoever this imaginary boy is, I'm sure he'll lose interest quickly."

I can't do this. I need for them to know the truth. "Bradley, tell them," I plead. I turn to look at him. I'm angry that I have to deal with this alone while he sits there and just watches. This is all his doing in the first place.

"Tell her what, sweetheart?" Bradley asks.

"Tell them about Alex," I say nervously.

"Well, I know she's met Alex Emerson. I'm not sure if she's seeing him, though. He's famous around campus, so it makes sense that she'd pick *him*," he says carefully.

"Bradley, what are you doing? Wait, I know. You're trying to make them think I'm delusional. Well, it's not going to work. I know my dad'll believe me, right, Dad?"

"Oh, sweetheart… are you talking about Alex Emerson, the all-American tight end for the Wildcats? The one that's supposed to go to the NFL next year? The one who's won—"

I don't let him finish. "I cannot believe this. I really can't. Not even my dad believes me? It's the truth, Dad. He wants to be my boyfriend."

I hear a scoff coming from my mom's end of the table. That's it! I'm going to have to tell them what actually happened here since Bradley isn't man enough to admit it. There's a burning behind my eyes. Hearing my dad sound almost sad that I'd make up someone like Alex does it. I clear my throat, and I start to tell them what a cheating snake Bradley is, but when he stops me in midsentence.

"Stella, don't!" Bradley interrupts.

But I keep going. I shouldn't be alone facing this… this interrogation. This is his fault anyway. "The reason I broke up with him was... he, um, he was cheating on me with my roommate, Brooke," I say quickly.

"What?" my dad shouts.

"Oh, Stella, you don't know what you're talking about," says Mom.

Unbelievable. "Mom, I caught him coming out of my bathroom wearing only a towel. His tongue was down her throat."

"I'm sure what you saw was just a little indiscretion. I'm sure he wasn't sleeping with her."

"Mom, I heard him say, 'Come on, baby, let's go get dirty again.'" I repeat his words in a mocking deep voice.

"That's enough," my dad yells. "I've heard enough. Stella, is this true?"

"Yes, Dad, it's true. He was in my dorm when I got back from helping Lily move into her new room. He didn't know I'd had to move into Shepard because he wouldn't return any of my calls or texts. Actually, he hasn't replied to any of my calls or texts since July fifth. I gave up expecting him to contact me."

"I was busy," whines Bradley.

"Bradley, I am ashamed of you," says Dad. "You've always been like a son to me. I expected much more from you, especially with regards to my daughter."

"I know. I'm sorry, sir. It's not what you think. Brooke means nothing to me."

"That's neither here nor there," my dad snaps.

"Jim..." My mom's voice is weirdly cautious. "Let's give Bradley the benefit of the doubt here. I mean—"

"You mean what, Candy?" I've never seen my father this angry before.

"I mean, Stella shouldn't be rash. Who else is going to take her on?" Mom always thinks she's the voice of reason.

"Take her on? What does that even mean?" Dad asks.

"Well, look at her—"

That's when I interject, "I know it's hard for you to believe that anyone would want to date me, Mom and Dad, but I'm not lying when I say that I have met Alex Emerson and he wants to be my boyfriend."

"Yeah, I'll bet!" scoffs Bradley.

I turn to him and glare. "What's that supposed to mean?"

"Well, he's just telling you that to get you into bed. He feels sorry for you because he was there the day everything happened with us," scoffs Bradley.

"I thought you said she wasn't seeing anyone, Bradley," my dad queries.

I ignore my dad's comment. "You didn't want me in *your* bed, so what's it to you?"

"That's not true," he snivels.

"Yes, it is, and you know it. Besides, I'm not having sex with Alex… yet. But we have feelings for each other. Not everyone thinks I'm ugly and disgusting, you know. It is possible for someone to like me just like I am! Alex thinks I'm beautiful," I say the last part quietly. That's it, I can't hold them back, the tears start, and I let them.

"We don't think you're ugly, sweetheart," my dad says.

"Of course she's not ugly, just overweight," Mom pipes up.

Yeah, like that makes it better.

"Candy, enough!" Dad yells. That gets everyone's attention. Number one, my dad doesn't yell, and number two, he never talks back to my mom. He lets my mom do whatever she wants and always has. "I've heard enough from both of you. Our daughter deserves better than a cheating boyfriend."

"Sir, I, uh, Brooke means nothing to me. I care about your daughter."

"You care about my daughter? Really?" sarcasm drips from my dad's voice. Honestly, I've never heard this side of him before.

"Oh, now, honey…" Mom is going to try to talk my dad down. Good luck.

With that, I decide I've had enough. The words start flying from my mouth. "Okay. I'm done. Mom, you've made me feel bad about myself my entire life. You've made me ashamed of my body and my appearance. It has to stop. I'm nineteen, and it's time for you to let it go. I'm not going to get any smaller. There's nothing I can do to change it aside from plastic surgery." I pause, thinking about my own words. "Actually, Mom, I'm surprised you haven't had me under the knife yet—I'm such an embarrassment to you."

That's the most I've ever said, to anyone, about how my mom makes me feel. It's sort of exhilarating. I might as well keep going because this chance isn't going to happen again. I know it. "And while I'm at it, I want to be an art major."

My dad is glaring at Mom, then he scowls at Bradley before turning to me. "We aren't embarrassed by you," my dad says.

Mom is silent. Of course, she is. Vicky's sitting silent, no doubt astonished by the whole thing. Heck, I actually forgot she was even here. But, when she finally speaks, she says, "Um, you know what, I think Bradley and I should go, don't you, Bradley?"

With a shrug, Bradley states glumly, "Yeah, I guess."

"Thank you very much for dinner. Stella, I'm sorry this has happened to you. I'll talk to you soon, sweetheart. I love you," says Vicky sympathetically. I'm not surprised by Vicky's words. While she's been my mom's best friend since high school, Bradley's mom has always been kind to me. It's strange that she and my mom are so close because Vicky's personality is the complete opposite of Mom's and Bradley's. She's quiet and reserved and loving.

Mom stands up abruptly and gives Dad a dirty look. Then she turns to Vicky and Bradley. "Let me walk you out."

"No, we know the way, Candy. Thanks again. Dinner was delicious."

"Good night, Vicky. Bradley," says Mom.

Dad stays quiet. I'd love to say it was strange that the only person who apologized and said they loved me was Vicky, but it's not. Once the front door clicks shut, I get up from my chair. It's time to pack my bag and head back to school tonight. Dealing with my parents anymore this weekend is more than I can take. Mom and Dad don't say a word. They stare at each other from either end of the table. It's beyond tense.

Funny, I sort of feel good about the whole thing—at least the part about me saying what I've wanted and needed to say for years.

I TIPTOE AWAY, leaving them to talk or whatever. I know I've said everything I need to say, but there are still parts of what just happened that are disappointing. Like the fact that those two people in my dining room are supposed to be on *my* side. I think it's possible for my dad to feel that way but not Mom. However, he still didn't believe me when I told him about Alex. He just couldn't believe I could meet someone like him or that someone like Alex would want me. Maybe I should have been more forthcoming while we watched the football game. But the stuff with Bradley hadn't been hashed yet—no, it wasn't the right time, and I'm not going to second-guess myself at this point. It doesn't matter when I told him about Alex, he should have believed me. He should know that I wouldn't just make something like that up. I've never been that kind of person.

Maybe Dad's right, though. That I *have* been living in a fantasy world. Alex Emerson is one of those guys who will end up on magazine covers next to supermodels, and I'm… well, I'm just me. Average Stella Matthews—future cat lady. It's okay. Cats are cool. I've never had a pet before. Mom wouldn't hear of it. So, that's something to look forward to.

In my room, I gather my things. I hadn't really unpacked, so it only takes a couple of minutes. After grabbing my bag, I walk quietly down the stairs. I don't even want to tell them I'm leaving. They'll hear my car pull away and get the idea. As I sneak toward the door, I hear their raised voices coming from the dining room. I hear my name, so of course I stop to listen. I know it's wrong, but I want to know what they think of me behind my back. It can't be any worse than what they say to my face, right?

"Candy, enough is enough," I hear my dad saying. "I've heard you talk about Stella in this disparaging way for too long. She's a beautiful girl. Does she really believe she's dating Emerson or is she just saying that to soften the blow of losing Bradley? It's hard to tell," Dad questions aloud.

"She could have Bradley back anytime she wants," Mom remarks.

"Do you sincerely want her to be with someone who cheats on her?"

"Well, no, but Bradley is a logical choice for her. He's willing to marry her."

"*Willing* to marry her?" Dad's voice sounds incredulous. "Is that what we want for her? Someone willing to marry her? I, for one, want Stella to be happy, even if that means she never gets married."

"I'd like grandchildren someday, *Jim*." Mom sounds snippy.

"Well, I want grandchildren too but not at the expense of her happiness."

"I don't know what you're talking about. Bradley would make her a fine husband. He could make her happy."

"Again, Candy, he's a cheater," my dad says angrily.

"Maybe she misunderstood what was happening? He's a normal young man—"

"Candy." There's a long pause. "I was young once too, and I never cheated on you. If it's normal for Bradley, it should be normal for every man according to that logic. That's not what we want for her. At least that's not what *I* want for her. What I want is for her to be happy."

"I want her to be happy too, Jim."

"Do you? Because it doesn't come across that way. You're extremely critical of her. It's been going on too long. I should have intervened before today. Then maybe she wouldn't feel compelled to make up all-American boyfriends," Dad mutters.

I scoff at that. He really thinks I'm delusional. I start to leave but stop again.

"I want the best for her too. I want her to look her best and present herself in the best possible way," explains Mom.

"She is all of those things. She's beautiful. Her manners are impeccable. And that's all thanks to you, Candy. But you go too far with her. I've watched you talk down to her and berate her when she doesn't deserve it. I've let you handle all of those things so far because you're her mom and mothers and daughters should work together, but it's gone on long enough. It's time for me to step in. We need to let her grow up and find her own happiness. Let's allow her to be who she's supposed to be."

"Well, I want that too. I'm not trying to stifle that, Jim."

"Actually, I think you might be trying to stifle that to create her in your own image. You've got to remember, she's five feet three inches tall, and she's built just like *your* mother."

"Oh, don't say that!" Mom sounds horrified.

"Candace, she's never going to be you—five feet nine and slim. She's never going to look like you. She's voluptuous. She's nineteen, and her body is what it is. It's not going to change no matter how much vegetarian lasagna and fresh fruit you make her eat."

Mom scoffs.

"She eats relatively healthy foods, and that's thanks to you. You've taught her how to do that."

"If she would exercise more——" Mom tries to explain.

"Candy, we all could exercise more. It's not just Stella. Let's give her the benefit of the doubt. We've kept a tight rein on her for her entire life. Maybe we need to trust that we did a good job and let her make some of her own choices now."

"Do you mean let her be an art major?" Mom scoffs again. "Where did that come from anyway?"

"She's always loved art. From the time she could hold a crayon, she's been making art. So, yeah, maybe I am. I could think of worse things she could do. For example, not finishing college because she hates what she's doing. That's number one on the list. How would you have liked to have your parents dictate what you studied in college? As I recall, your mom wanted you to major in home economics."

"Ugh, don't remind me, Jim."

"The point is, you did what you wanted to do, Candy."

"I know, but I chose mathematics, a solid degree."

"That you haven't used," he reminds her. "Don't look at me like that, Candy. You know what I mean. I want her to decide what'll make her happy. She's a talented painter. I know you've noticed."

"She is, but painting is just a hobby."

"Not to everyone it's not. I'm ready to let Stella make some choices. And you need to figure out a way to make things right with your daughter. If you don't, there'll be a cavernous divide in your relationship forever. If she has children, you may never get to see them if you continue treating her like she's not good enough. She may not want that type of attitude around her own children."

"Jim! What are you saying to me?" I can hear Mom sniffling. She's crying? She rarely cries. Even so, I find it hard to feel sorry for her.

After listening to their talk, I decide that I'm not as angry as I was and choose to stay overnight. But I won't go to the barbecue. I've endured enough for one weekend.

It was a fascinating conversation, though. I wonder if anything will change. Tiptoeing back upstairs, I make sure to be as quiet as possible. I don't want them to know I was in earshot of their little discussion. Once in my room, I plop down on my bed and sigh. What a night. What a day. I'm exhausted. I smile remembering how my day started—in Alex's bed with his arm wrapped around me. A shiver runs through me at the memory. My good thoughts are marred by the memory of Bradley in my dorm room. "What did I ever see in Bradley?" Or better yet, how did I let myself believe Bradley actually cared for me? I should have known on the 4th of July, the day my future was planned out for me, that something was amiss. I squeeze my eyes shut, trying to avoid thinking about that day, but no matter how much I try, the memories keep trying to weasel themselves to the surface.

After Bradley's sweet proposal and the fireworks, he and I walked down by the lake. He took my hand, and we strolled away from prying eyes. When we were far enough away, I stepped up onto my tiptoes and leaned in to kiss him. He's not super tall, probably five foot nine inches, but I'm only five foot three inches so, I had to stretch up to reach his lips. He kissed me back—no tongue, of course. I thanked him again for the beautiful ring and the romantic gesture. He told me that he wanted to show everyone how much I meant to him. That's why he did it so publicly.

After the kiss, I told Bradley I was ready for us to move on to the next level, and by next level, I meant sex. Heck, I think I would have accepted touching or groping of any kind. I mean, I was eighteen going on nineteen and still a virgin! We'd been together for almost a year. I thought it was time, especially since he was promised to me.

But Bradley wasn't convinced. He said he thought we should wait.

He wanted to do it at a special time and place. He said he'd plan something for us in the near future so that we could take that important step. Reluctantly, I agreed. I mean, what else could I do?

After our embarrassing little talk, we rushed back to join our friends. I went to join Lily while Bradley joined all of his fraternity brothers. Lily's known me since first grade. She could tell when something was wrong with me before I knew it sometimes.

"What's wrong?" Lily asked.

I shrugged, not ready to admit that Bradley turned me down, again. Lily didn't relent. So, I told her.

Lily rolled her eyes. "You know he's not a virgin, right?"

I shrugged again. I didn't know for sure, but I suspected. After all, he was two years older than me and going to be a junior in college. I assumed he had experience. "I know. I guess Bradley just wants to make it special."

After another dramatic eye roll—sometimes I thought those eyes of hers would roll right out of her head—she added, "He slept with, like, every female in his high school class, and I mean every female."

"Allegedly," I defended.

"Allegedly, my ass!"

I rolled my own eyes at Lily's dramatic response. It's not possible that he slept with every female. I know at least one girl who would not be interested in Bradley, or any other boy for that matter. I doubt he talked her into bed. Just saying. "I don't expect him to be a virgin. That just means that he will know what to do when the time comes." I nodded as I spoke. It made it look like I was on board with Bradley's plan.

I cringe at the memories. I mean, what a joke. My life is one big, stupid joke. I roll over on my side and stare at my Charlie Puth poster. "I bet you'd treat a girl better than that, wouldn't you, Charlie?" Yeah, I'm talking to a poster. I slide the pillow underneath my head and take a deep breath. Just as I start to doze off, I hear a ding from my phone. Wow, great timing. It's Alex.

Donnie: You there, sweetness?
Me: Sweetness? That's a new one, Donnie.
Donnie: Because you're sweet as can be.
Me: Really? Thank you.
Donnie: You're welcome. How has it been at home?
Did you deal with Brad?

I really don't feel like talking about it but I suppose I must.

Me: It went okay.

Maybe that's enough and he'll let it drop.

Me: Great game, by the way. You were amazing!
Donnie: Oh, stop. ;)

It's working.

Me: I also googled you.
Donnie: And? What did you learn that you didn't
know already?
Me: Everything. Do you know how many times you're
listed on Google? It's insane. You're like a celebrity.
Donnie: No, I'm not. I'm just me, Pixie. Now, I
noticed you switched topics on me. Tell me… how did
everything go tonight?
Me: Ugh, don't ask.
Donnie: But I am asking. Are you OK?
Me: It was about what I expected.
Donnie: You aren't back with Brad, are you?
Me: Of course not. It's just, well, my mom is not a very
nice person. I'll just leave it at that. I didn't mean to,
but I sort of, maybe, told them that you and I were
dating.

Donnie: Good. I'm glad. But do they know who I am?
Me: Of course! My dad's a huge Wildcat football fan. He knows about you. The sad part is that they didn't believe me. They thought I made you up to deflect some of the conversation about Bradley and me.
Donnie: What? Why wouldn't they believe you?
Me: They don't believe someone like you would want to be with someone like me.
Donnie: Someone like you? You mean beautiful, sexy, smart, funny, and amazing?
Me: Well, they don't see me like that, I guess.
Donnie: That's terrible. What do you want me to do, Stella? Can I help you in any way?
Me: No. You're already doing it. I was really happy to see your name pop up on my screen, Mr. Football God.
Donnie: Grrrr
Me: LOL. You seriously just text growled at me. The other good news is that I'm heading back early. After everything that happened today, I'm heading back to school first thing tomorrow. Screw the blasted barbecue.
Donnie: Really? That's awesome. So, what are you doing tomorrow night then? It's Sunday, and we don't have school on Monday….
Me: I've no plans since this was impromptu.
Donnie: Well, I'd like to ask… would you go on a date with me, Stella?
Me: To the caf?
Donnie: Nope. A real date. One where we dress up, eat at a fancy place with candles and what not. What do you say?

Oh, my gosh. Alex Emerson just asked me on a date. A real one.

Me: Sure. That sounds nice. What time?
Donnie: I'll pick you up at your room at 6:30 p.m.
Does that work?
Me: Yep. That works.
Donnie: All right, Pixie. Time for my beauty sleep. I
worked extra hard on the field today to impress my girl.
I hope it worked.
Me: You were trying to impress me?
Donnie: Of course.
Me: You are so sweet, Alex, thank you.
Donnie: Just thank me by going out with me tomor-
row. Sweet dreams, sweetness.
Me: Ha-ha. Night, Alex.

He has got to be the sweetest man that ever lived, I swear. I
lie back on my pillow and reread the texts that he sent to me. A
date? A *real* date? I've never been on an actual date. Bradley
never saw the need—either that or he just didn't want to be
seen with me. I think it was the second one, sadly. I fall asleep
clutching my phone to my chest. Alex made the bad part of my
day fade away. Poof.

Chapter Thirteen

Bzzzzzzz.

I awaken to a loud buzzing beside my head.

"What the hell?" I grumble. Whatever it is, it's making my head vibrate. Oh, wait, I fell asleep holding my phone. As it buzzes again, I run my hands over the top of my sheets and under my pillow. "Ah-ha! Found it!"

I look at the screen and read: Donnie wants to FaceChat. I push the green button and wait for his face to appear. "Uh, hello? Is everything okay?"

"Hey, beautiful. I thought I'd call and wake you up so you can get back home faster."

"Oh, well, gee thanks," I reply sarcastically. "What time is it?"

"Six," he says, like it isn't the ass-crack of dawn. "Actually, there was another reason I called."

"Yeah?"

"Yeah, is there any way I can talk to your dad?"

"My dad?"

"Yeah? You think he's up yet?"

"I'm sure he's up. He gets up at like four in the morning. He's a dork."

"Can you take your phone to him?"

"I guess. What's this about?"

"Just take me to him."

"Okay." I pull myself out of my bed. "I'm sure I look like a crazy person with my hair standing on end, but that's what you get when you wake a girl up *this* early," I grumble. Oh hell, I look like a crazy bag lady.

"You look beautiful, babe. I love seeing you first thing in the morning. I'd like to make a habit of it, actually."

"You're the sweetest. I'm just glad this isn't smell-a-vision. My breath is terrible."

Alex chuckles. When I reach the kitchen, I hear my parents chatting away. I hear the word "barbeque" as I push through the swinging kitchen door. I feel a little awkward after last night, but I'm not letting that get in the way of whatever Alex has planned. "Uh, Dad?"

He turns to look at me, surprise written all over his face. No doubt due to the time. "Yes, sweetheart?"

"Um, I've got a phone call for you."

"For me? Why did they call your cell?"

Too many questions this early, so I just hand him the phone. "Here, he's on FaceChat. Just look into the screen so he can see your face," I say that loud enough for Alex to hear.

My dad takes my phone in hand and says, "Hello?"

"Yes, hello, sir. This is Alex Emerson. I play football for the Northwestern Wildcats, and I'm your daughter's boyfriend. I thought I'd take the opportunity to introduce myself to you and invite you up to one of our games."

My dad's eyes have gotten huge. He's blinking at the phone, then at my mom, then at me.

I merely smile.

"Well, son, that would be wonderful. I'm a huge Wildcat

fan, and I've been following your career for several years. It would be an honor to be your guest."

"Well, technically, you'll be Stella's guest. I've signed over two of my season tickets to her, so she can watch me play each week. She can bring any guest she chooses."

Huh? That's news to me.

"Well, that's very generous of you, son."

"Not generous. I want my girlfriend in the stands to watch me play. It makes me want to impress her."

I look at my mom. She's actually scowling. When he says the part about impressing his girlfriend, I swear she scoffs. It's like a grown-ass version of Brooke living right in my own house. Why have I never noticed that before?

"Alex, it was nice talking to you. I look forward to meeting you next weekend," Dad says.

"Me too, sir. Can I speak to Stella again?"

"Of course." Dad holds the phone out to me. "Stella?" He has the biggest, cheesiest smile I've ever seen on his face. I wonder what makes him happier, that he gets to go to a game or that I'm dating Alex Emerson? Maybe both. I take the phone from Dad and walk out of the kitchen away from the stares.

"Alex?" I say.

"I'm here. Was that okay?"

"That was...." I pause to catch my breath. "Hang on, Alex." I rush up the steps to my bedroom because I need to get as far away from the kitchen as I can. I don't want my parents to listen to our conversation. "That was fantastic. Now they have no doubt. It's probably going to take my dad a week to come down from the high of talking to the amazing Alex Emerson," I say, giggling.

"What about your mom?"

"I have no idea what to expect from her. It's not going to be good. She's just realized that she was wrong—that she misjudged the situation last night. She isn't going to take kindly to being made a fool of."

"I'm sorry, Pixie."

"No need to be sorry. I'm looking forward to seeing you tonight. That means I need to get packed up."

"Okay, I'll hang up so you can get here sooner. I've got a team meeting this afternoon, so I won't be around. I'll just see you at six thirty sharp. Okay?"

"Yep. Six-thirty sharp."

"Drive safe."

"I will. Bye."

"Bye, Pixie."

As I pack up my things, I hear a knock on my door. It's Dad.

"Hey, pumpkin. What's going on? Are you leaving?"

"Yeah, I'm heading back early. Lots to do and all that."

"What about the barbecue?"

"I don't have it in me today. Yesterday was really the tipping point for me with Mom, and with you, to be honest. You didn't believe that I could be with someone like Alex Emerson. You thought I made him up."

"I know, honey, and I'm very sorry for not believing you. It's just that he's a, well, he's a celebrity, and you don't expect anyone you know to date someone famous. It's not that I think you're not good enough or pretty enough. I do. You're my beautiful Stella. As for your mom, I don't know what I can say about that. She's got some soul-searching to do. I can under-stand why you don't want to be around today. I don't blame you, actually."

"You don't?"

"No, I don't. I'll let your mother know. I don't think you need another confrontation with her today. Do you need any help with your bags?"

"No, I only have the one." I go up to him and wrap my

arms around him for a hug. Stepping back, I smile up at him. I can't say I'm completely okay with my dad's reasoning about me and Alex, but I want this to be over. "Thanks, Dad. I'll see you next weekend?"

"Yeah!" he says excitedly. "That's going to be great!"

The trip back to school goes quickly. Driving my own little car back is so liberating. Finding a parking spot is another story, though. It's almost impossible to find a place for long-term parking without an N.U. Parking permit. I find a parking garage a couple of blocks from campus that allows monthly parking. That will have to do until I get an assigned spot. I grab my bag and start the trek to my dorm. I've been thinking about the events from yesterday and the call from Alex this morning. Why was that so satisfying? I suppose it's just the fact that I was vindicated. Alex did that for me. Then, my mind turns to my roommate and the fact I can't wait to move in with Lily. I'm going to miss going to the cafeteria with Alex and Hank, but the rest of it can't end soon enough. I hope, after I move, I never see Brooke Clark again.

AS SOON AS I step into my dorm, I breathe a sigh of relief because it's silent, which means Brooke's gone. I set my things in my room and plop down onto my bed and send a text to Alex.

Me: I'm back. Going to unpack and do some homework. C u tonight! I can't wait!
Donnie: Same! Glad you're back safe and sound. ;)

After finishing my homework, I begin the fruitless search for something to wear on my date. Besides my graphic tees, there's not a lot to choose from. When I spy something dark blue, I grasp the hanger and pull it out. It's the dress from the July 4th party. The one where Bradly…. Never mind him. Lily told me I looked hot in this dress, like a 1950s pinup girl, so it's the perfect dress for my very first date.

At five thirty, I begin the process of getting ready. I hop in the shower and shave everywhere—and I mean everywhere. I've never shaved my lady parts before. It's not easy to do when you have a tummy—there was a lot of contorting going on, but I think I've managed to get it all taken care of. It's not like I expect Alex to try anything tonight. But he might. I want to be prepared for anything.

I pull out my fancy, blue, lace boy shorts and slip them on my smooth legs. What is it about a pretty pair of undies to make a girl feel good about herself? I decide to go braless because the dress is snug enough in the bodice that a bra is unnecessary. Besides, Alex will never know. I step into the dress and pull it up over my hips and slide my arms into the sleeves. Luckily, the long row of buttons that run down the front of the dress help open the dress far enough to allow me to put it on this way. I start the tedious process of buttoning it up. There are twenty-four in all, and it takes a bit of time. Once it's all cinched up, I turn and peer into the mirror above my dresser. Uh-oh, my chest is practically bursting from the top. "I don't remember my boobs being this obvious when I wore it last summer." I hold the dress with one hand and press my chest down into the top with the other. It's better, but they're still really obvious. It's going to have to do unless I want to wear my tee that says, *Every night's date night.*

After hooking the little belt at my waist, I peer at my reflection one more time and decide that I don't look *so* bad. My boobs are a bit obvious, but not in a trashy sort of way. I hope not anyway. Since I'm not sure, I send a selfie to Lily and ask her if it's okay. I'd talked with Lily earlier about my date tonight. She's excited for me. She writes back with two thumbs up emojis, which I take as a good sign. I finish up by flat ironing my hair. It looks shiny and sleek. I add a little pink eyeshadow, brown eyeliner, and mascara. Then I dab on some pink lip gloss. I don't want to wear flip-flops and definitely don't want to try heels, so I pull out some silver, practically new flats from the back of my closet.

When a knock sounds at the door, I gasp. "He's here." I reach for my small clutch person, throw in my ID card, my debit card, and a small brush, just in case. Oh jeez, I'm so nervous. I shouldn't be, but I am. When I walk out into the lounge area to answer the door, I spot Brooke standing in her bedroom doorway.

"Well, well, well, what do we have here?" Brooke mocks. "Where are you going all dressed up?"

"Out." I don't have time or energy for her snark. Just a few more weeks and I'll be free of her.

"Are you sure you want to wear that ugly dress? Can it be any tighter?"

Ignore her, ignore her, ignore her. Just then there's another knock on the door. Brooke moves so fast I don't have a chance to get to the door first. She pulls it open, revealing the hottest man in the universe. He's wearing snug, dark denim jeans, a blue button-down shirt, and a gray sport jacket—no tie. I kind of wish he had a tie. Just then, I see the tie in his hand. I wonder if he's trying to decide whether to wear it or not. His hair looks wavy tonight and maybe a bit too long, but I like it. He's clean-shaven, and I just bet he smells like heaven. He has such a beautiful face with his clear blue eyes, strong jaw, and nose. But his mouth is the best part. His lips are full, and the top lip has that sweet cupid's bow. I realize I'm staring, so I look at Brooke who's standing with her arms crossed and her hips jutting to the side like she's ready to say something evil. Her outfit is especially small tonight as well—only teeny tiny shorts and an equally tiny tank top.

She practically purrs, "Hiiiii, Alex!"

Alex doesn't even see her. His eyes find mine, and he smiles. His gaze travels from my eyes, pauses on my mouth, and then continues downward. When they reach my breasts, his eyes get huge and his smile turns to something else. Shock? Or does he just hate my dress?

"Jesus, Pixie. What are you wearing?"

Oh, he hates it. Maybe the Evil One is right.

"It's super tight, isn't it?" Brooke announces. "I told her she'd better go change. It looks ridiculous."

Once again Alex ignores Brooke and strides toward me. He stops directly in front of me and places his hands on my hips. My eyes tingle, tears beginning to find their way to the surface. I close them tight, fighting for control. *My dress is too tight.* Which means it's not appropriate for my date, and Alex doesn't like it.

"Pixie, baby, you look beautiful. I'm speechless. You look like a wet dream," he whispers in my ear.

"A wet dream?" I whisper back.

Just then I hear Brooke scoff. God, I'm so sick of her.

"I think we need to skip dinner and head back to my place so I can really get a look at you," he says, smiling.

I smile back. He likes it. "Alex."

"I know, I know, later. Let's get going."

Alex takes my hand and leads the way out the door. Before I shut the door, I turn to see the look on Brooke's face. It's the same ugly look I get every day. I shrug and smile at her. That's all I can do.

When we reach an enormous black pickup in the lot adjacent to our dorm, I exclaim, "Wow. That's a big truck!"

"I'm a big guy. I need room to spread out in there. Plus, I love trucks. They make me feel tough," he says, laughing.

"You don't need a truck for that."

Instead of responding, he leans down and kisses my lips

softly; then he runs his finger over the top of my chest—it's bulging out of my dress.

"Thank you," he says.

"Thank you for what?"

"Thank you for the compliment and thank you, thank you, thank you for wearing that dress. I'm going to remember you in this dress for the rest of my life," he says, still running his fingertip over the top of my breasts.

His touch makes my breathing speed up. How can this one little action turn me into a shivering mess? Those shivers reach all the way down to lady land again.

"Shall we go?" I ask.

"Sure. But first, can you help me with my tie? I can never tie these things."

My dad taught me how to do this years ago. I was always fascinated with all of the flips and folds that he did when he was getting ready for work.

"You're going to have to bend down or something."

Alex bends down so I can wrap the silk around his neck. There is something so intimate about tying a man's tie. I'm standing close enough to feel his breath on my face. His scent is all around me. When my fingers touch his neck, I've got the urge to pull him closer.

Instead, I flip the tie around, and it first hits my face then his. He laughs, and I giggle. Giving me the sweetest smile, Alex watches me closely. It's then that I decide to be a little flirty. I pull the tie ends toward me to bring him closer. I'd like to say that he was looking in my eyes at the time, but I can't. His eyes are staring right at my chest. I use my finger to lift his chin.

"My eyes are up here," I say, laughing. I lean in and kiss him softly on the lips. It feels perfect.

"I can't help it, Stella. Jesus, your tits are amazing in that dress."

I choke, surprised at his use of the word "tits."

"Sorry, that was a little vulgar. I'll watch my mouth."

I don't mind, really. I probably should, but he said it in such a genuine way—like he was in awe of them or something.

When I'm finished with his tie, Alex stands at his full height. "You look so handsome, Alex." And he does.

"Let me get your door, princess." He pulls his keys fob from his pocket and presses the unlock button. As he opens my door, I turn to get into the truck, but the seat is at about eye level for me. I look down to see if there are some steps to lead me up but no such luck. Just then I feel big hands on my waist lifting me up, up, up. I climb into the truck and slide into the seat. He's next to me before I get the chance to reach for my seat belt. His face is in my cleavage. Coincidence? I think not. I start to laugh.

"Pix, I can't help it. I'm only human, for God's sake. All I want to do is bury my face in there for the rest of my life."

Oh goodness!

He shuts my door and runs around to the driver's side, hopping into the truck easily. When the engine rumbles, he slides the shifter into drive and off we go.

"I thought I'd take you to a new steak place out in Oak Park. One of the guys said it was excellent and there are a lot of choices on the menu, so you don't have to eat steak if you don't want to. Is that okay?"

"Sure. That sounds good." Steak sounds great.

As we drive, Alex tells me a little bit about the team meeting and the big game against the University of Iowa next weekend. He tells me my tickets will be at the Will Call window at the stadium under my name. It's also the moment he warns me, "You'll be sitting with my parents."

"Y-Your parents?" I stutter.

"Yep, they have my other two tickets. Each team member gets four."

"What about your sister? Doesn't she want to see you

play?"

"Nah. She's too busy with her high school stuff to want to watch her big brother play football. Besides, I want my girl to have my tickets."

"If you're sure?"

"Positive. Plus, your dad will get a kick out of the seats. They're pretty good."

"Oh, he will. He's really excited. Thanks for doing all of that, by the way. You didn't have to talk to him about, err, us."

"I wanted to, Stella. It's not right that they didn't believe you."

"I know." It's all I can say before we pull into the restaurant parking lot. He finds a parking spot in the back of the lot with space enough for his huge truck.

I reach for my door handle but hear him say, "Don't even think about it."

"What?"

"I'm coming around to help you out. Sit tight."

I sit tight as he jogs around the truck, opens my door, and steps up again to unbuckle me.

"I am capable of unbuckling myself, you know?" He ignores this little outburst as he slowly releases the belt, watching it slide back over my chest. Seriously? I'm starting to think he's kind of a pervert which for some reason, makes me laugh.

"What's so funny?"

"Nothing."

He leans up and kisses my lips. It's a gentle kiss, but I want more, and yet I want to linger here too. His lips brush against mine, his breath heating me from the inside out. Why are we bothering with dinner again?

"I'm glad you're here with me, Stella."

"Me too."

He slides his arms around me and lifts me out of the truck

until my feet touch the ground. "Let's eat. I'm starving."

When we enter, we're seated immediately even though there's a long line to get into the place. They must have recognized his name on the reservation. The hostess seems to be lingering a little too long after seating us as well, batting her eyelashes at Alex and giggling like a fangirl. *Hello, I'm right here*, I want to say. What is it with women today? The girl blinks like twenty times. Her eyes move from Alex to me then back to Alex.

Then she has the nerve to point and ask, "*That's* your girlfriend?"

"Yes, it is. Can you leave us to our dinner? Please?" he asks politely.

She huffs, then stomps away. I roll my eyes while Alex apologizes. I assure him that it's not his fault. After we order, we sit in silence. It's not uncomfortable silence, but it's strange since we usually have so much to talk about. In retrospect, I don't think we've had any trouble talking to one another since the first day we met. I've felt at ease with him from the very beginning. Why is he so quiet now? I bring up several things about geology class, and he just nods and says things like "Uh-huh" and "Yep." The food comes, and that helps ease the tension that I feel. Alex orders the world's biggest steak, and I order a grilled chicken breast with a side of steamed veggies. Even though my mom is not my favorite person, I still can't seem to break away from her years of brainwashing—err, I mean guidance about healthy eating.

As we eat, there's more silence, and it's deafening. I've run out of mundane things to talk about, and I'm starting to feel self-conscious. Am I a terrible date? I must be boring as hell either that or he regrets bringing me. Or worse, he's embarrassed to be seen with me.

Why do I keep putting myself through things like this? I know it'll end in pain. Mine. Tears prick my eyes. Where did they come from? No matter, I can't stop them. He doesn't notice though because he isn't even looking at me. His eyes are roaming around the restaurant. Is he hoping he doesn't see anyone he knows?

I can't take it. It's too much.

I set my fork down and choke out, "I'm not feeling well."

I get up abruptly, grab my purse, and rush to the entrance of the restaurant. I wish I had my own car then I could get away from here. Maybe I can grab a cab if I head out toward the main road. As I turn to move in that direction, big arms wrap around my waist.

"Leave me alone, Alex. I need to go."

Lifting me off the ground, he carries me to a secluded spot at the side of the building. So embarrassing.

Setting me down, he turns me until I'm facing him. "Stella, what happened? Did I do something?"

"Did you do something?" Yes. No. That's just it. He didn't *do* anything. He didn't speak to me or look at me. "No."

"Then what's wrong?"

"Nothing." I shake my head, but I know he won't let me leave until I explain. "I guess I'm a boring date. I'm sorry for that. I've never been on a date before, and I must not have done it right."

"What do you mean you've never been on a date before? Didn't you date—"

"Yes, jeez, I dated him for a year, but we never actually went on 'a date,'" I say with air quotes. "He usually just came over to my house and watched television."

"What the hell, Pixie? What were you doing with that guy all of that time?" He sounds pissed.

That's when I lose it. "It's not like people were banging down my door to ask me out. They weren't, Alex. You might as well know that you're on a date with a fat loser. Wait, you already know that. You could barely look at me through dinner.

You wouldn't talk to me. I'm sorry I'm such an embarrassment to you too." I hiccup and start an all-out sob. I think the last time I cried this hard I was standing in front of Alex the day we met. Great. Just great.

"Embarrassment? Why would you say such a thing, Stella?"

I can barely talk through the bawling, but I try to get it out through rapid breaths.

"Because everyone is embarrassed to be seen with me." I've worked myself into such a crying jag that I can't catch my breath now.

He wraps his arms around me, pulling me into him.

"I'm sorry. I was the one that was the terrible date. Honestly, it was because I had a hard-on the size of Pike's Peak. I kept looking at you in that dress, and I couldn't concentrate on anything else. I started to look at other things in the restaurant to get the thing to go down, if you know what I mean. But then you were talking, and it seems even your little voice makes me excited."

"Huh?" I say through sniffles.

"Honey, I'm so sorry. I'm the one who ruined our date. My mind has been on getting you naked, not on conversation."

"Oh." What can I say to that? Do I look down at his pants to see if he's telling the truth? No, that's a bad idea, but I do it anyway. My eyes slide south until they reach his zipper, and yep, he wasn't lying. "Whoa."

"Yeah. See? That's what you do to me on a normal day. That dress has added serious voltage to him."

"Him?"

"Yeah. I don't have a name for my dick, so I just refer to it as him or the big guy."

I lower my head until it's against his chest and giggle. "Alex, you're such a dork."

"Yeah, I know." He takes my hand in his and leads me back

to the truck. "Let's head back. We can get cozy at my place and talk about you and that naughty little dress in private."

At the truck, he goes through the ritual of unlocking and opening the door and lifting me into the truck. As he's about to buckle me in, he places his hand on the back of my neck and pulls me forward to kiss me deeply. His tongue darts out into my open mouth as he tries to touch every spot inside.

He moans in my mouth. "Jesus, Stella, you're driving me crazy."

"I am?"

"Yeah, you are." He slides his hand down from my neck to the front of my dress, feeling my nipple harden under his touch. I arch into him.

"We'd better stop now. We're in the middle of a parking lot, after all," I reluctantly say.

Alex grunts. Instead of buckling me in, he shuts my door and slides in through his side. When I reach for my seat belt, he stops me, lifting up the center console. Then he pulls my hand so I scoot closer until I'm right next to him, thigh to thigh. Reaching back, he finds the center seat belt strap and buckles me into place.

After putting the truck into drive, he slides his hand just beneath the hem of my dress and rests it there. The warmth from his palm feels nice. Anytime this man touches me, I turn into a quivering mess. I decide that turnabout is fair play, so I reach over and touch his huge, muscled thigh. He jumps from my touch, but I don't move my hand. Instead, I gently rub back and forth from the outside to the inside of his thigh. I can't help noticing his breathing has started to pick up. His left hand is clutching the steering wheel so tightly I see white knuckles, and it looks like he's gritting his teeth. His jaw is so tense.

"Are you okay?" I ask.

Just then, he turns the wheel suddenly to the left and heads down a dark side street.

"Where are we going?"

"To finish what we started."

He finds a dark tree-lined street that almost seems abandoned and pulls off to the side. After throwing the truck into park, he roughly slides his seat back as far as it will go. After reaching over to unbuckle my seat belt, he grabs my hand, tugging it in his direction.

"What?" I squeak.

"I want you on my lap, Stella."

"Oh, no, I'll hurt you."

"Stella, please." He sounds sort of desperate. "Get on my lap."

I'm frozen in my spot. Looking down at his lap, I attempt to figure out how I'm going to achieve that goal. I guess I'm taking too long because, before I know it, Alex has his hands on my waist and I'm in the air, and then I'm straddling his lap a second later. I move around a little bit, attempting to get comfortable, when he growls. I feel his hardness between my legs and do my best to get closer. Man, it feels good.

"I need to see you, Stella. Can I?"

I'm not sure what he means by "see" me. I'm a little worried about it, to be honest, but I go ahead and say quietly, "Okay."

Next, he reaches up and starts to unbutton my dress, slowly, one button at a time.

"So many buttons, Pixie."

"Twenty-four."

"Twenty-four what?" His eyes are on the work he's doing on my dress.

"Buttons. Twenty-four buttons," I say, panting a little.

"You counted them?"

"Uh-huh" is all I can muster.

"Fuck!" he growls again. Alex is now working furiously on

the buttons. By the time he has six undone, he starts to pull the two sides of my dress apart.

"What? What's wrong?"

"Babe, no bra?"

"Uh, no. The dress was really tight, and I didn't think I needed one. Plus, I hate bras. They're uncomfortable. You should try wearing one. You'd know what I am talking about. Even though they make pretty ones and stuff."

I'm nervous but also full of anticipation. There's no other way to describe it. I'm watching him unbutton my dress. The girls are on full display now.

"Fucking beautiful," he says breathlessly. "Pixie, can I touch you?"

I breathe out a yes.

"Are you sure?"

I nod. "Uh-huh."

He slides both hands up from my waist until they meet my revealed flesh. He runs them up underneath each breast, feeling the weight of them in his hands. "These are spectacular. I knew they would be, Pixie," he says breathlessly. When his fingers brush across each nipple, I moan, so he does it again, along with more like pinching and tugging on each nipple. It's making me squirm in his lap.

"Oh, God," I moan out.

"You like that?"

I nod because I can't speak. Guttural noises are all I can muster. He squeezes each breast. They aren't small, so they overflow in his giant hands. He leans up and kisses me frantically. His tongue moves around in my mouth in an increasing pace. I meet him with my own passionate kisses. Feeling how hard he is, I have an uncontrollable urge to move my hips, so I slowly rock back and forth on top of him. He moans loudly and breaks away from the kiss. I feel a sucking sensation as he moves down to kiss and suckle on my breast. Holy moly!

Alex pulls away from my breast to say, "The way you're moving on top of me feels amazing. Don't stop."

"I won't," I pant.

With that request, I reach for Alex and run my fingers through his beautiful, wavy hair while kissing him hard and fast. My tongue darts out to meet his. He turns his head to the side and presses his tongue in again. His tongue is deeper now. As we kiss, I grind into him. I've never, ever, ever felt like this before—as if I'm going to explode. The orgasm he gave me the other day was nothing compared to this feeling tonight. This one is way more intense. I can't help but worry though. Should I be doing this? As I think about that, Alex grips my hips with his big hands and begins to grind up as I grind down. Oh my God!

I plead with Alex, "Don't ever stop."

"I won't. I won't," he chants.

And that's when it happens. I explode into a million pieces. It's so amazing. I've never felt so light—so good. I've read about this in my romance books—the French call it *le petite mort*, or the little death. I think I get the meaning now. As I slow my hips down, I hear Alex begging me to keep going. He's not done yet. Good to know. I continue to move. Oh crap, it's building up again. I never knew. I'll never be the same again. So, I rock back and forth and rub against him. I'm paying more attention to Alex's words now. My God, the boy talks dirty.

"That's it, sweetheart, grind into my cock." His hands reach up to squeeze my breasts. "You have the most amazing tits, baby. God, I want to fuck you so bad, Stella. I can't wait to sink into that tight little pussy of yours. It's going to be fucking amazing. I want you to come all over my cock and my face. I can't wait to taste you, honey."

Taste me? What does that even mean? I'm going to have to google this stuff later.

He's still talking. "I can't wait to have your sweet little mouth on my big cock. Okay, damn, are you close again, Stella?"

Wow! I mean wow! I'm almost there when he says, "Are you ready, Pixie? I'm not gonna last much longer. Come for me, now!"

That's it, that's all it takes is him telling me to come and I orgasm again. I don't know how it's possible, but it's better than the first one. Who knew dirty talk could put a girl over the top? I hear him shout out his release and my name. It sounds wonderful, having my name on his lips at this moment. He's still muttering dirty things, but it's quieting down.

"Holy shit, Pixie. I've never come so hard in my life. You turn me on so much. I'm hard the minute I see you. Shit, I don't even have to see you. If I just think about you or hear your voice, I'm done for."

"Um, thanks?" I say hesitantly.

Alex exhales. "I'm sorry, babe. Did that whole thing scare you? Once we started, I just couldn't stop. I hope you aren't upset. I don't want you to feel like you're not safe with me."

"No, I'm okay," I say with a smile.

"I still can't believe that douchebag never tried anything with you. The guy is an idiot."

"Well, we kissed. I mean, nothing like you and I kiss. He'd give me a kiss when he came over and a kiss as he was leaving. No tongue. He said French kissing was gross. I know now that he was just telling me that because he didn't want to French kiss *me*. He seemed to be okay with it when he kissed Brooke, though."

"So, for a year, the guy missed out on the sexiest girl on the planet?"

I laugh. "If you say so."

"Oh, I say so. I'm also one lucky bastard!" he says with a sigh.

Chapter Fourteen

When we get back to the dorm, Alex walks me to my door and invites me down to his place to watch a movie. I agree after I change into something more comfortable. He laughs and tells me he needs to change too. I may be missing something, but he winks at me as he says it. I'm relieved to see that my roommate is gone. I decide to hurry, though, in case she comes back.

It takes some time, but I get out of my dress. I change out of my panties, since they're kind of a mess from our tryst in the truck. I decide to wear some short pajama bottoms—not as short as Lily's were—a tank top, and another loose sweatshirt. He's already seen me braless, so no need to go through the trouble of wearing one of those, right? I run a brush through my hair and reapply my lip gloss, grab my keys, and take the stairs down to his floor.

I knock, but the door is ajar. When I push it open, I hear music playing. It's coming from Alex's room. I walk to the sound, and what I see takes my breath away. Alex Emerson. Naked. Granted, it's from the back, but H-O-L-Y shit, the guy's ass should be bronzed. He's got muscles bulging everywhere—like in his legs and back, my goodness, his back. Who knew a man's back could be that sexy? I could honestly and sincerely look at this man for the rest of my life. I suspect I could find something new and beautiful each and every time I look. I stand still with my mouth agape. As I lick my lips, I hear someone clear their throat. Oh shit! Busted!

"Like what you see, Pixie?"

"Hell yeah! Who wouldn't like it?"

He gives a deep, trembling laugh. "I don't really care about anyone else, Stella. I just want to know if you like it."

Nodding like a fool, I speak the truth. "I definitely like it."

He hasn't turned around to face me yet. He's looking over his shoulder. If the back looks this good, I can only imagine the rest of him.

"I need to put some clothes on. To do that, I need to walk toward you to get to my dresser. Do you want to stay there, or would you like to wait in the lounge?"

Huh? What? Oh, he's asking me if I'm ready to see the rest of him. Am I? "I'm not sure."

"Well, maybe this will help. If I turn around and move toward you, I can't promise you I'll stop at my dresser. I'll want to come to you. I'll want everything, Stella."

"Oh. Okay. Um, I'm not sure I'm ready for that. Yet."

"No, I don't think you are. Soon though." He grins.

With that, I turn toward the lounge and slowly walk away. Did I make the right decision?

"You made the right decision, Pixie," he says, walking out of his room in his loose athletic shorts and a white tee, "You're not there yet."

How did he know that's what I was thinking?

"I saw the expression on your face. The one that looks like it's overanalyzing everything. I've seen it quite a bit in the last week."

"It's possible I tend to overthink things."

He nods. "Don't get me wrong, I would have been more than happy for you to have chosen to stay put, but I don't want to do it when you feel pressured. I want it to happen organically."

I know what he means. It needs to happen naturally—at the right moment.

"Which movie should we watch? We didn't get a chance to see *Saw* the other night…."

"Ha-ha, hilarious!" I punch him in his hard-as-a-stone arm. Ouch, I think I hurt my hand.

"What about… *Bridesmaids*?"

"That's good," I agree, but then I ask, "Do you have *Pitch Perfect*? I love, love, love that movie. They sing and everything."

"I think we do, but I've gotta ask, are you going to sing? Because if you are, I'm going to insist on *Bridesmaids*."

I punch him again. "Jerk," I mutter.

He laughs. I know I can't sing, but it doesn't stop me from doing it. I'll try to refrain though. It may scare him off for good, and I'm having too much fun to let that happen. "Fine, I'll keep the singing to the confines of my head."

"*Pitch Perfect* should be on Netflix. Let's check it out. We can watch it on my laptop in my room. Let's go in there and get cozy."

We cuddle up in his bed with my head on that perfect spot on his shoulder as we watch. I'm going to have to say that this, right here, is my new favorite place to be in the entire world. Alex wraps his arm around my shoulders and pulls me closer. I fall asleep not long after the movie starts. I sleep, dreaming of happy times and Alex Emerson.

Chapter Fifteen

ALEX

Someone's watching me. It takes me a few seconds to figure out what day it is and who that warm body is next to me. When I look down, I see the back of a blonde head, and it's peering into my shorts. She's pulled up the waistband to sneak a peek. I can't resist.

"Whatcha doin', Pixie?"

I startle her so much that she squeaks and lets go of my shorts with a snap. Ouch. She's busted.

"Uh, I was just, uh, seeing, um, what kind of underwear you liked. I was going to buy you some for your birthday."

"Were you, now?"

"Yes. Yes, definitely. That's all I wanted to know."

My God, she's adorable all flustered like that. Let's see if I can get her going here.

"Well, that's unfortunate since I'm not wearing any underwear."

"I noticed that," she mutters.

"What else did you discover?" I ask with a look of innocence on my face.

"Well, I did see your, um, manhood."

"My what?" I can't believe it. She can't say dick.

"You know, your manhood. Your penis, johnson, willie, dick...."

Well, maybe she can, plus a few others.

"Okay, that's enough." I laugh. "I get the idea."

"It twitches and grows. You knew that, right?"

She is so funny. Has she never seen a dick before? Oh, wait, probably not. Douchebag Brad didn't get around to it. So, I ask, "You haven't seen a man's coc—err, manhood before?

"Of course I have! Well, not in real life. I've seen a few on YouTube."

I'm going to shock the crap out of her. "Well, would you like to see mine, Pixie?"

"You wouldn't mind?" she responds so innocently.

I get the feeling she just wants to see it for the purposes of scientific discovery. After last night, I know she's not looking to start anything sexual yet, but if she wants to see him, it's going to happen. She'll figure that out soon enough. I reach down and slowly place my fingers beneath my waistband.

Before I pull them down, I ask, "Are you sure about this?"

She nods quickly. No words from my nervous girl. I continue pulling my shorts down. My dick is as hard as a rock now, which is not surprising since so much of this morning's focus has been on him. It's not possible for me not to get hard when Stella is around anyway. When I get past my junk and my dick pops straight up, she gasps. That's not going to help me get this thing to go down.

"Wow!" she says with awe in her voice.

That's not going to help either. I chuckle because this whole thing is surreal. First, I can't believe she wanted to do this, and second, I can't believe I'm letting her analyze my dick like she's my doctor.

She whispers, "Oh my gosh, there it is! I don't have

anything to compare it to, but I have a feeling yours is especially big. Is it?"

"Oh yeah! He's huge."

"It's not as hideous as I imagined it to be. And see, it's moving!" she says excitedly.

"Yeah, it twitches. He can't help it when your face is inches from my co—manhood."

I swear, if she had a pen, she'd be taking notes. It feels very clinical right now. That is until she asks, "Can I touch it?"

Oh shit! I'm not going to be able to take this if she's just going to poke and prod. It's going to take all of my restraint right now. "Uh, sure, Pixie, you can touch it," I say reluctantly.

She reaches over and runs a finger over the head. I hiss. Damn, that feels good.

"Oh, am I hurting you?"

"No, definitely not. You're definitely not hurting me," I say, holding my breath. What is she going to do next?

She continues to touch me, gently running her finger over the head and straight down the vein that runs to the base. Oh, God, this is killing me. "I'm not going to be able to handle much more. It's getting too hard to hold back."

"Tell me what to do, Alex. I want to make you feel good."

"You don't need to do anything, Stella."

"But I *want* to," she pleads.

I'm going to let her because it's that or I have to go jump in the shower to finish this. I take her hand in mine and show her how to grasp my cock, explaining that if she holds firmly, she won't hurt me. I guide her up and down my shaft. Oh, God, it feels amazing. Her tiny hand on my big cock is a sight to behold. Her mouth would be even better, but she's not ready for that, not by a long shot. She is a fast learner, though, thank God.

She asks me if she should move fast or slow. I can barely

speak, but I tell her either is good. I'm panting like I've just run a marathon. Damn, she's good at this.

"What is that?" she asks as precum spreads out of the tip.

"Precum. I'm… I'm excited." Hard. To. Talk.

"Oh. I could already tell you were excited." She smirks, getting cocky.

"Grip it a little harder, Stella. You won't hurt me."

She grips harder, and then my brain explodes because she's leaning closer and closer to me. She sticks out her pretty little tongue and licks the tip.

"Oh fuck, Stella!" I shout. I think I startle her, but I can't help it. That sight will be burnt into my brain for all eternity.

"What? Did I do something wrong?" She looks terrified.

"God, no, you just surprised me."

"I just wanted to see what you tasted like. It was salty, but not in a bad way," she reflects.

This girl is going to kill me. "Keep going, baby. I'm almost there." I start to ramble. I'm saying shit like, "Oh, God, Stella, that feels amazing, baby. Don't stop. Please, don't stop. Oh shit, I can't wait to sink into you, Pixie. It's going to feel so fucking amazing. Keep going, honey. I'm not going to last long. Damn, you're good at that. Don't stop. Keep going. That's it. That's it. I'm going to come!"

It takes only a few more of her little strokes until I explode. Last night, when I told her I came harder than ever before, I was wrong. *This* moment is the most intense orgasm in my life. Cum is spurting out onto my chest and abdomen like it's never going to stop. Stella just watches as she continues to pump me. She looks shocked. Oh, hell, I hope I haven't scared her shitless. I take her hand, and gently pull it away from me. I bring it to my mouth and kiss it, making her smile. I grab the top sheet and wipe myself off before rolling it into a ball and tossing it across the room, right into my laundry basket. Two points.

I reach down and take her face in my hands. "Thank you,

Stella. That's the most amazing way to wake up in the morning. Do you want me to make you feel good now?"

She shakes her head and says she's fine. She tells me that she's happy that she can make me feel as good as she did last night. "Actually, it made me excited to make you feel good."

"I know what you mean. Making you come is sexy as hell, Pixie. It turns me on too."

I pull her to me into our favorite spot. I'm exhausted. I need to sleep some after that. As we doze off together, I whisper, "Best. Weekend. Ever."

Stella softly laughs.

ith Tuesday morning dawns the realization that the fun is over, and classes begin again. It started off as an emotional weekend but ended up being relaxing and romantic. Alex and I lazed around watching television, mostly football games, all weekend. Part of that time was spent kissing and touching. We also ate and talked. It was sort of perfect. Now that Tuesday's here, reality has also set in. Time to get back to work.

Tuesday flies by. Actually, the entire week goes really well thanks to my routine. I go to class, go home, and work on my homework. I do my best to get everything done before Alex picks me up so I can hang out with my man. I giggle to myself when I think about calling him "my man." He's more than I ever hoped he'd be. He's sweet, thoughtful, funny, kind, affectionate, and sexy—*really* sexy.

He usually has homework too, so I can sit with him and read my psychology textbook or sketch while he works. Sometimes, we sit in companionable silence, and it doesn't freak me out. I think I would worry if I just sat quietly with anyone else, but not with him. Every once in a while, he'll rub my leg or squeeze my hand. Sometimes I'll even lean over and kiss him on the lips. He has amazing lips. I'm careful not to get too into it though. I know he's got to concentrate on his studies and the big game this weekend. When he's not in class or with me, he's practicing, working out, and watching film. He's got even less time in the day to get things done than I do. I want him to focus.

Hank isn't around very much. Since we're usually at their place, I know he's been hanging out at Lily's. I'm sure part of it is to give us some privacy, but he may also use it as an excuse to go see her. According to Lily, her roommate is never home, so that works out. It won't be long, though, until Lily and I get to live together. I'll miss my evenings with Alex, but I'm sure we'll see each other just as much. We haven't fooled around yet this week. We've kissed a lot, and he's always touching me. I think it's okay that we haven't done more. Besides, I'm not sure I'm ready for more just yet.

On Friday, Alex says he wants to give me something before I head up to my room for the night. "Here." He hands me a purple shirt.

"What's this?" I hold up the giant top. It looks like part of his uniform or something.

"It's my away jersey. I want you to wear it to the game tomorrow," he's says, beaming.

"You want me to wear this? Why?"

"Why? Because you're my girlfriend, Stella. I want everyone to know you're mine."

"You do? You want people to know?" I look at him doubtfully.

"Stella, of course, I do. I wouldn't have asked you to wear this if I didn't."

"I would love to wear your football top."

He laughs. "Jersey. It's a jersey, sweetness."

I smile. I knew it was a jersey. Now that I know football

lingo a little better, I like to mess with him. He leans down and gives me a sweet good-night kiss.

"I'll see you tomorrow. Wave to me from the stands; I'll be watching for you, Stella."

"I will. I hope you have a great game tomorrow. Kick their asses all over that court." I laugh so hard I have to bend over. "I'm just messing with you. I know it's a diamond."

He laughs that beautiful laugh that fills me up. "I'll do my best—not because I want us to beat Iowa but because I want to impress my girl."

"I'm already impressed by everything about you. You don't need to do anything special."

"Let me walk you back to your room."

He holds my hand all the way up to my floor and kisses my cheek at the door before telling me "sweet dreams," just like he always does.

As I get ready to sleep, my phone dings. A night doesn't pass that Alex doesn't send me some type of a text.

Donnie: Good night, sweet Pixie. Sleep tight.
Me: You too. I had a great time with you this week.
Good luck tomorrow! I'll be cheering you on with all of my might!
Donnie: With all of your might? We can't lose then, angel.
Me: Good night, Alex. Get a good night's sleep.

I'M ready for some football. Today's game starts at eleven in the morning. I guess I should say kickoff is at eleven. I wake up at seven thirty to get ready since my dad will be here in an hour. Dad wants to tailgate. He's wanted me to come to football games with him in the past, but I wasn't interested. Now I am.

The weather is sunny and warm, so I decide to wear shorts with his jersey. I slide on some old cutoff jeans shorts along with a tank top to wear underneath the top. I tried the jersey on last night, and it's actually huge on me. It goes down past my knees, so I need to either tie a knot in the bottom or tuck it in a little bit. I opt for tucking. I pull a lot of it back out, so it's not all stuffed into my shorts. I choose my lucky purple Converse tennis shoes. I don't actually know if they're lucky, but they are Wildcat colors. I guess we'll see after today's game. I don't bother with makeup since I'll probably get hot and sweaty out there, but I do put on some clear lip gloss and mascara. I stick my keys, ID, and some cash in my front pocket, even though I know my dad will pay for everything. It's impolite to assume that, even if he is my dad.

I walk out into the lounge to wait and spot my roommate and resident Leviathan standing in the kitchen. Ugh. I just can't deal with her today. Luckily, she's hung over—not that it makes her any more pleasant. I've come to realize that she's much less talkative on those mornings after a long night of drinking and whatever else she does. A quiet Brooke is the only good kind of Brooke.

Alas, she's not going to remain silent this morning. "What the hell are you wearing?"

"It's called a jersey," I speak slowly since she seems to be having a tough morning.

"I know what it's called, you twit. Is that Emerson's jersey?"

"Well, since it says E.M.E.R.S.O.N. on the back." I point to my back with my thumb while turning around for her to see his name. I'm facing her again in no time. "I'm going to go out on a limb and say that, yes, it is his jersey."

"Is that his frigging away jersey?" she asks, sounding perplexed.

"Yes, yes it is." I know I'm acting smug but who cares?

"Since when did you get to be such a smart-ass?"

"It beats being a dumb-ass," I say, looking at her, hoping she hears the insult. Catty, I know.

"I can't believe he's letting you wear that today. What did you do, beg him?"

"Why would I beg him?"

"Don't you know the significance of wearing his jersey?"

"I'm wearing his jersey because he wants me to wear it, so everyone knows I'm his girlfriend."

"Girlfriend? You've got to be freaking kidding me. That's hilarious. That guy would never, and I mean *never,* have you as his girlfriend."

"Yeah, you're right. As usual." I nod. It feels great to mock her. A knock on the door brings the conversation to a halt, thank goodness. I greet my dad with a kiss on the cheek. Brooke keeps her mouth shut. At least she can figure out that she shouldn't be rude to parents. My dad doesn't even look at her. He was really nice to her when I moved in, but he probably remembers she's the one Bradley cheated with. While he pretends she's not there, he asks me if I'm ready to head out. He's got everything packed in the cooler that we need, along with a grill for hot dogs. That's when he notices my shirt.

"Say, isn't that Alex's away jersey?"

Brooke groans.

"Yes."

"Did he ask you to wear his jersey to the game?" Dad has a look on his face like a kid on Christmas morning.

"Yep. He sure did." I smile in Brooke's direction.

"Wow! You know what that means, don't you?" His grin is going to take over his face if he doesn't watch out.

"It means that he likes me, Dad, he really likes me," I say with a laugh. "Come on, let's get out of here. I'm ready to watch some football."

Dad, as a donor to the school, has a parking pass for special events. So, we get to park in the lot right next to the stadium. While Dad sets up the grill and other tailgate necessities, I walk over to the Will Call window to pick up our tickets. By the time I get back to our parking spot, Dad has the hotdogs on the grill. He's drinking a can of beer and sitting in his fold-out chair in the sun. He's totally decked out in purple and white—purple baseball hat, purple polo, white shorts, white tennis shoes, and purple footie socks. Yep, purple footie socks. I'd be embarrassed, but why bother? He's excited to be here with me, and that alone makes me happy. He could be painted head to toe in purple, and I wouldn't care. Wait, I might care about that.

"Got 'em." I wave two tickets above my head.

"Let me see." His giddiness is contagious.

I hand him the tickets.

"Wow, these even look different than regular tickets. There's gold leaf or something on them. Holy shit, Stella, did you see the seat numbers?"

I hadn't paid any attention. Apparently, we are sitting on the fifty-yard line. I guess that's a good thing.

"We're sitting right behind the team!" he exclaims. "Best seats I've ever had, sweetie."

I smile because I'm happy that he's happy, but I'm starting to get nervous. I'm meeting his parents today. What if they don't like me? After a little over an hour in the sun, we clean up our tailgating supplies and pack them into Dad's SUV and head for the game.

"By the way, we're going to be sitting with Alex's parents. I've never met them, but their names are Jack and Jill," I explain to Dad.

"Really?" Dad looks surprised. He must be able to tell I'm nervous, because he says, "It'll be okay. They'll love you, Stella."

I'm not so sure about that. I'm not the ideal girlfriend for a guy like Alex. I hope his mom isn't like mine. I couldn't take two women in my life who thinks there's something wrong with me all because I'm not thin. We weave in and out of people and down the rows of steps to our seats. Dad was right, the seats *are* fantastic. The players are all down on the field doing stretches and throwing the ball around. I want to look for number eighty-five but think I'll do it after I sit down. I could just see myself face-planting on these steep steps.

We find our row and slide down the aisle until we spot our seats smack-dab in the center of the whole stadium. I look over to see two really attractive people. They see us and stand. I reach the woman first. She raises her hand to shake mine and introduces herself as Jill Emerson and then introduces me to Jack Emerson, Alex's dad.

Wow, Alex looks exactly like his dad. Alex is bigger and a little taller, but I can see how he will look when he's older. It's a good thing, a *very* good thing. I introduce my dad to both of them. We sit, and Dad leans over to ask them questions about their family, what they do, where they live, and more. He is a lawyer, after all, so he's used to questioning people. I'm not too worried because as soon as the game starts, his focus will be 100 percent on the game.

I take the opportunity to look out onto the field, but I'm unable to find Alex, so I check the sidelines, scanning down from one end zone to the other—see I'm learning lingo. I finally spot him directly in front of me. He must have seen me, because he's come closer to the stands and is looking directly at me. He's smiling from ear to ear. I smile back, and I'm sure my dimples are at full strength.

He waves and mouths, "Hi! You made it."

I mouth back, "We did."

He points to his jersey and gives me a thumbs-up. I think he's telling me he likes my jersey. I like it too. He waves again and returns to his teammates on the sidelines. Sighing, I watch as he goes about his pregame preparations. Alex's mom interrupts my thoughts. "You're even prettier than Alex described," Jill says, smiling. "He said that you were the most beautiful girl he's ever seen. I can see why he feels that way."

I'm blushing so hard I bet I'm purple.

"He said you were a tiny little thing."

"Well, I'm short but not tiny."

"Sweetheart, you're a beautiful girl," she assures.

I try to smile, but it's a weak attempt. I turn to watch the activity on the field, hoping to stop the conversation. I'm not tiny, jeez.

"You know, Alex hasn't dated anyone for a long time. And he's never let anyone wear his jersey before."

Hearing those words make my heart flutter in my chest. It's too good to be true. "I've been told that this gesture is significant. I've never had anyone do anything like this for me before, so it's significant for me too."

Jill grabs my hand and squeezes. It's reassuring and intimate. I think she likes me so far. Changing the subject, I tell her that I hope it's okay that Alex let us use these two tickets and that I hope his little sister hadn't wanted them.

"No worries. She likes to have the house to herself for a day now and then," Jill explains.

I feel better after that. Alex's dad nods as he listens to our conversation and smiles at me every once in a while. He hasn't said much, but he seems like a nice person. I hope he doesn't think I'm distracting Alex from his goals. I would never want to do that.

The game is exciting. We beat Iowa by twenty-four points, and Alex plays even better than he did last week. He scores two touchdowns and runs for another hundred yards. Apparently, he does a great job protecting his quarterback too. I don't notice that part as much.

"I think you might be a good influence on my son, Stella. I believe he was playing for you," Jack Emerson says.

"Oh, no, I'm sure he's always that good."

"Not always," says Jack.

The thought of me helping him with his goals fills me with overwhelming happiness. Before we leave, Alex's parents invite me and my dad out for pizza. Apparently it's a family tradition to meet up with Alex and a few of the other guys after the game. While my dad was going to head out right afterward, he changes his mind when the offer is extended. I think it's because he wants to meet Alex, even though he says he wants to spend more time with me. Whichever it is, it's fine with me. We agree to meet downstairs in front of the dorm building at five.

"That will give Alex enough time to finish up any postgame interviews, shower, change, and talk to his teammates," says Jill.

I hadn't thought about postgame interviews. I bet the media loves him. He's so handsome and talented—not to mention his amazing voice. When we get back to the dorm, Dad's adrenaline is still pumping. We turn on the television to watch the postgame show and get to see Alex conduct his interviews—he's so good at it. I can tell he's comfortable in front of the camera. He's very polished.

I imagine him doing these types of interviews after he makes it to the professional league. He'll draw in slews of adoring fans, especially women, with his charm and charisma. Oh dear, I hadn't really thought about his adoring female fans. He's got a million of them on campus. Imagine the entire world as his fan base. Could I handle all of that? Oh, shoot, this is a ridiculous thing to ponder. I'm sure he'll be done with me by the time he goes pro. I just need to focus on the here and now.

While Dad is camped out on the couch, I start to freshen

up. I got hot and sweaty in the stands, so I decide to take a quick shower. I'm not sure if I should wear his jersey tonight. What's the correct protocol for jersey-wearing girlfriends? I decide to change my tank top for a clean one and put on the jersey again. I hope that's the right way to go. While I get ready, Dad calls Mom to check in and to tell her he's having pizza with Alex and his parents.

I can hear him talking to her.

"Candy, yeah, I'm staying for dinner, so I'll be a little later than I first thought. Yeah. What? What's wrong? Your head hurts? Do you want me to pick anything up for you on the way home? Yes, I'm still staying for dinner. It's just pizza. I won't be too late. I think you'll be okay until I get there, Candace. Right. I'll call you on my way home to see if you need anything. Great. Goodbye." He hangs up and sighs.

"Everything okay, Dad?"

"Sure. Your mom has a migraine again."

"Has she been having those a lot?"

"Only when she isn't getting her way," he mutters under his breath, but it's loud enough for me to hear.

"Thanks for coming today, Dad. I've really enjoyed having you here. We need to do it more often, just you and me." I make a point of saying that last part because it wouldn't have been nearly as fun with my mom here.

"Yes, we certainly do."

Chapter Seventeen

STELLA

At exactly five, Alex knocks on the door. The boy is prompt; I'll give him that. He introduces himself to Dad, again, calling him sir. Dad tells him how impressed he was by the game and his stats. They continue to talk football on the way out as Alex guides me to the elevator with his hand on the small of my back.

We all ride together in the Emerson's Suburban. It's big enough to hold all of us. When we walk into the popular pizza place, I can see that it's packed with people. A lot of the customers are from the team. The hostess sees Alex and, without a second glance, grabs menus and motions for us to follow her. My first thought is there's no way there's an available table, but I'm wrong. I hope they didn't kick anyone out to make room for all of us.

When we reach a large round table, Alex holds a chair out for me, and I sit. Alex sits to my right, my dad to my left next to Jill.

Alex leans down to whisper, "I missed you, Pix."

I whisper back, "I missed you too."

"You look perfect in my jersey, babe."

"Thanks."

As we place our pizza and salad orders, the conversation turns to today's game and Alex's performance. They also talk about the NFL combine—whatever that is—and the NFL draft. I try to pick up new pieces of football knowledge, but my mind has turned to mush ever since Alex started rubbing little circles on my thigh with his finger. It's very distracting. To make things fair, I place my hand on his inner thigh and rub it back and forth. He immediately stops touching me and pulls his hand back. His eyes are closed, and his breathing has picked up speed. I snicker. He turns toward me and gives me that sexy, heated look. His lids are hooded, and his eyes have turned to a stormy blue. I gently pull my hand away from his leg. I don't want to give him the wrong idea when my dad is sitting to my left.

He nods and whispers in my ear, "Later, Stella. Paybacks are a bitch."

My breath hitches, but he just chuckles. The pizza and salads arrive, and I try to stick to just my salad but, of course, that doesn't fly with my guy. He reaches over me to grab two huge pieces of pizza and puts them on my plate, giving me a look that tells me to eat some damn pizza.

"Alex, please, I can't eat all of that." And I mean it.

"I'll eat what you can't finish, sweetie."

Blushing, I look over at my dad. I'm waiting for that look of embarrassment that I've seen my whole life, but he's smiling. First at me, then at Alex, then back to me. He nods and digs into his pizza. Alex's mom is watching too. Jill and my dad make eye contact, and they smile courteously at each other. The pizza is delicious. I really can only eat one piece because it's about the size of my head. Alex grabs the other one off my plate and eats it in three bites. He's already eaten an entire pizza by himself. My goodness the man can eat.

"Stella, what's your major?" asks Jack Emerson.

"Well, it's business, sir."

"Really, do you want to be a small business owner someday?"

"Actually, Dad," Alex interrupts, "Stella wants to be an artist or an art teacher."

I take a deep breath and hold it. My dad is going to burst a blood vessel. I look over at him, and he's grinning at me. Maybe he's going to wait until we're alone to let me have it.

"Art, really? What media do you prefer?" asks Jill.

"I love to paint and draw. I also enjoy art history and would love teaching art someday. But I'm focusing on my business degree right now." I dare a look over at Dad. He doesn't seem upset.

"Well, if you like art history, you could work toward your Ph.D. and teach at the college level. A friend of mine is an art historian. He actually works as a curator at a big museum out east, but he was a professor for a long time," says Jill.

"Wow, really? I've never thought of that." Maybe Mom would see the potential of a Ph.D. and think more about it. This is something to consider. As I risk a glance at Dad again, I see him nodding as he chews on his food.

"We should talk more about all of that, sweetie," my dad says.

"Really?" My heartbeat flutters in my chest.

"Yes. Really."

I smile so big I think I might burst. I turn that dimpled smile right back to Alex. He's the most awesomely spectacular boyfriend in the entire world. I rub my palm over his thigh under the table again, but I remember what happened earlier and pull my hand back quickly. I want him to know I appreciate what he did, but it will need to wait. After dinner, Alex and I walk Dad to his car. Alex and my dad exchange pleasantries about how happy they are meeting each other and how Alex hopes to see him at future games.

Then the most shocking thing happens. Dad reaches out to hug me and says, "I love you, honey."

I know that he loves me, but I never hear those words from him. Nor does he ever hug me first. I hug him. No matter, I thank him for coming before assuring him that I'll call him this week. It's the first time in my life I've felt close to James Matthews. It's a good feeling. As he drives away, Alex and I stroll hand in hand back to our dorm.

"Did you have fun today, Pix?"

"Yes, and my dad did too. Thanks for everything! Today was amazing!" And it was. I'm not ready for him to drop me at my door. I don't think Alex is either. Instead of going up to my room, we walk silently to his.

"Are you tired, Alex?"

"A little but not too tired to be with you tonight, Stella. I have missed having you in my bed this week—even if it's only to sleep. I seem to sleep much better with you in my arms." He squeezes my waist. "Did I tell you how good you look in my jersey, Stella?"

"You mean my top?" I laugh at his scowl. "I know it's a jersey, big man."

"Big man?" he repeats as we reach his door.

Turning us, he pins me to the wall with his hands on either side of my face. Leaning down slowly, I close my eyes, waiting for his lips to touch mine. When they do, my entire body relaxes into his. My goodness, just a kiss is all I need to make me melt over this guy.

Pulling back slowly, his voice is deep, husky. "I like that you think I'm your big man." Reaching behind me, he opens his door and pulls me inside. "You know, I love you in my jersey… but I'd prefer you out of it," he says in a sexy drawl.

"Are you sure you're not too tired?" There's slight worry in my voice. I think I know where we're headed tonight.

"Nah. I'm never too tired to love you, Stella."

Love me? Huh? "What?"

"You heard me."

"You, um, love me? We just met."

"How long do you need to know someone before you know? I didn't realize there was a set time period."

"Alex, I've never been in love before. I'm not sure how it's supposed to feel."

"I think it's just intended to feel good, feel right, princess."

That term of endearment sends jolts into my panties. Standing directly in front of me, he touches my face as we stare into each other's eyes, his expression revealing his feelings. He slowly moves his head closer to mine, and when our lips meet, I shiver. I'm not cold. It's a different kind of shiver. It's one of those that take over your body when you know something good is about to happen. I reach both arms up around his neck and pull him to me. He practically has to bend in half at the waist to make it down to me. There's static electricity in the air. I want him. All of him. From the hardness that's pressing into my stomach, I can tell he wants me too.

"Alex."

"Yeah, babe?"

"I want you."

"I want you too."

"No, I mean I want you now, Alex."

"You do? Are you sure?"

"Babe, I've never been as sure of anything in my entire life."

"Shit, you called me 'babe,' Stella."

"You like it too?"

"I love it. Say it again."

"Babe," I whisper in his ear as he picks me up and strides to his room.

He sits down on the bed with me straddling him. I look down and wonder what he wants me to do. When he wraps his arms around my waist and pulls me closer to him, I feel how excited he is. I'm shaking with nervous anticipation. I have no idea what to expect. I'm not worried though; I trust Alex to be the kind of lover that's caring and gentle when he needs to be.

He leans in and kisses me with so much vigor it makes me dizzy. I kiss him back with equal force, our tongues intertwining. Making sure I don't fall, he moves his hands down to the hem of his jersey and lifts it up over my head, leaving only the white tank top, but that doesn't last long either. It's on the floor before I know it. I reach up and pull his T-shirt from him as well. His chest and stomach are solid and ripped. I run my fingers over his pecs and nipples.

He gasps at my touch. "I've wanted your hands on me since the second we met."

This encourages me to explore all of his peaks and valleys. His abdomen is insane. I count the bumps—eight. Damn, he has an eight-pack. I slide my hands lower to the waistband of his cargo shorts and reach for the button, but he stops me.

"Not yet, Stella. I need to make sure you're taken care of before I get ready."

I nod as he slides his hands up to my breasts. He takes his time playing with each nipple, pulling and sliding his fingers back and forth over their pebbled surface. Since I've never really tried to pleasure myself, it surprises me what just touching my breasts does to the rest of me. I can feel it everywhere, and it's better than the last time because now we're skin to skin. Leaning forward, his chest is against mine. I rub my breasts back and forth over him.

"Damn, that's hot, Stella."

He reaches down to unbutton my shorts and pauses before he pulls them down over my hips. He looks into my eyes, making sure I'm okay. I nod.

"Lift your hips."

I lift up onto my knees so he can pull my shorts and panties down to reveal my secret garden. I giggle aloud.

"What's so funny, Pixie?"

"Secret garden," I snicker.

"Secret garden?"

"Yeah, that's what I decided to call all of my lady parts." I nod down at myself. "Secret garden was the first thing to pop into my head."

Alex chuckles. "I believe that 'secret garden' is the perfect name for your beautiful pussy, Stella."

I gasp. He's such a dirty talker. When he runs his fingers through me, that's when I know this is getting real.

"You shaved for me." It's not a question.

I smile.

"You didn't need to do that, Pix. I love it natural. But this is nice too. It doesn't matter what is growing in your, um, secret garden. I'm going to love it. But you'll like this. You'll be even more sensitive here." He cups my mound.

I let out a breathy laugh until he takes a finger and sinks it slowly into my center.

"Oh, God, Alex."

"You like that?"

I nod furiously. "Uh-huh."

"You're already so wet for me. I love it." He lifts me off his lap and lays me down onto my back. Standing up to his full height, he looks down at me. I'm lying there with my shorts down around my knees and nothing else. He scans me from the top of my head down to my secret garden then back up to my face. "That is the fucking hottest thing I've ever seen, Stella. You all spread out on my bed. Damn." He rubs his crotch while he talks. It's then I notice his hardness pressing up against the fly of his shorts.

"Take your shorts off," I plead.

"Not yet. If I take them off now, I won't last."

He reaches down and pulls my shorts off the rest of the way and tosses them onto the floor with the rest of my clothes. He kneels next to the bed and reaches up to grasp my hips, pulling them right to the edge of the bed so that he's eye level with my garden. My eyes feel so huge; I know they are bulging out of my head. "Wh-What are you doing?"

"I'm looking at your pussy, babe. It's beautiful. I want to taste you now. Okay?" He doesn't wait for a response from me as he reaches down and gently pushes my knees apart. He's getting a serious look at my lady parts. When his head leans in closer, I begin to squirm away, but he holds my legs and hips in place with his big hands. "Shhh, it's going to be okay. Trust me." He leans in again and swipes his tongue along the entire seam of my garden.

"Oh. My. God!" I yell.

"Feel good?"

"Oh, God, yes!" I groan. *Please don't stop.*

He leans in again and repeats. It's like he's French kissing me down there. When he starts to focus on specific areas, like my golden ticket, it takes me to that place of sheer euphoria. He then uses one of his thick fingers to rub inside of me, in and out. The two things combined are overwhelming. Four swipes with his finger while he sucks on my clit, and I literally detonate. I scream out his name over and over again. He continues to use his mouth on me even after I've come down. My legs are shaking.

"You're delicious. Your sweetness and spice, Stella."

He slowly stands up, then leans over to kiss me. His face shiny with my wetness. It should be gross, but it's not. I want to taste myself on him. He made me feel so good. He deserves a kiss for that. Leaning up, I put my hands on either side if his head and kiss him passionately. He's right, I do taste like sweetness and spice. As I kiss him, I reach down to rub his hard length over his shorts. When he moans into my mouth, I unbutton his shorts and slowly unzip his pants. He's wearing boxers, so I reach inside to stroke his erection. Pulling back, Alex slides his shorts down the rest of the way.

Standing in front of me completely naked, he makes me speechless. I've referred to him as a Greek god and a better statue than Michelangelo's David, but seeing him like this— so real— those other two things don't hold a candle to this man in front of me. I sit up so I can really see him—so I can touch him. His skin is smooth and tight, and as I run my fingers down his abdomen to his manhood, his muscles tighten and flex even further. So much muscle. I grasp him and run my palm up and down just once. After releasing him, I lie back onto the bed and reach out for him. I want him to come to me, to rest that amazing body between my legs.

"Are you sure about this, Stella? We don't have to do anything until you're ready."

"I'm sure. I'm ready."

He's stroking himself now, and if it's possible, he's getting even bigger. I'm not sure I can handle all of that.

"You and I will fit together perfectly, Pixie. You were made for me."

How did he know that's what I was thinking? Damn telepath. He walks over to his dresser to retrieve a box of condoms. He tears open the box and pulls one tab out. After ripping it open with his mouth, he brings the ring to the tip of his penis. I sit up so I can watch him. He holds on to the tip of the condom and slowly rolls the rest of it down his length. I reach out to help, but he shakes his head.

"I'll go too fast if you touch me right now. It's more than I can take that you're looking so closely. Lay back on the bed now, Stella."

I lay back and scoot up toward the pillow so that my feet aren't hanging off the bed. He kneels onto the bed and climbs up slowly until his hips are between my legs and we're face to face.

"I'll stop at any time, Stella. Just say the word. I'll be as gentle as I can be, but I suspect that you're going to be very small in your… in your secret garden."

"It's okay. I'm ready, Alex." And I am. I've never wanted something so bad in my life.

He kisses me with such love and tenderness it nearly makes me weep. That is until I feel him. The head of his penis is pressing against my entrance. He's not pushing yet, but it's enough that I know he's there and that he's about to start. Slowly, he pushes the head into my opening, and I start to pant. I'm not going to lie, I'm scared shitless.

"You okay, Pixie?"

"Uh-huh," I pant out. I can feel him pushing further and further inside of me until it stops. I feel very full. He's so big. "Well, that wasn't so bad, was it?" I say, relieved.

"I'm only in halfway, angel. Is it too much? Do you want me to stop?" Alex is speaking slowly, like he's holding his breath. He's actually wincing and gritting his teeth as he talks.

"No, keep going."

"It's going to hurt a little right now, but it won't last. Okay?"

"So, um, have you popped a lot of cherries or something, Alex?"

He laughs. "Well, no, you're my first, but I googled it."

That's it. A laugh bursts out of me so hard I didn't even feel him push the rest of the way in—until I did. "Holy shit, that's hurts like a motherfucker," I yelp.

"I'm sorry, baby. I'm so sorry."

"It's okay. Really, it's okay." I'm breathing in and out like I'm in labor.

"Damn, Stella, you're so tight."

The pain begins to wane, and I have the overwhelming

need to move. So, I shift my hips up toward him to give him the sign that things are okay now. He slides out almost all of the way, then back in. Alex repeats that several times until I feel the urgent need for things to move fast.

"Can you go faster?"

He doesn't need any other invitation. He starts to pump in and out of me with powerful thrusts.

"Oh, Stella, I knew you'd feel amazing. Your pussy is so tight, baby. I never want this to end. Damn. This pussy is mine, Stella. You're mine."

He says those last two things while thrusting in so hard it moves me up toward the headboard. His words, albeit a little territorial, only add to this surge of adrenaline. His dirty talk doesn't hurt either. Moaning, I lift my hips to meet his thrusts. I can't believe I've lived this long without this unbelievable feeling of pleasure.

"You like that, angel? You like knowing that I claimed this pussy?"

I whimper a little bit at that and nod. It's the best I can do under the circumstances. Then he shifts around slightly, hitting a spot that makes my nipples hard and brings tingles to my spine. I feel it. An orgasm of epic proportions is heading my way. I can't wait! He's moving and groaning. Even that's sexy with Alex. I could listen to his noises every day. "Don't stop, Alex. Please don't stop." The sensation is reaching a fever pitch.

"I won't, but you need to hurry. I'm not going to last much longer." His movements become shorter and more focused on that special spot inside of me.

"I'm almost there. Don't stop," I urge.

"Come for me, Stella."

I do. How does he do that? Just as I scream out my release, so does Alex. He yells out my name along with other expletives that tell me he feels good about what we just did. My smile is huge as I wrap my arms around his neck and as he flops down on top of me. He's heavy, but the sheer weight of him is good. It doesn't matter that I can't breathe easily. It would be worth dying in his arms. He lifts his body up a little bit and rolls over to his side. Apparently, he heard my gasping breath. Keeping his arms around me, he pulls me so that I am on top of him.

Panting, he says, "That was, hands down, the best sex of my life, Stella."

"Mine too." I giggle.

"Smart-ass."

After a moment, he points to the condom and says, "Hang on, I need to take care of this."

He returns quickly and settles back onto the bed, pulling me into his arms where I fall asleep in that special spot.

Chapter Eighteen

STELLA

I wake up first. Alex is doing his cute little snoring thing, but he's rolled over onto his side away from me. It feels strange not waking up wrapped in his arms. Then I remember… I had s-e-x. Yep, I just spelled it out in my head. It was incredible. He was amazing. Looking down, I see blood. I'd heard that you could bleed when you have sex for the first time. It's not much, but I feel like I should take his sheets off and throw them in the washer because it's kind of embarrassing. I hope he doesn't mind. Did he know there was going to be blood? I'm sure he did, since he did google it. I giggle softly, not wanting to wake him. I stretch my arms above my head and feel the pain a little more acutely. It's not terrible, just general muscle soreness. I move carefully in the bed. My lady parts are as sore as the rest of me. He *was* very physical, which isn't surprising since he's so big and strong—just like Adonis. The bed shakes beneath me, making me realize that he's shifted around a little bit. Is he waking up too? His head lifts a little bit; then he turns it toward me.

"Oh, hey," he says. He's not smiling, but I am, like an idiot.

That is until I see his face. I drop the big smile and change it up to a small one.

What's wrong? He's usually so cuddly and affectionate in the morning.

Oh no. Is he sorry he had sex with me? I've read about this kind of thing a million times. Once the guy finally gets the girl in bed, he's over it. Besides, it's me we're talking about, and now that he's seen me completely naked *and* he's gotten what guys always want, he's done with me. I should have expected it.

Now that these thoughts are running through my head at a frantic pace, my little smile is completely gone now.

Alex raises his arms above his head to stretch and rolls over toward me. He still hasn't touched me.

"How are you this morning?" he asks.

What, no "babe"? No "Pixie"? No "angel"? Shit is getting worse and worse. I decide to go into protection mode.

"Uh, yeah. I'm fine. How are you?"

"I'm good, but I need to get up and get out of here. We have a team meeting bright and early today. We need to get ready for the homecoming game next weekend against Ohio State."

"Oh, right," I mutter.

He still hasn't touched me. What the hell? He rises from the bed—still naked—and reaches down to the floor to locate some of his shorts. After he's gotten those on, he picks up my tank top and my jean shorts for me. Luckily my panties are still intertwined with the shorts.

He hands me the jersey, saying, "By the way, I'm going to need this back after next week's game."

What is happening? A burn builds behind my eyes. Damn it, I'm *not* going to cry in front of him. I've done that too much already. It's starting to make me feel weak, and I am *not* weak.

"Oh, then just keep it. No need for me to take it now."

"No, I want you to wear it next weekend."

"It's okay. I'll wear some of my own Northwestern gear. Thanks for letting me wear it, though." All the time I'm talking, I'm getting dressed, attempting to hide beneath the quilt. It's not working very well, but it hides enough. I dress quickly and scoot off the bed. Now, where are my shoes? I think I took them off at the front door. As I rush from his room into the lounge, I hear his footsteps behind me.

"Stella, I want you to wear this jersey next weekend."

I ignore him, pretending I'm looking for my shoes. "Ah-ha, there they are." Deciding that speed is more important than anything else, I slide my feet into the shoes, leaving my heel exposed and squishing down on the back of the shoe. "Okay, well, I'm off. Good luck today." I wave behind me as I open the door and rush out.

I pull the door shut and rush toward the stairwell just as the tears trickle down my cheeks. In my entire life, I've never felt so sad and humiliated. I thought he was special. I figured he felt the same way about me. I guess all of his talk about love and all of that bullshit was just so he could have sex with me. Cringing, I recall the entire event. I groan when I think about "secret garden" and begging him to keep going. If a virgin could be a slut, I'd be one of those. Holy shit, I'm doing the walk of shame. What the hell have I just done? Now I'm going to have to see him in the cafeteria. Then there's the fact that I'll probably run into him when Hank is hanging out with Lily.

I finally reach my door, pull out my key, and enter quietly. It's still super early, so I know Brooke won't be up yet. I tiptoe to the bathroom. It's time to shower off the night before. The sooner I get rid of his scent from my body, the better. I scrub myself thoroughly and wrap a towel around me. I head to my room and slip on one my favorite T-shirts, the one that says: F. U. T. K. It's an old Dixie Chicks reference, and it fits my mood.

I slip on yoga pants because I just want to wear stretchy clothes. I'm exhausted. I have homework to do, but that can wait until I get some sleep. Yeah, right. Like I'm going to get to sleep. Who needs sleep when I can lie here and cry all day?

By lunchtime, I've given up on any possibility of sleeping. I decide to get up and eat something completely unhealthy. I deserve it. I recall having a microwave pizza in the freezer, so I head out into our common area to cook. I spy the pod coffee maker and decide coffee is just what I need. I peek over at Brook's door and sigh because Beelzebub's door is still closed. I'm in no mood for her crap today. Oops, spoke too soon. Just then her door opens, and a guy's head peeks out. When the rest of him steps out, I want to laugh. He's naked? He's perfect for her. The man—a tall, blond—looks at me as he exits her bedroom and winks as he strides to the bathroom. He has no qualms about walking naked through our suite. Shaking my head, I hear the microwave ding. I pull the pizza out, grab my coffee, and start to head back to my room.

"Do you think you should be eating pizza, Miss Piggy?"

"You know what, Brooke—"

I don't get to finish. The skinny guy comes out of the bath- room and heads back to her room where he starts to dress. We're both watching him. He slips on his shirt and slides his feet into some checkered Vans and walks toward the door.

"Later, baby," he says as he nods toward Brooke.

"Yeah, later," she mutters in response.

After he leaves, she says snidely, "Much later."

What a bitch. I can't help but notice that the guy called her "baby." I guess that's the way guys talk to girls. It doesn't mean a damn thing, sadly. I continue to ignore her and walk back to my room. I turn on my music, eat my lunch, and get my books out to study. Time to get caught up. It looks like I'm going to have plenty of time to get things done now. It's probably for the best. My homework was suffering because all my attention was on the drama with Bradley then on Alex.

Yep, it's for the best. It's time for me to focus on the real reason I'm here—to get a college degree. Instead of jumping right into my work, I get online to google art history degrees and jobs related to that major. There are a surprising number of opportunities for art history degrees, especially if I decide to get my doctorate. It's something to think about. I hope my dad meant what he said, that we'll talk about it.

The entire day passes without a word from Alex. It's okay. I think if I had heard from him, it would have made me relive the night before. It's not like I needed him to contact me for that to happen; I mean, it could have made it worse. By the time I get most of my homework done, I'm hungry again, but I don't go down to the cafeteria for dinner. Sadly, Alex doesn't pick me up. I think that's the first time he hasn't stopped by to get me. That tells me more than I wanted to know. Instead of risking another Brooke sighting, I choose snacks to eat from my stash in my closet for dinner; plus, I have juice and water in my mini fridge. If I only had my own bathroom, I could stay camped out here for days.

As I get ready for bed, I hear my phone ding. Maybe it's Alex.… Nope. It's Lily checking in on me. I quickly reply that things are great. We make plans to meet for lunch on the quad tomorrow. I need to catch up with my friend. I've neglected her. Well, she's neglected me too. She must be completely immersed in everything with Hank like I was with Alex. Still, I need to talk to her. She's the one person who gets me, and she'll tell me what the hell I did wrong with Alex

AFTER A FITFUL NIGHT, I oversleep on Monday. I tossed and turned until I was exhausted. Then, when I finally did fall asleep, my dreams were all about Alex. In one I was walking across the quad but stopped when I saw Alex with his little group of friends. A leggy brunette was leaning up to him, whispering in his ear. He laughed at something she said, then he leaned down and kissed her—with tongue. He wrapped his arms around her as he pulled away from the kiss. Just then, they both turned to look right at me. It was Brooke, and they were both laughing at me.

Hands down, it was the worst dream in the entire world. I woke up from it with tears pouring down my cheeks. Waking up crying sucks. And you can't stop crying once you wake up. It's like you have to relive the dream over and over again with your eyes open, and it causes you to get sad all over again.

I drag myself out of bed and hurriedly grab my towel. I shower fast, brush my teeth, and throw on sweatpants and a sweatshirt. Who cares what I look like? Stretchy clothes are perfect to wear on a day that is dark, gloomy, and depressing. No, not really. In reality, it's actually quite a pretty day for mid-September. My personal weather forecast has more to do with my mood than the actual weather. I grab my book bag and walk to class, even foregoing my pod of coffee—too much effort.

My classes drag. During my Introduction to Business class, I check my phone repeatedly. I'd turned it off the night before because I kept looking at it hoping Alex would text. I gave up looking at about midnight and turned it off. Like that helped me get to sleep. I just kept wondering if I should turn it back on. I mean, what if he'd texted me? I turn it on and hear several beeps. I did get some text messages. Scrolling through, I see a text from Lily about canceling our lunch plans, another one from Lily just saying "Hey," and then my eyes see one from Alex. I'm excited! He'd finally written. But it was sent at three in the morning? What was he doing up at three? I don't think I want to know. I click on his message.

Donnie: Night, Stella.

That's it? That's all it said? No "sweet dreams"? No "Pixie"? Without warning, the frigging tears start up again. Where the hell did they come from? I thought for sure there was absolutely no fluid left to cry out. I was wrong. I sniffle and cry during the class I dislike the most. I'm trying to be quiet, and I don't think anyone can see me, as it's dark in the auditorium. The professor is showing us a thought-provoking PowerPoint about small business entrepreneurship. Riveting.

By the time the lights turn back on, I've gotten myself under control. The girl next to me hands me a Kleenex. I guess I wasn't as quiet as I thought. She's got a look of sympathy on her face. I take the tissue and dab my eyes. I'll wait to blow my nose until I'm outside. No need to gross everyone out. I gather up my things and head out the door. I'm just about to blow my sniffling nose when I see a big guy leaning against the wall outside of my classroom. Alex.

"Oh, hey," I say, trying to act cool.

"What's wrong? Have you been crying again?"

Again? Oh crap, he must think I'm a crying, whining harpy. "Oh, well, the professor just told us some sad news."

"What sad news?"

"Oh, just how over 50 percent of all small businesses fail within the first year. Devastating news," I say, attempting a smile.

He laughs. He thinks I'm so fucking entertaining. And when did my language take a turn for the worse? Who the fuck cares? "So, what brings you this way?"

"Well, I knew you had class, so I thought I'd stop by and say hello."

"Oh, that's nice. Hello," I say, smiling a little bit. Not a lot, mind you.

"What are you doing for lunch?"

"I was just heading to meet with Lily. I haven't seen her for days, and it's our chance to catch up."

She actually canceled on me earlier. But I'm not going to give Alex the opportunity to end things, for good, in public. I know that's what he's going to do. Let me down gently and doing that in a public place is ideal. "Oh, okay. Maybe I'll see you tonight?"

Is he asking to see me or is he just saying that I'll see him if I'm lucky?

"Sounds good. I've got to run; Lily's waiting," I say in a fake singsong voice. I rush away before he even has a chance to say anything else and before my traitorous tears start up again.

Chapter Nineteen

STELLA

I didn't hear from Alex last night. Not even a text. Why does it hurt worse today than it did yesterday? Maybe it's because it's starting to sink in. The realization that he screwed me and dumped me. Maybe I was part of a joke. One of those "fuck the fat girl" jokes. I don't really think that was it, but how am I supposed to know for sure? I still haven't talked to Lily either. I have class with her today. I'll try to talk to her then, but today is the big day. She'll be a little distracted because Hank's going to pose naked for the class for the first time. I'm confident that Lily's already seen him in all of his glory, but *I* haven't. I'm not looking forward to knowing that much about Hank. I mean, he's great looking, but I've eaten dinner with the guy. Now I'll know about his you-know-what. One good thing about the breakup with Alex is that he's not going to care if I see anyone else naked. He probably didn't care before, but I know now for sure that he won't care.

It turns out that Hank is indeed built like a tank—with a big gun. I giggle at myself for that last part. If it's crude, I apologize. What if I just say that Hank is very well-endowed? It was actually a pretty hilarious class. Usually, Hank can't take his eyes off Lily. But today he did everything he could *not* to look at her. When he did look her way, she would wink and lick her lips. Her little teases were making him a little too excited for a nude painting class, if you know what I mean. Hank did a nice job keeping his junk in order. He had sweat on his brow the entire time, and I could see how hard, no pun in intended, he was concentrating on his, err, pose. I'll remember this day for a long time—and laugh. It feels good to laugh.

The rest of the week continues on in much the same fashion. I'd like to tell you that I was feeling better, but I can't. I'd also like to tell you that Alex came around and picked me up for dinner every evening and texted me every night before bed, but he didn't. He didn't completely ignore me though. I did have a few texts here and there. He sent one on Wednesday asking how my week was going. I just replied that "It's good." I asked him how his week was going. He said it was fine and that they were working like crazy at practice to prep for the big game.

On Thursday he sent a text offering up his football jersey one more time. I told him I was fine with my N.U. gear. I didn't get a reply to that one. On Friday he texted to remind me that he left tickets for me at the Will Call window. I said "Okay" to that. He wanted to know if I was bringing anyone. I said that I was going to ask Lily to come. Again, no reply. I'm not sure if it hurts more to be completely ignored or to get these tiny little reminders that this guy is still out there. I think it's the second one. I think cold turkey is the way to go with a guy like Alex Emerson. It's all or nothing. I want all of him, or I want none of him.

IT'S HOMECOMING, and I'm not excited about it at all. I know I should be. I should be rooting for the home team. I should be looking forward to seeing Alex's parents again. I'm not though. Lily can't go to the game with me after all. She's going to be sitting with Hank's parents today. I'm happy for her. I really am. Hank is a good guy.

The game today is at noon. I woke up early again to get ready. I should try to find someone else to take with me to the game. It's a great seat. Alex will probably be angry to see that I've wasted it. Oh well, there's nothing I can do about it now. I have about an hour to kill before I leave, and as I'm finishing up with my mascara, I hear frantic knocking at the front door. It's a knock that immediately makes me take notice. I rush to the door and wrench it open to Bradley panting and sweating.

"Bradley? What's wrong?"

"Stella, oh, thank God you're home. It's your mom."

"My mom?"

"Yeah, your dad rushed your mom to the hospital. My mom called me and asked me to get you and take you home right this minute."

"B-But what happened?" I'm looking around the room, frantic. What am I even looking for? My purse? My keys?

"Stella, focus! I need to take you home. Right now!"

Just then Brooke sticks her head out of her door. "What the hell, you guys? It's ten in the fucking morning. On a Saturday!" she yells.

"Shut up! We've got an emergency situation here," snaps Bradley.

"Whatever," Satan's mistress mutters. She slips back into her coffin and slams her door.

"She is such a bitch," spits Bradley.

"Bradley, what's going on? What happened to my mom?"

"I don't know. Your dad called my mom from the car and asked her to call me so that I can drive you home safely. He was worried you'd be upset and wreck your car."

"Let me get my purse." I run back to my room and return to Bradley in seconds. "Let's go."

He takes hold of my forearm and drags me toward the elevator.

"Stairs. The stairs are faster!" I exclaim. We turn and take the stairs down to the first floor and rush toward the main door. As we exit the building, I see Alex's mom getting into their Suburban. She sees me and motions her arm toward the car. I think she's asking me if I need a ride. I just wave and smile weakly, shaking my head. Bradley is still clutching my arm, pulling me toward his waiting car. He opens the door for me. I look back at Jill as I slide into his passenger seat and see her smile fade a little bit. Bradley rushes around and gets into the car. He starts it up and squeals out of his spot.

From the corner of my eye, I can tell Bradley's worried. It's right then I see my old family friend again. The one I grew up with. The one that cares about my family like it's his family too. We ride in silence the hour that it takes us to reach the emergency ward. Bradley pulls up to the emergency entrance, telling me to go on ahead while he parks the car. Racing inside, I search right and left for anyone who looks familiar. I spot my dad sitting in the waiting area next to Vicky. His leg is bouncing up and down rapidly.

"Dad! What happened? How's Mom? Have they told you anything?" My questions are rushing from my mouth so fast, he doesn't have a chance to answer any of them.

Reaching out, I take hold of his hand and sit next to him.

"I don't know, sweetie. When we got here, they took her back right away. They had her breathing with oxygen."

"I don't understand. What happened?"

"I'm not sure. She woke up clutching her chest, and her breath was short. I panicked. Instead of calling 911, I picked her up, carried her to the car, and came right here. I called

Vicky so she could let you know. I'm sorry I didn't call you myself; I just didn't want you to hear the worry in my voice."

"It's okay, Dad. I'm here now. It all worked out."

"And you're missing Alex's homecoming game today. I'm so sorry."

"Dad." I take his hand. "This is where I need to be. It's more important." And it is. It's way more important than a silly game.

Chapter Twenty

ALEX

Where is she? I look up at my mom and point to the empty seats next to her. Mom shrugs and shakes her head. Even though things have been so weird with Stella this week, I didn't think she'd blow off my game. The morning after we made love, she acted so nervous, so coy. I didn't want to scare her by attacking her first thing in the morning, even though that's all I wanted to do. She looked and acted so tentative. Shit, she couldn't get dressed and out of there fast enough, and since I've never deflowered a girl before, I wasn't sure what to expect or what to do afterward. I've been with plenty of girls, but they all knew what they were doing. This was all new for Stella, and I didn't want to frighten her away. I decided to give her space. She needed time to process everything. I did tell her I loved her, after all. Maybe that freaked her out. She didn't say it back.

Shit. *Maybe she's not ready for all of this with me.*

But where is she? Stella's not the kind of person to bail on me, is she? She said she was coming to the game in her text. But while she didn't promise; it still makes me angry. *Angry?* No, not angry. I feel sad, depressed, bitter, and worried all rolled into one. What if something happened to her and she couldn't get a hold of me? Surely she would have called or messaged me. The thought eases my mind a little. The second I get into the locker room at half time, I'll check my phone.

HALFTIME and no message from Stella. What the hell is going on? Even though we aren't supposed to be on the phones during our halftime meetings, especially *this* halftime, one where we're down twenty-four to three, I can't help staring at my phone. Needless to say, this midgame pep talk is more like a bitch-out session. I really need to listen to the coach. I'm playing for shit—like a high school freshman. Coach is yelling, and I think he's yelling at me, but I can't focus on that right now. I need to be sure she's okay. All I need is to know that she's okay. Right before we head back out onto the field, I grab my phone and quickly text her. *"Stella, where are you? Are you all right?"* Not only that, I call her number and hope to hear her voice, but I get her machine. So, I leave the message. "Stella, it's Alex. Where are you? You're not at my game. You're worrying me." Because I'm the last one out of the locker room, I hang up and spring back out to play the worst fucking game of my career.

Chapter Twenty-One

STELLA

It seems like we've been waiting forever. I try to keep Dad from going completely nuts by turning the game on the television. I can't stand to watch it myself. Dad doesn't notice my lack of interest. His mind is elsewhere. I sit as far away from the television as I can get so I won't see number eighty-five. I do hear them say his name a few times. One time I hear them say something about number eighty-five and a fumble. Actually, I hear that a couple of times.

Close to halftime, the doctor finally comes out. He sits right in front of Dad and me. Vicky and Bradley are close by, but you can tell they don't want to impose. "Your wife is stable, Mr. Matthews. We're still running some tests, but it appears she had a cardiac episode. Her heart is slightly enlarged, and she has built-up fluid around her lungs and her heart muscle. We've given her something to help diminish the fluid levels as well as something that will help regulate her blood pressure. We'll need to do additional tests to see if she has what we call cardiomyopathy. It's very rare but treatable with medication and a low-sodium diet."

"So, it wasn't a heart attack?" I ask.

"No, it wasn't a heart attack. She was feeling pressure in her chest and had a difficult time breathing due to the fluids. Her reaction was more like a panic attack rather than a heart attack. It's not uncommon to be scared when you can't catch your breath." The doctor continues, "I think she's battled the worst of this episode, but I'd like to keep her here overnight for observation and to make sure the diuretic is working. I hope you agree with that plan of action."

My dad nods and asks when we can see her.

"We have one or two more tests to run; then we'll get her into a room on the cardiac floor. If you want to go on up to that floor, there's a separate waiting room there. The nurse will get you when she's settled into her room."

"Okay, that sounds good. Thank you very much, Doctor," says Dad mechanically.

We all head upstairs. This waiting room is much smaller than the ER waiting area, but we're in there by ourselves, which is nice. The game is already playing on the TV, so Dad resumes watching.

When it's over, Dad looks dejected. "They lost, honey."

"Oh, what was the score?" I ask.

"Thirty-four to seven, Ohio State."

Yikes. That's not good.

"Your boy had a bad game, sweetie. He's going to be cranky when you see him."

"Yeah, you're probably right." I can't break the news about Alex and me to Dad today. He's going through enough. Once Mom gets situated in her room, they let Dad and me go in to see her. She's pale, almost ghost white. She's dozing, but she opens her eyes when she hears us.

"Jim. Stella. It's good to see you. That whole thing was really scary." Her voice is tired and raspy, so different from her usual tone.

"Yes, it was, sweetheart. We were having a time out there waiting for news. You scared the daylights out of me, Candy."

My dad has tears in his eyes. She's okay. He doesn't have to keep a brave face anymore. She smiles weakly at him. He reaches out to hold her hand. They just stare at one another for several minutes. Maybe they really do love each other. Maybe they always have.

"Mom? Can I get you anything?" I ask quietly.

"Stella, sweetie, I'm so glad you're here. No, I'm fine. I'm just happy to be alive." Then she smiles at me, like really smiles. I can't remember the last time I've seen her do that when it was directed at me. She smiles at Dad sometimes.

"I'm glad you're alive too, Mom." I wipe away a stray tear that found its way to my cheek.

"Oh, sweetie, don't cry. Everything's going to be okay." She's pulled her hand away from my dad's and reaches her arms out toward me. Does she want to give me a hug? I slowly walk toward her, extending my arms. "Come here, sweetheart," she coos.

I rush over to her and wrap my arms around her. I try not to hug her too tight as she still has a bunch of tubes and things attached to her.

"Mom?"

"I know. I know. Shh," she says, comforting me.

I don't know how long we stay like that, but after a while, I hear a female clearing her throat.

"Ladies, I need to get in there to check vitals. You can resume that in a few minutes."

Nodding, I wipe away the tears dripping on my cheeks and back away. "I'm going to go get Vicky, Mom. I know she's been worried sick about you too." I exit the room to let Vicky know that it's her turn. Bradley is still seated in the waiting area when I arrive.

"How is she?" he asks.

"Fine. Well, as fine as can be expected. I think this really scared her."

"I bet. It's surprising. She's so fit and healthy."

"I know, but it's all going to be okay," I say with confidence. "You should head back to school, Bradley. I'm going to stay the night here. I'm sure you have lots of fraternity things going on for homecoming weekend."

"No, it's okay. I mean, I do have a lot going on with ΣAE, but I'd rather be here. Besides, you'll need a ride back to school tomorrow, right?"

"Right, I could rent a car though."

"No need to rent a car. It's not a problem," he says as he squeezes my arm.

"Thanks, Bradley. Thanks for everything." And I mean it.

As we sit in the waiting area watching for Vicky to emerge, I think about texting Lily. I should also text Alex to let him know what's going on. I search through my purse for my phone. Not there. I must have left my phone back at school. It doesn't matter. I can let them know about it tomorrow. It's probably best to wait now that I know Mom is okay. After all, Lily's going to be busy all evening with Hank and his family.

As I'm thinking about all of that, Bradley says, "I texted Lily, by the way. I told her what was going on, and I let her know that your mom is going to be okay and that you're doing okay too."

"Oh, really? Thanks," I say, surprised.

"She used to be my friend too, Stella," he whispers.

No, I really don't remember that. "Thanks, Bradley. I appreciate it since I think I left my phone sitting on my bed at school. Can you tell her I'll call her tomorrow when I get back?"

"Sure, no problem."

Chapter Twenty-Two

ALEX

After the bloodbath that was our loss today, the team trudges back to the locker room. I'm not looking forward to the screams that'll come out of Coach's mouth. I mean, we lost, epically, and it's homecoming. I fumbled the ball three times, let my quarterback get sacked so many times I think he's going to have permanent bruises on his ass, and I didn't score one damn point. Worst. Game. Ever.

I get to my locker and grab my phone, hoping that she's responded to my texts. Nothing. There've been no texts and no voice mails from her. It doesn't make sense. There has got to be something wrong. After the coach has his say, I quickly shower and dress so I can book it back to the dorm. Not bothering to go to my room, I take the stairs two at a time to the fourth floor. I bang on Stella's door. No answer. I knock again. Footsteps. Finally! The door opens, it's her roommate.

"Oh, hey, Alex," she says seductively.

No time for that shit. "Where's Stella?"

"Stella? You're looking for Stella?" She's got a bitchy smirk on her face. "She didn't tell you?"

"Tell me what, goddamn it? Where is she? Is she okay?"

"Oh, she's okay, all right. I can't believe she didn't call you. I told her to tell you, but she just shrugged it off. The girl doesn't ever listen to me."

Why would she? Brooke is no friend of Stella's. "What are you talking about? Spit it out."

"It's terrible that she didn't tell you…" She pauses. "About her and Bradley."

"What about Bradley and Stella?" I yell.

"Calm down. Jeez. Okay. I'll tell you, but remember, don't kill the messenger."

I stand there with my hands on my hips, waiting for the bitch to speak. This day has sucked so hard.

"They're back together."

"What? Who's back together?"

"Stella and Bradley, silly. Apparently, her family put enough pressure on her, and she finally agreed. They went home together this morning. He picked her up bright and early."

"That makes no sense. I just talked to her last night."

No, wait. I haven't spoken to her. I sent her a text earlier in the day, but I haven't actually spoken to her. Come to think of it, we haven't actually spoken all week—well, except outside of her Intro to Business class. Damn it. She'd been crying. I bet it wasn't over some stupid class either. I'm such a dipshit. I've been so focused on the game this weekend. My mind was on that. It was on her too, but I guess I thought things were fine. I was just giving her space. Maybe I gave her too much space— just enough time to think about what she was missing with the douchebag. She probably compared us and decided that Bradley was a safer bet. Whatever. *Fuck it.* Jesus! Women. Who needs them?

Brooke's watching me as I think about everything from this past week. The more I think, the more pissed I become. "God-damn it. This is bullshit!" I yell.

"So, Alex, what are you going to do right now?" she asks, flirting.

"The hell if I know." The guys are all going out to drown their sorrows. Maybe I'll go along. "I'm gonna get drunk."

"Well, can I come along? I could use a drink too. It's been very dramatic here. My heart's broken too. I'm so sick of Stella getting everything she wants. I knew it the minute she walked into my dorm room. Talk about a spoiled princess. If it isn't Bradley fawning all over her, it's her dad and then you. Well, it used to be you. I mean, the girl is fat and ugly. What is it about her that draws you all like flies to that shit?" She's literally got her lip pushed out like she's a pouting little brat.

I only heard a few words out of that entire thing. Stella and spoiled princess doesn't ring a bell, but I can't seem to find it in me to argue with her tonight. "Fine, whatever," I spout. "Everyone's going to Changes." I turn and stomp down the hallway toward the elevator.

As I walk away, I hear, "Hang on. Let me grab my purse, Alex." I pause for several minutes until I hear her feet tapping on the concrete floor. At the elevator, she starts jabbering on again. "The other football players hang out at Changes, don't they? This'll be great. We can go commiserate with them over your loss."

I've tuned her out at this point. She can get her own ass to the bar. Not my responsibility. Fuck women.

At the bar, I leave Brooke at the front door. Sure, I gave in and let her ride with me, but she's on her own now. At the bar, I order two shots of whiskey and a beer. All for myself. I watch as a skinny arm reaches past me to grasp one of the shots. I glare down at her. "Mine." Luckily, Brooke takes the hint and moves away from me. "Time to get drunk," I mutter before I slam the first shot back.

I guess my angry growling has no effect on this woman because not thirty minutes later, she's shouting, "Come on,

Alex. Let's have some fun," all while attempting to pull me out onto the tiny dance floor.

I pull my arm free. "No, thanks. I don't dance." And why would I? There's nothing to dance about.

She stops moving toward the dance floor and comes back to me. Reaching up, she wraps her arms around my neck, and she coos, "Poor Alex. I know just what you need to feel better."

"Oh yeah? What's that?" I'm hoping she says she'll disappear, but that's nothing close to what she suggests. Nope, she offers me the "best blowie of my life in the bathroom."

"No, thanks," I mutter. "Jesus. I just want to hang with the guys. Go talk to Smitty or someone on the defensive line. They're always looking for head."

"Oh, well, that's rude!" She stomps away and directly in the path of none other than Smitty.

I step toward the bar in time to see Hank grabbing a beer. I didn't even see him come in.

"What the hell are you doing here, man?" Hank asks.

"I needed a drink. No, I needed a shot. Let's get drunk and forget this day ever happened. Where's Lily?"

"She's back at the dorm freshening up. I'm here for one beer before I walk over to get her. She met my parents today, man."

"Yeah, how did that go?"

"Awesome. They loved her. I mean, what's not to love?"

Just then Brooke strolls over and hands a shot to me, then one to Hank. "This should cheer you up, babe."

Ignoring her words, I throw back the shot and slam the short glass back onto the bar. I needed that.

"What the hell are you doing here with *her*?" he says, pointing at Brooke who's now dancing all by herself on the makeshift dance floor. "Actually, why are you here at all? You never go out," Hank asks, concerned.

"She dumped me, man."

"Who?"

"Stella, she dumped me."

"No way." He shakes his head. "That chick was completely into you."

"Apparently not. I don't want to talk about it. I just want to drink, heavily."

"All right. I would probably want to do the same thing. Here, I'll help you with your quest." He hands me the shot Brooke just gave him. "I've got to warn you though, Alex… that girl, right there," he says, pointing at Brooke, "is bad news."

"I know, man. She's not here with me. She just followed me here." Damn, I need more to drink. I can't stop picturing Stella with dickface Bradley. "Yo! Waitress? Shot me again!" I yell.

Chapter Twenty-Three

STELLA

Mom had a good night. I feel comfortable going back to school knowing that she'll be okay as long as she follows doctor's orders. The nurse said she's responding well to the new medications and that they've reduced a lot of the fluids that she'd built up around her heart. Things are looking much better.

"Mom, Bradley will be here soon. I'm going to take off now. You going to be okay?" I ask.

"Stella, can I talk to you before you go?"

I nod and smile at her even though I'm a little leery of what's about to happen. What if she still thinks Bradley and I should get back together?

Mom looks over at my dad who hasn't left her side all night. Smiling, she asks, "Jim, can I talk to Stella alone for a second?"

Dad's been dozing over in the world's most uncomfortable recliner. "Sure, I'll go see about some coffee. I'll take my time," he says, winking at both of us.

Stepping over to her bed, I grasp one of the railings next to her. "What is it, Mom? What's wrong?"

"Nothing is wrong, sweetie. I just wanted to tell you something." There's a long pause before she speaks again. "Yesterday, when I realized there was something seriously wrong with me, I started to panic. Lots of things were running through my head. I suppose it's normal when one has a near-death experience... but I kept thinking about you, Stella. Do you know what I thought?"

"Um, that you hoped that I'd remember to eat my vegetables after you're gone?" I snort out a little laugh. Awkward. "Sorry, that was morbid. I like to joke when I'm in stressful situations."

Mom gives me a warm smile. "Oh, I know you do. No, I realized at that moment that I was the world's shittiest mother."

"Huh?" I cough.

"Yes, it's true. I'm sure you know that already. It struck me that I was going to die and that I wouldn't be able to tell you that I loved you and that I was sorry for treating you abominably over the years. You are an extraordinary young woman, Stella. I'm so proud of all of your accomplishments. You have blossomed into such a beautiful woman, one who's smart, funny, loving, and a very talented artist."

"Who are you and what have you done with my mother?" I tease.

I half expect her to laugh, but she doesn't. "I'm serious. I've always loved your artwork but was hesitant to encourage that in you. I had my own ideas about what you should be when you grew up. But you *are* grown up. It's not up to me to make those important choices for you. Your dad was right about that. I'm just sorry it has taken me so long to figure things out."

"Wow. So, are you saying you won't mind if I change my major?"

"I won't fight you on it, no. But I wish you'd considered

either a double major in business and in art or going for the art history route that your dad mentioned."

"He told you about that?"

"Yes, he did. He likes the idea. I was hesitant at first, but the more I thought about it, the more I liked the sound of Dr. Stella Matthews," Mom says, winking.

A Ph.D. would give me that distinction. "Yeah, that sounds pretty good."

"Well, Dr. Stella Emerson sounds even better." She winks again.

"Uh, yeah, well, it's much too soon to be talking about that." I laugh nervously.

"I know. I know. Wishful thinking on my part."

I'm so not ready to tell them that there is trouble in Alex Emerson paradise.

Mom breaks my little moment of silence with "Stella, I promise I'll work harder on the mother-daughter thing."

"Me too, Mom. I'll even tell you when you are acting like old Mom."

"Hey, I'm not old!"

"I just meant—"

Reaching out, I watch her take my hand in hers. "I know what you meant. Yes, please tell me if I revert back to pre-heart-episode Mom. Okay?"

I nod. I will definitely do that. It's strange that something so good can come out of something so frightening. Just as we finish our heart-to-heart, Bradley appears in Mom's room. "Ready to start back, Stella?" he asks.

"Yep. I'm ready. Love you, Mom."

"I love you more, Stella."

Oh gosh, I'm going to cry. I reach over and hug Mom. As I start toward the door, Dad enters. I hug him goodbye and leave the hospital with a big ole smile on my face. Outside, I can't help noticing the sun has barely risen. It's still early, but

Bradley has to get back to his fraternity. His frat threw a big party last night, and he wants to be sure it's still standing. I don't mind. I need to get back.

Bradley drops me off in front of Shepard, and I make my way up to my room. I take the elevator instead of the stairs because I'm dead on my feet. Sleeping on a hard hospital sofa isn't for wimps. When I enter the suite, it's silent. Satan's mistress's door is closed, thankfully. I go straight into my room and start to get my things to shower but stop. Coffee! I need a coffee first, shower second. I grab my coffee pod and add the water. I'm about to put my cup under the nozzle when the bathroom door opens. I freeze as I watch Alex emerge.

What is he doing here? Wait, what is he doing here at nine in the morning? And why is he shirtless? He's holding his tee in his hand. His pants are unbuttoned but zipped, and his hair is a complete mess. He looks like shit, actually.

"Alex?" I whisper.

He looks at me with hate in his eyes—with contempt. "Have a nice time at home, did ya?"

"What?"

"No need to answer," he spews. Then he says, "Whatever," and walks out, slamming the front door behind him.

My mouth hangs open like a damn fish. I look over at Brooke, who's now standing in her doorway wearing only a tiny red tank top and a black thong. She looks like the cat who ate the canary.

"Well, it looks like Alex prefers thin women after all."

With that comment, she turns and walks back into her lair, slamming the door behind her.

In all of the drama, I had forgotten to put my cup under the pod nozzle. Coffee is running everywhere—on the counter, on the floor. But I don't care. I start to cry and run to my room. I throw myself onto my bed and cry so hard I think I'm going to throw up.

There's vibration under my leg. My phone. I'm glad it's here. I'd hate to lose it. As I pick it up, I see a text from Lily asking me if everything's okay. I quickly reply that things are good and let her know Mom is heading home later today. I'm in no frame of mind to talk about what just happened here, and I'm not sure I'll ever be.

I see a red number on my message icon and tap it to open and see a bunch from Alex. There are at least fifteen text messages and it looks like four voice messages. All of the texts are asking things like "Why aren't you at the game?" "Are you okay?" "I'm worried. Please write back a.s.a.p." It makes me nervous to listen to his voice messages. Reading a text is not as personal as hearing his voice. I've got to listen though.

The first two messages are frantically asking where I was and if I'm okay. Another one is asking me to call him back with more of the same questions. He was so worried—at least he was at first. The messages that came in later in the evening were a different story. On one, there's a lot of background noise. He must've been out. He's just breathing at first, then I hear him say one word: "Why?" And then he hangs up. The last message from him was left at two thirty in the morning. It's obvious he's drunk. His speech is slurred and angry; I'd go so far as to say he's downright belligerent. That's not typically how he talks to me. Something's definitely wrong, and I can't see it having anything to do with the loss yesterday. No, this is personal. I know this when he says, "Stella, it's Alex. I just wanted to say that I thought you were different, but you're not. You're just like all the rest of the bitches in this world. Well, good riddance. I don't ever want to see your fat, err, ugly, round face again." I hear a giggle coming from somewhere in the background of his message and then a girl's voice. "Come on, baby, let's go. I can't wait to get you into my bed."

I'd recognize that voice anywhere. It's Brooke Clark.

Not gonna lie. Hearing him call me ugly was more than

this girl can take. *Fat, ugly round face?* Really? He had to say the most hurtful thing he could think of at that moment. I caught the first word—fat—even though he tried to change it to ugly. Too late. The damage is done.

The thing I don't understand is why? What did I do to deserve that? Is this all because I didn't go to his game? I could clear all of this up right now, but if what he said last night and just now in my dorm, what's the point? He never wants to see my fat, ugly face again.

I *knew* I shouldn't have trusted him so easily. I should have learned from Bradley that guys don't like soft, round girl. Alex may have thought he did, but I guess once he saw the entire package, he was repulsed and wanted to move on to skinnier (and meaner) pastures. Well, if he wants a woman like my roommate, he can have her.

Chapter Twenty-Four

ALEX

Holy shit. *What have I done?* Waking up on that bitch's couch was bad enough. Having Stella catch me coming out of her bathroom like Bradley on the day we met was completely fucked up. I didn't fuck Brooke. I don't think I even touched her. She pulled me down the hall from the elevator last night, begging me to make sure her room was safe. It was total bullshit. Once she got me in there, she pushed me onto the couch and tried to shove her hand down my pants. I was able to push her off me and literally growled at her to get away. By the time she finally slithered back into her hole, I was passed out on her tiny-ass couch. I was so wasted, all I wanted to do was sleep.

In the morning, I took a quick shower to wash off the stench of bar from my body. I slid my jeans back on but not my shirt. Fuck. Why did Stella have to be there? Even though she doesn't want me, she didn't deserve that, even if she is dumb enough to go back to that jerk.

And yet, the asshole part of me is glad she saw that. She broke my heart. Maybe it bothered her at least a little. Besides, eventually she'll figure out that Bradley is the same douche he was a month ago, and she might come crawling back to me. But I won't be able to handle her messing with my head. This should put an end to any of those ideas she may have later. This whole thing sucks beyond words. God, I fucking hate my life right now.

Chapter Twenty-Five

STELLA

I spent the entire week after all the stuff happened with Alex in my bed. I mean, who the hell cares if I make it to class? No one, that's who. Who cares if I don't shower and only eat Twinkies for sustenance? No one. Lily has texted me throughout the week. I just reply with "I'm fine—just busy with Mom stuff."

With that thought, I email all of my professors and tell them about my mom and that I'll be back soon and will catch up at that time. There, that seems to appease everyone. Now I can lie here, cry, eat junk food, and feel sorry for myself. This is exactly what I need. Alone time. But after a week of alone time, I'm pretty sick of myself. I smell, I feel like a bloated whale from all of my processed snacks, and I don't think I can cry another drop for the rest of my life. Did I mention that I stink? I just don't feel like showering. What's the point?

GOOD NEWS! No, *great* news! I received a letter from the NWU Department of Residence Halls that says our dorm will be ready next Saturday. Yeah, *finally*. No more Brooke Clark! If that doesn't turn my frown upside down, I don't know what will.

Is it too soon to pack? I pick up my phone and send a text to Lily about the good news. She's thrilled too! Lily's roommate turned out to be a nightmare too. Apparently, she's very needy and borrows Lily's things secretly. Yeah, creepy.

I send a text to my dad next. When I first moved in, he'd said he'd come up and help me move over to Hinman Hall when the time came, but I'm not sure if he still can with Mom and all. Even though she's doing much better, he may not want to be away from her. He replies saying he'll be able to run down and help me. He wants me to be all packed up though. He doesn't want to be away from Mom for very long. Vicky can stay with her while he's helping me. He asks me if Alex is going to help, but then he remembers that there's an away game. *Phew*. I don't want to get into all of that. I'm not ready to confess to them the total and complete disaster my life has become.

Chapter Twenty-Six

STELLA

The weekend went by at a snail's pace. Even with a week of wallowing, I still can't shake the melancholy. I hope time will make that go away. On Monday, I meet up with Lily over lunch to update her on my mom's recovery. She still thinks I was home all last week. I'm not about to tell her where I really was. As for today, I need to track down all of my professors to pick up my missed assignments from last week so I can I try to get back into the swing of things and pretend like nothing is wrong with me.

Good luck with that, Stella.

Luckily, I did get a little homework done last night, but I've got much more to do. Now, I sort of regret my week of solitude. A lot.

I pick at the blueberry muffin I chose to buy for my lunch. It's the only thing that looked remotely appetizing, and now that I've got it, I don't want it. Lily's looking at me with concern. "So, is everything okay? You know, with you and Alex?"

I know she's fishing. She's been with Hank nonstop since

they met. She has to know that Alex and I are no longer together.

"Um, well, I think things are over with Alex," I say quickly.

"I'm not going to lie," she reveals, "Hank told me that you dumped Alex."

"Me? Dump *him*?" I scoff. "Well, that's convenient."

"Why? What do you mean?"

"I didn't get the chance to end things last Sunday when I caught him coming out of my bathroom, shirtless with his jeans undone. He saw me and just stormed out of my suite before I got the chance to do any dumping."

"What? Wait, you were back last Sunday? I thought you just got back this weekend?"

That's when I confess my self-induced isolation.

"I'm confused. Hank told me that Alex showed up at Chances to party with the team, which he never does, and Brooke was in tow. Anyway, Alex told Hank that you dumped him that day."

"That's not even possible. I ran home with Bradley that morning—as soon as I heard my mom was taken to the hospital. I forgot my phone in my room and missed Alex's calls and texts. I never spoke to him that day. I did get texts and one pretty nasty voice mail from him though. But I didn't hear those until Sunday afternoon. So, no, I did *not* dump him. He's full of crap," I say, exasperated.

"None of this makes any sense."

"It's over. That's all there is to it. He made it clear that he wants to be with other, thinner girls. I need to accept that it's over and move on. I should focus on my degree and forget about men. They're nothin' but heartache. Let me tell you. It's going to take time, but I'll feel better soon," I say, trying to give myself courage.

Lily sits, tapping her fingers on her leg. I don't know what's going through that head of hers, but she needs to forget it. I'm in no way ready or willing to get mixed up in the guy drama again. I couldn't take another heartbreak, not in this millennium anyway.

The rest of the week is better. I don't run into Alex, and I avoid Brooke like the plague. I do see Hank, but only naked in my painting class. I pack up my stuff a few minutes before class is dismissed so I can rush out of class. I make it my mission to avoid him because he'll just talk about Alex, and I do *not* want to hear about Alex Emerson. And even though I know Alex doesn't want me, I can't help but wonder about him. I don't think it's healthy for me to continue harboring feelings for him. On the bright side, I get to move in with Lily in a few days. I'll use all of my free time to pack up so I can be waiting by the door for my dad to get here. I can't wait!

THE DAY HAS ARRIVED. *Finally*. I get to move in with my best friend. Funny, now that it's happening, I feel like I'm getting a fresh start with school, with everything. I packed up all of my stuff, and instead of waiting by my door, I lugged all of my boxes down the stairs one by one to the main level. I set them next to a girl who's studying on the main floor in the lounge area. The girl was nice enough to watch my things as I trek up and down the stairs. Once it was all there, I sent a text to my dad to let him know I was waiting for him in the main lobby. I'm sure I've left something behind, but I don't care. Anything that's still up there can be replaced, or not—I don't care. I hope to never see Brooke Clark again. Worst. Roommate. Ever.

Dad shows up, right on time, and he's super happy to see that I've gotten everything downstairs. Being away from Mom is making him nervous, I can tell. So, I jump up, give him a quick hug. and grab my first box.

"Got a parking spot right out front. This will be a piece of cake," Dad says cheerily. He grabs two boxes, and we start loading up the truck. We make quick work of it and head off to Hinman. After we move all of my boxes up, my dad takes off. I know he wants to help me get settled, but home is where he needs to be right now. Besides, the fun part is setting things up with Lily. We can finally put our room décor that we planned out last summer to good use.

As we unpack, we play fun, fast music to keep us moving. We dance and sing along. When I belt out a song, Lily stops working and stares at me. Slowly, she shakes her head back and forth. "No. Just no, girl."

She makes me laugh so hard. I need that. "I know. I can't sing."

"Oh, no, it's not that you can't sing; it's that you *shouldn't* sing. Remember that, okay?"

"Yeah, yeah, I've heard that before." From Alex.

After we've unpacked, Lily and I figure out where the closest cafeteria is located. It's literally been weeks since I ate in the cafeteria, having avoided Shepard Hall's. I started to go down once, but I ran into Alex in the stairwell. It was awkward, to say the least. I nearly tripped and fell on my face when I saw him coming toward me.

When our eyes met, I could see Alex's internal struggle through his tense jaw. He was gritting his teeth. He must really hate me. The question is, why? I just stood there staring at him. I couldn't decide if I should keep walking forward or turn around and head back upstairs. I didn't need to make that decision because, after a couple of seconds, he nodded, turned around, and walked back out onto the main floor. He went out of his way to avoid me. He probably couldn't figure out how to squeeze past my fat, ugly face.

Chapter Twenty-Seven

ALEX

When I get home from practice, Lily's sitting in the lounge with Hank.

"Hey" is all I can muster.

I don't want to see anyone associated with Stella right now. It's been a couple of weeks since she dumped me, and I still feel like shit. That shit feeling has infiltrated into my entire life too. I've been choking at all of my games, so much so Coach is about ready to bench me. I flunked a test in my communications class, and I'm going to flunk one in calculus. I don't care anymore. When will I ever fucking use calculus in my life? Never, that's when. It's all fucking bullshit.

"How are you doing, Alex?"

Oh crap, she's talking to me. "Fine."

"Just fine?"

Please make her stop. "Yeah, just fine."

"Did you know that Stella and I finally got to move into our dorm at Hinman?" she mentions in a singsong way.

"Good for you." I can't muster up any excitement about that news. I haven't seen the girl but once in the stairwell. I figured she'd fallen off the face of the earth. Fine by me.

Lily interrupts my internal rant when she says, "And her mom is doing much better, by the way."

"Oh yeah, good to know." What is she talking about? What was wrong with Stella's mom? I want to know, but I don't want to ask. That'll start an entire conversation that I don't want to have. But today isn't my day, I guess. She keeps going.

"Yeah, they were all scared. They thought it was a heart attack. It was touch and go. Her dad rushed her to the ER, you know, on the morning of the homecoming game. You knew that's why she wasn't at your game, didn't you?"

"No, I didn't know that," I reply curtly.

"Yep, Bradley got a call from his mom and rushed over to Stella's place to get her. They didn't want her driving herself because she was so upset. Can you imagine?"

What is this girl up to? "Sure. I can imagine," I say as deadpan as possible.

"It's a good thing too. She was beside herself. Then, when she realized that she left her phone back at her dorm, she was really freaked out. I had no idea anything was happening until late Sunday night."

"Uh-huh," I mutter absently. So, that's why she didn't get a hold of me. It doesn't explain why she got back together with —wait a second.... "That bitch!" I shout.

"What?" Lily says, startled.

"Brooke. That fucking bitch told me that Stella left with Bradley because they'd gotten back together that morning."

Lily looks completely shocked. "She did? Why would she do that? Well, besides that fact that she's the fucking devil."

"Dude, I told you she was bad news," Hank reminds me.

"So, Stella didn't get back together with Bradley? All this time I thought they were back together." I'm rambling now and talking to no one in particular.

"She never got back together with Bradley. Why would she? She loved *you*."

"Loved?" I say weakly.

"You broke her heart, Alex. She's been a wreck. I can barely get her to leave our dorm room, and it's been days. Hell, it's been weeks. She missed an entire week of class after she caught you coming out of her bathroom. Brooke told her that you two—"

"No! Nothing happened. I passed out on the couch. That's it."

"He's been miserable too, baby," says Hank to Lily.

"I know, but he had Brooke to help soothe his wounds."

"I didn't sleep with her! I didn't touch the bitch."

"I don't know if Stella will believe that. You were pretty mean to her on the phone. You left her a very nasty message."

"I did? I was wasted. What did I say? Do I want to know?"

"Probably not, but you should so you know what you're up against. You told her you were glad to be rid of her 'fat, ugly face.'"

"No! No way! I love her face. It's not fat. And it sure as fuck isn't ugly. It's beautiful." I actually whine that last part.

"You're trying to convince the wrong person, Alex. But if it were me, I don't think I'd believe that you didn't mean it. Stella has heard negative things about her body all her life. She's got thin skin when it comes to the people who are supposed to love her saying shit like that. She's not going to rebound from that one like normal girls."

Normal girls? What does that even mean? Stella's a regular girl. Well, not regular—she's special, and I totally fucked up with her. I feel burning behind my eyes. I've been miserable for weeks, and it's all my own fault. I could have prevented all of this. "I have totally and completely fucked up. What do I do? Where is she? What's your room number? Is she home?" The questions pour out of me as I beg Lily for information.

"Hold on, Alex. You can't just run over there and expect

her to just accept what you're saying. You need a plan, man," says Hank.

"Fuck the plan. I need my girl back. I've been such an idiot. What happens if she doesn't take me back?"

I'm crying? I'm actually crying right here in front of Hank and Lily, but I don't care. This has been the worst time of my life. I love that girl so much, and she loved me—past tense. Surely she still loves me somewhere down deep. I mean, I was her first. *And I will be her last, goddamn it.*

"Where is she, Lily?"

"Room 216."

"Thanks."

"Don't fuck this up, dude," warns Hank.

I hope I don't. I throw on my hoodie and race out the door. I'm going to have to figure out a way to convince her to take me back. She has to. I pick up the pace as I rush to Hinman. I can't get there soon enough. *Stella, please be there. Please be there.* I enter Hinman and search for the stairs. I take them two at a time to the second floor and race down the hall, searching for room 216.

When I find it, I stop to catch my breath. A plan. Hank said I needed a plan. But I can't think of anything but seeing her face. When I raise my hand to knock, I hear music coming from her room. Aw, fuck, it's Adele. I can hear her singing along with the music. I hate that she's listening to heavy shit instead of her happy Meghan Trainor playlist. I know I'm the cause of her sadness. I haven't been the guy she deserves. But that's all going to change right now.

I can't wait any longer. Instead of knocking, I try the doorknob. It turns. It's not locked. Damn it. She needs to lock her damn door. It's not safe. Gingerly, I open the door, revealing the view of Stella's back. I stand there for a few seconds to really look at her. She's wearing some type of baggy shorts and a T-shirt. They're both paint stained; she looks beautiful. Her hair has grown a little since I last saw her. I like it, but I liked it shorter too. She's holding a paintbrush in her right hand as she sways to the music and sings along. Man, that girl cannot sing, but she can move that body of hers. As I slowly walk up behind her, she visibly stiffens. I don't want to scare her. Maybe I should have tried to call first? She stops moving and stands with her back to me. I move as close to her as I can, our bodies almost touching.

"Stella," I whisper that so softly I'm not sure she can hear me.

She takes a deep breath; she heard me. I wrap my arms around her waist and sway to the music. She crosses her arms in front of herself, stiffening slightly. I can tell she's uncomfortable with my hold on her, but I don't let go.

"What are you doing here, Alex?"

"I'm a fucking idiot, Stella."

"Yeah, that's true. But you didn't answer me. What are you doing here?"

I laugh a little at that as I take her right hand. I place the paintbrush on her dresser and turn her around to face me.

"I just saw Lily. She told me that you'd moved over here. She also told me about your mom. I hope she's doing better."

"She is, thanks."

"She also told me why you missed my game that day and why you hadn't called or sent me a text."

"I would have told you those things if you'd given me a chance. Even when you came out of the bathroom, you could have asked me. I would have answered even though my heart was shattering into a million pieces. I would have told you."

"I went to your place after the game. I was worried about you. I knew you wouldn't miss it without a good reason. I thought you were hurt or sick."

"I wasn't. My mom was."

"I know that now. But when I came to your door, Brooke

answered. She told me that you had gone home with Bradley, that you had taken him back."

"What? Why would she say that?"

Oh, I know why. "Because she's a jealous, evil bitch," I spit.

"You seemed to like her just fine that night."

"I didn't do anything with her, Stella."

"Uh-huh."

"I understand why you would hesitate to believe me, but I would never touch that girl. I was drunk, and I passed out on your sofa. That's it."

"Your shirt was off, and your pants were undone."

"Yes, they were. I took a quick shower at your place and hadn't put my shirt back on when I saw you. But I sure as hell didn't touch her." I look into her eyes. I need to know. "Stella, you avoided me the entire week after we made love. I thought you had changed your mind about me after that."

"Me? I wasn't avoiding you. That's not how that happened. When we woke up the next morning, after we… you know, you could barely look at me. You didn't try to touch me. You practically threw my clothes at me to get me out of there. What was I supposed to think? I'd never had sex with a guy to know what the protocol was the next morning."

"I'm sorry, babe," I plead.

"Do not call me 'babe.'" Wow, I've never seen Stella this angry. "You don't get to do that anymore."

"I don't?" Damn, that makes me feel like shit.

"And you said I had a… a…"—I watch her attempt to hold back tears—"f-f-fat u-ugly f-f-face."

Holy hell, she's shaking. I don't know if she's shaking with anger or sadness. What the hell do I do?

"Leave. That's what you do."

I guess I said that last part out loud.

"No, let me—"

"Alex, please leave."

"I can't leave you, angel."

"Nope, no 'angel' either. No 'angel,' no 'babe,' no 'princess,' and no 'Pixie'! Just go. I can't deal with this again. I can't go through it again. I was starting to get back to normal. Now I have to start all over again. Fuck!"

I swear to all that is holy, I want to fix this. I want to pick her up and cradle her like a baby. So, that's what I do. I reach down and pick her up and draw her to my chest. I turn and sit on her bed.

"Stop it, leave me alone. I'm too heavy. My fat, ugly face is going to break your legs."

"Stop saying that, damn it. I was drunk. I was trying to say something, anything that would hurt you as much as you'd hurt me. That's all. I love your face. It's not fat, and it's definitely not ugly. I told you. You're the most beautiful girl I've ever seen. I love your face, almost as much as I love you."

Now I'm fucking crying. Jesus. I need to hand in my man card. But she's worth losing it for. I don't care. I love this girl. If something is meant to last, we'll have to see each other at our best and at our worst. This is a worst, for sure. I lift her so she's straddling my lap and pull her as close to my chest as I can as I wrap my arms around her. I hear her sniffle, but I don't think she realizes I'm crying too. After a few minutes, I can tell she's started to calm down a little bit. I reach up and move her hair from her beautiful face. That's when she sees my tears.

"You're crying?" she asks, looking surprised.

"Yes, I'm crying because our breakup could have been avoided if I had just talked to you that Sunday morning. And I'm crying because I love you and because the last weeks without you have been the worst of my life. I thought I'd lost you forever to Brad. I fell in love with you the second you wrapped your little arms around me, Stella. You make me feel like I can do anything as long as you're with me. I can't sleep without you. I'm so tired, ba—sorry." I almost said "babe."

"I'm just so tired and lost without you." I *am* lost without her. Everything I said was the absolute truth. "God, Stella, I'm so sorry that I hurt you."

"You are?"

"Yes, I am, ba—please, can I call you 'babe'?"

"Okay," she says hesitantly.

"What about 'Pixie'?"

"Yeah."

"Angel?"

"Maybe."

"Princess?"

"I guess."

"Thank God, I hope this means that we can start from here. Are you taking me back, giving me another chance, Stella?"

"I guess so. But I'm scared, Alex. I'm not sure I trust your feelings yet. I mean, I'm always going to wonder if you really like how I look after what you said on the phone that night."

"I know. I'm so sorry for that, angel. You're so beautiful, every single part of you. I just lashed out at you and used the one thing that I knew would hurt you the most. I promise I'll never say or do anything like that again."

"You should know, I may get even bigger. There are no guarantees that I'll ever lose weight or even stay the same. I can't be with you if you're going to make my appearance an issue. I've lived with someone like that my entire life, and I won't do it again. So, if you have any reservations, you should leave now," she says confidently.

I place my hand behind Stella's head, beneath her hair, and pull her to me.

I whisper in her ear, "Stella, I don't care if you gain a thousand pounds. It's never going to change how I feel about you. I suspect you'll gain weight when you're carrying my babies. I can't wait to see you like that, to be honest," I say, smiling.

"What? Babies? I, uh, can't even think about that right now."

"I know. I just wanted to let you know that I want those things with you, Stella. I've never felt this way about anyone else. I've imagined our life together, and it makes me excited about our future. God, Stella, I've missed you so much. I've missed kissing your beautiful lips. I've missed everything about you."

"Kiss me, Alex."

I lean down slowly. I want to remember this moment. The moment my girl took me back. I'll never let her get away from me again. Stella is it for me. She's my beginning and my end. I just hope she'll come to realize that. I hope I'm her beginning and her end. My lips touch hers, and it's like fireworks. It's been so long since I've felt her against me and since I've touched her. Too damn long. She's kissing me back like she's been in the desert and I'm water. I feel the same.

Chapter Twenty-Eight

STELLA

Well, it's official. I've lost my ever-loving mind. A week ago, I took Alex back. I guess I could say we took each other back since the whole thing that split us up was a misunderstanding—a misunderstanding caused by a pit viper named Brooke Clark. I had to give us another chance though, even though I'm still wincing from the comments about my face. He's tried very hard to show me how much he loves me. I'm going to keep reminding him though, even though it makes him feel guilty. Guilt is much easier to deal with than self-loathing, let me tell you. But, also, I sort of like the groveling. I deserve some groveling.

During our breakup, he lost weight. I don't know how much, but it's enough that you can tell. I'm sure his coach is on him about it. He's also sporting a beard now. He must have decided to do that Octobeard thing, or is it Novembeard? It doesn't matter; he looks damn good in a beard. It makes his eyes seem even bluer. His hair has gotten pretty long too. He could totally pull off one of those man buns. On other guys, I think they look kind of dumb, but on Alex, it's hot.

Speaking of looking good. I need to get ready. Alex is

taking me out tonight; he's picking me up at five. I don't know where he's taking me, but he wants me to wear my blue dress. I know why he wants me to wear it. He likes what it does for my girls, and since all we've done is kiss this week, he may be hoping he can unbutton me again. It is a definite possibility, but I used it as leverage. I told him I'd wear the dress if he kept the beard and wore a man bun. I giggled when I asked. He, reluctantly, agreed. I can't wait to see him.

Chapter Twenty-Nine

ALEX

It's been a week since Stella took me back. I'm still so thankful that she did. I can't wait to see her tonight. I'm surprising her by taking her to the Meghan Trainor concert downtown. Even though that's not my favorite music, I'm looking forward to seeing it with Stella. She's a big fan. I've asked her to wear the blue dress. It'll fit perfectly into the event; plus, I have big plans that relate directly to twenty-four buttons. I had to agree to wear something called a man bun. Sure, some of the guys on the team sport those, so I knew what she was talking about. I for one, am not a man-bun kind of guy but for my girl, I'll do just about anything.

I get to her place at exactly five. When she opens her door, my breath catches. It's been forever since I've seen her in the dress, and it looks just as good as it did then. Maybe better now because I know what lies beneath the blue fabric. I want to reach out and touch her breasts. They're just so plump and full. Damn, she's got beautiful tits, and they're all mine. I smile and lean in to give her a soft kiss on her lips. "You look beautiful, sweetheart."

"Thank you. So do you!" she squeaks. "Holy crap, you look

so good with the man bun. Promise me you'll keep it like that forever! And don't shave the beard."

She's practically breathless now. She reaches up and wraps her arms around my neck and pulls me down for a kiss. Damn, I like it when she takes the lead. I can get into that. I'll keep the fucking bun for this. Suddenly, she pulls at my neck to get me into her room. Once inside, she turns and kicks the door shut and locks it. Her hands slide to my chest, and she pushes me toward her bed.

"Uh, is Lily here?" I ask.

"Nope. Out. With Hank." She presses her palm on my chest and says, "Lay down, Alex."

I do as she says.

"What time do we have to leave?" she asks impatiently.

"Well, we need to get on the road by five forty-five to make it."

"Great," she says distractedly as she climbs up onto the bed.

She scoots up to straddle me but stops to unbuckle her little belt first. I watch as she slips the little belt out of the loops sewn into her dress. Placing my hands behind my head, I can't help but enjoy this little show especially when she starts to unbutton the first button.

"One," I say with a smirk.

She looks at me a little surprised, but I can tell she likes it. When her fingers move down, I say, "Two."

She looks right into my eyes as she undoes number three. I keep counting as she undoes each button. When she gets to eight, I sit up and pull off my suit jacket, throwing it on the floor. I unbutton my shirt and cuffs, and by button twelve I'm shirtless. She stops what she's doing to look at me.

"Don't stop, babe, please," I plead.

She nods.

"Thirteen," I count.

We're both panting, and I'm as hard as a fucking spike. I reach for her breasts, but she slaps my hand away, giggling. She slowly opens the dress for me. Her eyes haven't left mine, but I can't look at her eyes anymore. I stare at her glorious breasts. They are fucking perfect with her little pink nipples. I can tell they're hard and aching for my touch. I reach for her, and she lets me this time. Pulling her down, I rise up and let our mouths touch. The kiss is one I never want to forget because it's the kind that tells me she loves me, again. Rolling us over, I lean back and open up her dress again and stare.

"You have fucking beautiful tits, Stella."

"Thanks," she says excitedly.

Leaning down, I lick the nipple on her left breast. She gasps and arches up toward me, pressing her nipple into my mouth. I don't want to miss this chance, so I lick her hard nipple again then suck and bite just a little bit, making her squirm beneath me. I slide my hand underneath her skirt until I feel lace. I've got to see what she's wearing under her dress. I hike her skirt up to her waist to get a view of some fucking sexy lace short things.

"Jesus, Stella, you're killing me."

I want to rip them off, but I can't do that to her, so I move down her body so I can slide those little shorts down her legs. She lifts her hips to help me.

"Alex, I want you. I've missed you so much."

"I want you too. I've missed you. So much."

I know we're going to be late for the show, but who cares about the opening act? Sitting up, she starts to unbutton my pants, and I let her. She unzips me and reaches in to pull me out of my jeans. Damn, her little hand feels so good. She rubs my cock just like I showed her before. She leans down to lick the head to taste my precum.

"Damn, that's sexy, angel."

She starts to put her mouth on me, but I lift her up.

"I want to be inside of you. I need to feel you around me."

"Okay," she whispers.

Stella can be a little timid, but tonight she seems to be much more confident. I let her settle back while I reach for my wallet. Fuck, no condom. I honestly didn't think she'd be ready for this again so soon.

"It's okay, Alex. I'm on the pill. I have been since I was sixteen to regulate my period."

"Are you sure, Stella?"

"Yes, I'm sure. I need you, Alex," she says frantically.

I'm holding myself above her while my cock rests between her legs. Wanting to make sure she's ready for me, I play with her breasts while I run my fingers through her pussy.

"You're so wet for me. You have no idea how good that makes me feel, honey."

"You do that to me, Alex."

While looking into her eyes, I place myself at her opening. She nods, and I press in all the way. "Wow." I've never gone bareback before. "Nothing in the world feels as good as you do, Stella."

We move together. She's in tune to me, and it's only our second time together. Her movements match mine, which makes this so much more intensely erotic when we work together for our mutual pleasure. Damn, I love this girl. Thinking about that makes me thrust even harder. I need to get as close to her as I can. When I feel her tighten around me, I know close.

"Don't stop, Alex, please. I'm almost there," she moans.

I fuck her in earnest now. This is only the second time we've had sex, and it's the best I've ever had. Nothing compares to having sex with the person you love. Nothing. I thrust in three more times, and that's it. I come inside of her like it's a fucking cannon, and I can feel her come at the same time. She's squeezing my cock so hard I think I might black out.

"I love you," I whisper in her ear.

She smiles up at me with those beautiful dimples, and I know. I just know. I'm going to marry this girl. And when we do, I'm going to hire her favorite designer to create a wedding dress for her that looks exactly like her blue dress, but with more buttons. Then, on our wedding night, I'll unbutton every single one of them to reveal my wife. Holy shit. The thought of that makes me hard again.

Incredibly, we make it to the show in time. We skip dinner and miss the opening act, but Stella's so excited to see one of her favorite singers in person. She knows all of the songs, and I don't complain when she insists on singing along. Hell, it's worth hearing her sing just to watch her dance to the music. Her dance moves make me want to have a repeat of earlier. My girl's got moves.

Chapter Thirty

STELLA

I can't believe I'm sitting here with Alex and his parents waiting to hear where he'll play football in the National Football League next year. We're hoping the Chicago Bears pick him so he can stay nearby, but honestly, wherever he ends up will be amazing. I'm so proud of him. Even though the season was a bit rough for him, having had a few games where he wasn't focused, he still ended up with a fantastic season. His grades suffered a little too, but he'll still be an All-Big 10 Academic All-American this year. He's also on track to graduate with honors next month.

We've seen the first ten teams pick their number one draft pick; the Chicago Bears pick next. I cross my fingers and toes for him and for us. Even though we've only been dating for eight months, it feels like we've always been together. If he has to play ball in another city, I know we can manage the long-distance thing. I'd be willing to transfer schools if he wanted me to, but I won't invite myself. He would need to ask. There are plenty of excellent art history programs around the country.

Yes, you heard that correctly; I'm working on my Bachelor

of Arts degree in Art History. I plan to continue until I earn my doctorate or Ph.D. I'm not sure which area of art history I want to focus on, but I have plenty of time to figure that out. Alex is happy that I switched majors. Plus, I still get to take plenty of studio art classes, like painting and drawing, so it's the best of both worlds. Oh, hang on… it's time!

"With the eleventh pick in the NFL Draft, the Chicago Bears select Alex Emerson, tight end from Northwestern University." The crowd erupts with cheers as Roger Goodell, the commissioner of the NFL, announces Chicago's pick on national television.

When Alex hears his name, he stands up, shakes his dad's hand, kisses his mom and sister's cheeks, then picks me up and wraps his arms around me. He kisses me like we're the only two people in this room instead of the hundreds in attendance.

"We did it, babe. I'm going to be close to you while you work on your degree."

"I know!" I squeak. "But, Alex?"

"Yeah, angel?"

"I think they're waiting for you up on stage so you can get your new Chicago Bears top with the number one on it," I say, smiling sweetly.

"Jersey, babe. It's a jersey."

I wink at him as he turns and strides up to the stage. I'm so happy for him, and I'm not the only one. His family is beaming with pride. On the stage, Alex holds up his Bears jersey. He's so happy. I know because he's smiling right at me. Even though there's a room full of people here, I feel like, in this moment, it's just the two of us. How did I get so lucky to literally run into the love of my life? It had to have been fate.

AFTER THE NFL DRAFT CEREMONY, Alex's parents decided to head back to the hotel. We had all planned on having dinner together, but they decided they were too tired. Strange, considering tonight was so huge for Alex. But that just means I'll have Alex all to myself.

He chose a fancy new restaurant in downtown Chicago. I think it's another steak place. He loves steak places. It's fine with me; I'll find something that I enjoy. I considered wearing "the dress," but in the end, I decided it was a little worse for wear since the last time I wore it, so I called my mom to see if she'd go shopping with me for a new dress from that same vintage store. She was really excited to go with me.

Since her heart episode, she's been working very hard to mend things between us. I've been trying too. I want to have a good relationship with my mom. It's not easy though. I'm so used to her insults that I tend to expect them and become a little defensive with her. But this shopping trip was good for both of us. When we found the store again, I told her how much I liked the blue dress and that I'd like to look for something similar. We found the coolest red dress there. It was even sexier than the blue one but with no buttons. This one has an exposed zipper that runs from the top of the back all the way to the bottom. It completely unzips and comes off in one piece. The skirt is a little more fitted too. It still flares out at the waist but not as drastically. It feels more like a dress from that show *Mad Men*. You know, like a sexy secretary from the 1960s. It's low cut in the front too. I knew Alex would like that a lot. When he saw me in the dress, he nearly passed out. I giggled when I saw his reaction because his parents were with him and he could do absolutely nothing about his, um, manhood. I could tell he was struggling to remain composed. Poor Alex.

"Pix, later you, me, and that dress have a date," he whispered in my ear as he hugged me.

Now, as we sit at the table in the restaurant, I notice that

Alex is doing everything he can to not look at me—just like our first date. I refuse to take it personally this time. I know he's happy to be with me. Maybe he's nervous about everything that happened today. I reach out to hold his hand on the table, and he flinches a little bit. Uh-oh, what's going on? Is he going to break up with me? Maybe I *do* need to be concerned. What if he just wants to focus on his career now? I wouldn't blame him. I'm holding him back. I should have known. Why do I constantly do that? The second I feel secure and happy about my future, shit slams to a halt. Deciding to make my escape before I'm humiliated in such a public place, I turn to get up and almost trip over Alex. He's on the floor—well, not *on* the floor. He's on his knee on the floor in front of me.

"Alex? What are you doing on the floor?" Is he doing what I think he's doing? Maybe he's not going to break my heart after all.

"Stella, you are the most beautiful girl I've ever seen. The minute you touched me that day in September was the moment I knew you were meant for me. I know that sounds strange, but it's true. It only took me a week to figure out that it was love. Getting a job with the NFL today was great, but it wouldn't compare to you saying 'yes' to my question."

Oh my goodness, is this really happening? Is Alex actually on his knee in front of me holding out a little blue box? I blink at him as he speaks. I hear him, but my focus is on his handsome face. When I peer into his eyes, I can see he's nervous. I recognize the signs, having been with him almost daily since we got back together. Watching him go through all of the steps to earn his place in the NFL, I saw his nerves. His smile quivers just a little bit, and his left eye twitches. It's adorable. *He's* adorable.

"Stella Nicole Matthews, will you make me the happiest man in the entire world and be my wife? Marry me, Stella."

Doing my best to calm down, I nod furiously. I reach out to

hug him around the neck, but he stops me first to show me the ring. It's the most beautiful ring I have ever seen. It's a square-shaped diamond, and it's silver in color. If I could pick any ring out in the entire world, it would be this one. He knows me so well. I reach my hand out toward him so he can slide it on my finger. It sparkles so much, I swear it's blinding me. I try to grab him around his neck so I can kiss him, but he wraps his arms around my waist and lifts me up from his kneeling position and kisses me first. It's full of love and passion and happiness. It's a kiss I will never forget.

I hear the crowd around us clapping and cheering. People must've been watching us and were waiting to see what my answer would be. *Come on, people, look at the guy. Who would be crazy enough to say "no" to that? Not me.* I know what a catch he is and how special. I'm the luckiest woman in the world. We kiss once more, and then he sets me back on the ground, but it feels like I'm still flying. To think I was ready to run out of here fearing he was breaking up with me. I couldn't have been more wrong.

Epilogue

FIVE YEARS LATER

So much has happened in the last five years, I'm not sure where to start. Oh, I guess I should start with our wedding. *Sigh*. It was beautiful and intimate. Okay, maybe intimate isn't the right word. Once we invited his family and mine, our best friends, his football teams, both of them, and the staff from the Chicago Bears organization, it became a "rather large affair." At least that's what my mom called it. Side note: My dad nearly expired when he found out the players from his beloved Bears were going to attend. Jim Matthews was one happy man.

We sincerely wanted to keep it small, having considered eloping to Vegas or planning a destination wedding somewhere sunny, but when it came down to it, I wanted everyone with us. Alex agreed after he thought about it awhile. When he said, "You're right, Pix. We're only getting married once; we might as well have the wedding to beat all weddings."

So, that's what we did. We were married in the same venue we had the reception—the ballroom on the top floor of Chicago's Cultural Center. It's a spectacular space with a glass dome in the center and amazing tile work throughout. It's fitting that we chose a place that supports the arts so beautifully since I'm almost finished working on my Master's in Art History.

My mom took the lead organizing the event. Seeing what she was able to do in only two months is astonishing since we wanted to hurry and get married before the football season started. She may have missed her calling. Actually, the events staff the Chicago Cultural Center asked her if she wanted a full-time job. She declined the full-time position but said she'd consider working part-time. Four years later and she's now a sought-after wedding planner. I don't think she's ever been happier.

After the wedding, Alex and I moved into a beautiful Chicago brownstone near the university. There are three floors, but we only live on the first and second floors. The third floor is devoted to visitors like Grandma and Grandpa Emerson and Nana and Papa Matthews.

Oh, I gave away the surprise, didn't I? No matter, I was going to tell you anyway. Alex and I had a son almost three months ago. We named him Finnian—or Finn for short. I know that name is a tad strange, but the meaning is perfect for him. It stands for handsome, fair, and warrior.

Finn is a great mixture of both of us. He's got my coloring, blond hair and blue eyes, but he's a big boy like his daddy, weighing almost ten pounds at birth. He's Daddy's boy in more ways than that though. I didn't think I could love Alex any more than I did, but after Finn was born, I saw another side to my husband—a father. He's amazing. Every time I see them together, I want to cry. There's nothing to compare to the love I see between my two fellas.

As for the rest of the gang, sadly, Hank and Lily split up after a two-year relationship. They're both still single and, in my opinion, still in love with each other, but Alex disagrees. He said, "You're just a romantic, angel. Not everyone is meant to be like us." He kissed me after saying that. It was sweet and sexy, but just between you and me, Lily and Hank still love each other. I'm crossing my fingers and toes that they pull their heads out of their you-know-whats and get back together.

The other two people you're probably curious about are no longer in my life. Bradley is an attorney at a firm in Ohio. He didn't even apply to work in my dad's firm. Bradley and I are on good terms. Friends, I guess. He came to our wedding, and he's even met Finn. I'm happy things aren't strained with him because his mom means so much to Mom and me.

As for Brooke? I have no idea what happened to her. I take that back. I saw her a year or two ago at a CVS pharmacy on South State Street. She was a cashier. There's nothing wrong with being a cashier, but because it was Brooke, part of me wanted to relish in the fact that she had a not-so-glamorous job, but I didn't. Actually, I've never spoken to anyone about seeing her there, not Alex or Lily. So, you heard it here first. I don't wish her ill. To do so would mean she has some sort of power over my life, and she doesn't. Not anymore.

So, what's next for us? Well, the biggest change in our life revolves around Alex's job. He's retiring from the NFL after this season due to several injuries, one of which required surgery. His body has had enough of professional football. Now he's moving on to broadcasting. He's been hired by a major sports network to cover Big-10 football games. He'll travel about the same as he has as a player, which stinks, but Finn and I will be able to go with him on some trips when I'm not working on my Ph.D. starting next fall.

In all, my life is sort of perfect—charmed, I guess you could say. I feel very lucky and blessed to have met the love of my life so early. I'm confident I can say the same for Alex. It's still a little surreal to wake up next to him every morning. Sometimes I want to pinch myself, but I don't. Instead, I roll over and pinch my tight end. ;)

IF YOU ENJOYED THIS BOOK, you may also enjoy:

Quinn Maxwell. Student. Dork. And a woman in love with a guy who doesn't know she exists.

Cooke Thompson. British. Hottie. Rugby Star. Chick Magnet. And a guy trying to FaceChat with his old mate Maxwell Quinn.

Sure, it was a wrong number but sometimes, wrong ends up being so-so right.

For more information: www.kaytmiller.com

Hopeful Romantic

Thanks to Margie Dill (Coming soon.)

Acknowledgments

Thank you to everyone from Hot Tree Editing for editing this book from start to finish.

And an extra special thank you to Becky Johnson at Hot Tree Promotions for your advice, expertise, and positivity.

And to my beta readers. Your feedback and patience is essential to this process. Thank you!

And to my mom who is the wind beneath my wings. Literally.

About the Author

Kayt grew up in the midwest surrounded by a loving family which included three brothers, one sister, and parents who always fostered her creative side.

Kayt wrote her first book when she couldn't find a story about a certain type of a woman and a specific kind of man. She called it *Game Changer* and it couldn't have been a more appropriate title. It changed her life in many ways.

Her goal, as a writer, is to write stories that relate to all of us, to make readers laugh and maybe cry sometimes. Kayt hopes her readers can escape into a fantasy, one that's actually possible. Sure, some of the stories are dubbed "Insta-love" but that's okay. She fell in love with her husband pretty damn fast and with her daughter the second she saw her. So, it's a thing, she swears.

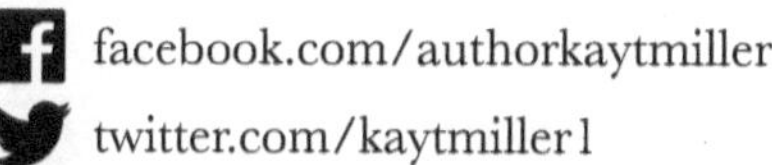

facebook.com/authorkaytmiller

twitter.com/kaytmiller1

instagram.com/kaytmiller1

bookbub.com/profile/kayt-miller

Thank you so much for reading! When I start a story, it begins with an outline, notes, and lots of crazy thoughts running through my head. When I actually start writing, the characters take over, leading me through the story like they're holding my hand—guiding me. The process is exciting and cathartic. With that said, I hope you enjoy the story.

If you did, please go to my website, www.kaytmiller.com, and join my newsletter so you can be the first to know what's coming up next. And…

Please, leave a review!

Chapter 1

Happy Frigging New Year

"Yo! Mac. Hottie at three o'clock," my best friend says as she approaches me.

Looking to my right, I scan the crowd. "I don't see any hotties."

"No, I said *three* o'clock," Lauren clarified, annoyed. "Don't make me point. It's bad manners."

"I know. I looked at three o'clock and saw only Father Time." Seriously, there's a guy dressed up as Father Time. Ah, New Year's Eve in Chicago. It brings out the crazies.

"No, dork, *my* three o'clock."

"That would be my *nine* o'clock, not my three o'clock."

"Crap, girl, just look to the right."

"Wait, my right or your right?" Lauren can be so confusing.

"Jesus, now he's gone. You missed him. He was your dream man."

"Ooh, you mean he looked like Jason Momoa?" I look frantically around the room.

"What? No. Jason Momoa is your dream man?"

"Uh… yeah. After *Game of Thrones*, he's *everyone's* dream man. Ooh, did you know he's the new *Aquaman*? He was perfect for that part. The man is a god."

"Well, this guy was hot, and he was actually *here*," Lauren says, rolling her eyes. Even at the best of times, the girl barely puts up with me. She continues, "He's got blond hair, and he had that faux-hawk fade haircut that's so in right now. Plus, he had on nerd glasses."

"Holy shite. I love me some faux-hawk. Add the nerd spectacles, and I can feel it in my pantaloons, *giiirrrl*. Gimme. Where is he?"

Lauren giggles. "God, you're such a dork. Spectacles? Pantaloons? Where do you come up with that stuff?"

"I read a lot of Regency-era romances."

"You mean Regency erotica. You're a pervert," she deadpans.

I let out a surprised giggle. *Lauren, Lauren, Lauren.* "It's not erotica. It's *romance*. Sure, there are some naughty little debutantes types in the books and even some wicked rakes, but it's all in good fun."

"Whatevs. I'm going back to Blake. He'll be lost without me."

I snort, rather unattractively, I'm sure. But the truth is, she's right. Blake is her husband of almost a year, and he would literally be lost without her. I'm not sure the man can choose his own clothes, to be honest. I think she chooses his outfit for the next day and sets it all out before they go to bed. It works for them, and I guess there's nothing wrong with it. He adores her and she him, no matter how creepy their love seems to me.

Now that I'm on my own again, I decide to move around the ballroom with eyes peeled for the mysterious "hottie at three o'clock." While I do, I do my best to put this into perspective. Even if I find him, Mr. Hottie would not be interested in me. There's nothing extraordinary about MacKenzie Blue Parker. I'm just your average woman with an average face and a larger-than-average ass, but who *does* have an interesting middle name.

"Thank you, Mom," I say softly, looking up toward heaven. I'm not sure why she used a color for my middle name. When I asked Pops about it, he just said she was whimsical. I love that he used that word to describe my mom. I don't remember a lot about her, but I do remember that she was pretty and lots of fun.

I squeeze through the throng, turning my body this way and that, saying "excuse me," "pardon me," and "oh, I'm sorry my ass knocked your drink out of your hand." After all that, I'm grumpy, my feet hurt, my head hurts, and I'm still hungry even after nibbling on the delightful spread they've got here. I'm trying to look on the bright side but *ugh*, New Year's Eve sucks.

Are you wondering why my feelings about such an optimistic holiday have taken a nose dive? Personal history. Yep, personal history tells me New Year's Eve is a night filled with loneliness, sore feet, and worst of all, shattered expectations. I'm referring specifically to the promised kiss at midnight that never seems to happen—at least not for me. *Why did I let Lauren talk me into coming to this fancy-schmancy party tonight?* Oh, I remember. It's because I'm a sucker for my best friend's charms. I'm a grown-ass woman. You'd think I could turn her down, but Lauren Jacobs-Warner practically guaranteed that I'd have the time of my life tonight *and* I'd get a kiss at midnight.

I don't know why I let her do this to me time and time again. Yeah, my dress is fabulous. I actually feel sort of pretty in it. Pretty but pained. I've been thrust into fashion purgatory with four-inch heels and a too-tight Spanx undergarment.

Ugh. I seriously think the people that invented Spanx are sadists—not to mention strange. I mean, who says "undergarment"? No offense, Spanx Incorporated, or whatever you call your business.

To be honest, I'd rather be home watching Netflix and eating junk food. That's my usual activity on holidays like this one, but my best friend sweet-talked me into this. I told her I didn't have the appropriate clothes for this part. I even modeled my best outfit, a pair of black leggings and sparkly top. But that wouldn't do for my friend, the little socialite. So she gave me a dress, an old one of hers that she "didn't really like." I don't believe her for a second. I mean, how could she not *love* this dress? This dress is *Ah. Maze. Ing.*

Imagine a dress that Audrey Hepburn might wear in *Breakfast at Tiffany's*. It's black with a delicate lace overlay. Beneath the lace overlay is a satin dress with a sweetheart bodice. The lace top has a boat neck that is open to my shoulder. Simply put, it's spectacular. Itchy, but spectacular. Oh, and it's got pockets. It's perfection. It has three-quarter sleeves and a flirty skirt that's lined with tulle so that it flares out at the waist and stops right above my knee in a 1950s style. It's a flattering silhouette, because it hides my larger-than-average rump. The truth is, that's the only reason this dress fits me, because Lauren's got a perfect bod. She's five-feet-eight with an hourglass figure in perfect proportion. I'd be jealous if I didn't adore her. But I do, so I'm not.

To ensure I'd attend this little shindig, Lauren even provided me with a date—her cousin, Frederick. He's not really my type, though. Not that I have a type. I haven't even had an actual boyfriend, per se, so maybe *type* is the wrong word. I have book boyfriends, sure. Television and movie boyfriends, of course, but nothing in the flesh. Yeah, so *type* is the wrong word. Perhaps I should just say he's not my dream man. He's short, only an inch or two taller than my five-feet-five-inches. He's also a tad doughy. I know that's not at all nice to say since I'm a bit doughy myself. But he's got a paunch on him like a sixty-year-old man, and he's only in his thirties. He's a little too young to have the dad bod, if you ask me.

Too judgy? If so, I'm sorry. I'm sure Freddy is a great guy.

He seems nice enough, though. I've met him at a couple of the Jacobses' family gatherings. The Jacobses are rich as Croesus. That's what Pops used to call rich people. It fits. He's rolling in it. So, this is more *his* kind of party, not mine. Lauren means well—she really does. But I'm so *not* this girl. I'm a starving artist. Figuratively. Not literally. No, *literally*, I live off of forty-cent packages of ramen noodles and macaroni and cheese in the blue box, so, no, I've got lots of carb-induced meat on my bones.

Case in point. Right this minute I'm surrounded by hundreds of rich people, famous people, important people, and politicians. I think I saw the governor a few minutes ago. We're in a huge ballroom in one of the five-star hotels in downtown Chicago. The ballroom is practically the size of a football field. Above me are the most spectacular chandeliers I've ever seen. They're enormous and appear to be dripping with jewels. The way they glitter and sparkle makes the entire space feel like a scene from a fairy tale. Because I'm no princess, and this place is so beyond anything I've ever seen, it makes me feel self-conscious.

Everyone is dressed in tuxedos and beautiful gowns or cocktail dresses like mine. Thankfully, I don't look completely out of place here. Waiters and waitresses dressed in penguin suits are walking around with trays of finger foods and flutes of champagne. There's a relatively large orchestra sitting off in the far corner near the huge dance floor. Several couples are already out there cutting a rug; not the kind of dancing I'm used to. This is fancy, grown-up, ballroom dancing, not the grind-your-ass-into-the-guy-behind-you dancing that I've done at clubs. No matter, I won't be dancing tonight unless I want to make a complete fool of myself.

As my eyes scan the room, I notice the long table filled with endless amounts of food and delectable-looking desserts, and my stomach rumbles. *Of course, I'm hungry.* In the center of the table is a giant ice sculpture of a swan. If it were sitting on the floor, it would probably stand taller than me. The swan's neck is bent down as though it's ready to take a bite out of all of the deliciousness below it. The main bar is nearby, while other smaller bar stations are located throughout the ballroom. Deciding a drink is in order, I cross my fingers that it's an open bar. I brought a little money with me, but I'd rather save that in case I need a taxi home.

Walking to the bar, I look to my right and spot Lauren standing with her husband, Blake. I recognize the people they're with as old family friends. I scan the other way in search of my "date." *Now, where did he go?* I spot him standing near the bar with a group of guys. They're in a small circle, and each man has his phone in his hands, texting.

I walk toward Frederick in the hopes that he'll be fun tonight. He hasn't proven to be much of a date thus far, but he *is* doing me a favor, I guess. I'm sure Lauren had to coerce him into bringing me. I move to stand next to him and wait for him to notice me. Should I tap him on the shoulder so he knows I'm here? Do I stand and wait for Frederick to ask me to dance or if I'd like a drink? I decide to do my best to be a good date. I wait. And wait. And wait. Nearly ten minutes pass, and Frederick does nothing but text and talk to his buddies. None of the guys even look at me. It's annoying. What? *Am I hideous?* I don't think I'm that tragic-looking. I've got cool hair that's naturally reddish-auburn and cut bluntly just past my shoulders. I've also got the ends tipped with blue tonight, like my middle name. It's only temporary color, but I'm an artist; we artists need to have funky hair at special events. It's the law. I giggle, which draws several pairs of eyes to me. Oh, *now* Frederick notices me.

"You okay?" he asks. He doesn't make eye contact with me, and before I can respond, he's back to his phone. I hear him mutter to his buddies, "Chick is weird." The men chuckle at that little slight, and that's it? That's all I get? Whatever.

"Asshole," I grumble as I start to move around the room again. I can keep *myself* entertained. I'm used to doing things alone. That's probably why I hate stuff like this. I'm much better on my own, in my own world, in my own head. There's nothing wrong with being alone. It's being lonely that sucks.

9 781951 162214